ONE DARK NIGHT
Ivy Bishop Mystery Thriller
Book 5

ALEX SIGMORE

Dark Woods Press

ONE DARK NIGHT: IVY BISHOP MYSTERY THRILLER BOOK 5

Copyright © 2025 by Alex Sigmore

All rights reserved.

This is a work of fiction. Names, characters, places and incidents are products of the author's imagination and are used fictitiously and are not to be construed as real. Any resemblance to actual events, locales, organizations or persons, living or dead, is entirely coincidental.

No part of this book may be reproduced in any form or by any electronic or mechanical means, including information storage and retrieval systems, without written permission from the author, except for the use of brief quotations in a book review.

1st Edition

Print ISBN 978-1-957536-88-0

Description

One dark night changed everything. Now Ivy Bishop must face the truth she's spent a lifetime outrunning.

Haunted by the fallout of a case gone tragically wrong, Detective Ivy Bishop is forced to confront the one mystery she's never been able to solve—her own. When new evidence resurfaces about the night her family was destroyed, Ivy is pulled into a web of secrets that stretches deeper than she ever imagined. But the truth won't set her free. It might even break her.

As she investigates the shadows of her past, Ivy is also reckoning with a failure she can't forgive: the young victim she couldn't save. With the weight of two tragedies threatening to consume her, Ivy must decide if she's still the protector she set out to be—or just another ghost left behind by the darkness.

Some wounds never heal. Some answers only lead to more pain. But Ivy Bishop isn't done fighting.
Not yet.

Prologue

THE RAIN NEVER SEEMED TO STOP.

Detective Natasha "Nat" Buckley drove down the soaked streets, the drone of the police radio nothing but white noise at this point. The streetlights reflected off the slick roads, pinpricks of light in the dark pavement only to ripple and disappear in the constant rain. She adjusted her windshield wipers and continued through the industrial district, part of her normal patrol.

At twenty-eight, she'd been working the night shift for two years, long enough to know that the quiet hours between two and six AM were the most uneventful and boring hours of the day. But, as the newest detective on the force, she'd expected the graveyard shift. And until someone else retired or was injured in the line of duty, she'd be on this patrol for a while, so she had gotten comfortable with the idea.

Nat liked the night. Things were generally quieter, less crazy. But when something did happen during these hours, it was usually something serious. Which meant even though it was unlikely as hell, she couldn't let her guard down. Not ever.

The radio crackled with occasional dispatch calls—a domestic disturbance on the east side, a possible break-in at a convenience store—but nothing in her sector. Nat preferred it that way. The industrial area was mostly warehouses and auto repair shops, places that emptied out after five and stayed that way until morning. It gave her time to think, to process the cases that had been weighing on her mind lately.

As she approached the intersection of Braswell Street and Sixteenth something caught in her peripheral vision. A flash of white against the dark asphalt, moving erratically near the loading dock of Peterson's Manufacturing. Nat slowed the cruiser and squinted through the rain-streaked windshield.

A figure stumbled into the cone of light cast by a streetlamp. Small. Child-sized.

Shit. She pulled to the curb, grabbed her flashlight, and stepped out into the rain. The cold droplets hit her face as she approached the figure, her hand instinctively moving to rest on her service weapon.

"Police," she called out, her voice cutting through the sound of the rain. "Are you all right?"

The figure turned, and Nat's breath caught in her throat. It was a girl, maybe twelve or thirteen years old, wearing what looked like pajamas—now soaked through and clinging to her thin frame. But it was the dark stains across the fabric that sent Nat's stomach plummeting. Even with the rain washing some of it away, she could tell it was blood.

"Hey there," Nat said softly, approaching slowly with her hands visible. "My name is Officer Buckley. What's your name, sweetheart?"

The girl stared at her with wide, unfocused eyes. Her lips moved, but no sound came out. She was shivering violently, though whether from cold or shock, Nat couldn't tell. Probably both.

The girl wasn't much shorter than she was, but Nat found herself crouching down to meet the girl's eye level, careful not to make any sudden movements. "You're safe now, okay? I'm here to help you." She scanned the girl's visible skin for injuries but saw none. The blood wasn't hers.

"Can you tell me your name?" Nat tried again.

Still nothing. The girl's gaze seemed to look right through her, as if she were seeing something else entirely. Something terrible.

Nat stood and keyed her radio. "Dispatch, this is Unit Seven. I've got a juvenile, approximately twelve to thirteen years old, appears to be in shock. Requesting ambulance to my location at Mill and Fourth."

"Copy, Unit Seven. Ambulance en route."

Nat returned her attention to the girl, who had started to sway on her feet. She caught her gently by the shoulders just as the child's knees buckled. The girl didn't resist the contact, didn't even seem to register it.

"I've got you," Nat murmured, supporting the girl's weight. "We're going to get you somewhere warm and safe."

As they waited for the ambulance, Nat studied the scene around them. The loading dock was empty, no signs of struggle or disturbance. Whatever had happened to this child, it hadn't happened here. But where had she come from? And whose blood was she covered in?

The ambulance arrived within minutes, followed closely by Nat's partner, Officer Mike Torrino. Mike was a twenty-year veteran with graying temples and the kind of steady demeanor that made him invaluable during crisis situations.

"What do we have?" he asked, approaching as the paramedics began their assessment of the girl.

"Found her wandering the industrial district," Nat explained. "Appears to be in shock, covered in blood but no visible injuries. She hasn't spoken a word."

Mike's expression darkened as he took in the girl's appearance. "Any idea where she came from?"

"No clue." Nat watched as the paramedics loaded the girl

into the ambulance. "I'm going to follow them to the hospital, see if I can get anything from her once she's been examined."

"You do that," Mike said, looking up at the rain that continued to fall. "Gonna be hell to track with all this." He turned away and began examining the area.

"You really think you can find something?"

"Just let me know if she starts talking," he replied, his back to her. Mike never had been one for conversation. At first Nat thought it had been something *she* had done. But it turned out Mike was that way with everyone.

"I'll be in touch." Nat headed for her cruiser. At the hospital, she sat in the emergency room waiting area while doctors examined the girl. When Dr. Patricia Hayes emerged from the examination room two hours later, her expression was grim.

"No physical injuries," the doctor reported. "But she's in a severe state of psychological shock. We've cleaned her up and run some preliminary tests. The blood on her clothing isn't hers—it appears to be from multiple sources."

"Multiple sources?" Nat felt her stomach tighten.

"Different blood types. At least two, possibly three different people." Dr. Hayes lowered her voice. "Whatever this child witnessed or experienced, it was traumatic enough to essentially shut down her conscious mind. She's slipped into what appears to be a protective coma."

"Will she wake up?"

"We don't know. Her vitals are stable, but her brain activity suggests she's retreated somewhere deep inside herself. It could be hours, days, or…" The doctor trailed off, leaving the unspoken possibility hanging in the air.

Nat spent the next hour sitting beside the girl's bed, hoping for some sign of consciousness, some clue about what had happened. The child looked so small and vulnerable in the hospital gown, her dark hair spread across the white pillow. Whoever she was, someone was probably looking for her, worried sick about where she'd gone.

Her radio crackled softly. Mike's voice came through: "Buckley, you need to get back out here."

Nat looked at the sleeping girl one more time, then spoke quietly to the nurse. "If she wakes up, call me immediately."

She met Mike at the edge of the industrial district, where he was standing beside his cruiser with a flashlight in hand and a troubled expression on his face.

"Found a trail that ran off past fourth, tall grass that had been split by something large. Could have been a coyote. But probably the kid," he said without preamble. "Found two footprints further down, a couple of broken branches. Small feet, about the right size for our girl. It leads back into the woods behind the Henderson property."

Nat felt a chill that had nothing to do with the continuing rain. The Henderson property was a sprawling piece of undeveloped land that stretched for miles into the forest. If someone had done something to this child out there, they'd chosen their location well—isolated, difficult to access, the kind of place where screams wouldn't carry.

"How far does the trail go?" she asked.

"About a mile. There's an old cabin back there. It's not accessible from here," Mike's gravelly voice dropped. "Better if we drive around and approach from the front."

It took almost a half hour to circumvent all the way around to the other side of what made up the Henderson property, but they managed to find a dirt and gravel road that led up to the cabin from the front.

The cabin emerged from the trees like something out of a nightmare. It was a small, single-story structure with weathered wood siding and an old shingled roof. Light spilled from the windows, casting yellow rectangles across the forest floor.

They approached carefully, weapons drawn, communicating through hand signals. Nat moved to the front door while Mike circled around to cover the back. The door was slightly ajar, creaking softly in the wind.

Nat pushed it open with her foot and stepped inside, her flashlight beam dancing across the interior. She checked her corners, but as far as she could tell, the small cabin was empty. "Police!" she called out. "Show yourselves." But there was no response.

Mike emerged from the back door, both of them doing a quick sweep of the two-room cabin. It was little more than a living room connected to a kitchen with only two other doors. One led to a bedroom and small bath while the other led to what had to be the basement.

There were no lights on down there.

"Flip you for it?" Nat suggested.

Mike just gave her an exasperated look and made his way down the stairs first, not bothering to argue the point. If there was something she could say about her partner, it was that he wasn't timid.

The basement was little more than four concrete walls that opened up into a garage space that probably led up to the gravel road outside. But as Nat shone her flashlight on the concrete floor and stairs, her stomach lurched.

"Mike."

Her flashlight landed on the drops and streaks on the ground. Blood.

Her partner bent down, scanning the floor. The trail led to what looked like an old wooden shelving unit up against one wall.

That didn't make sense. There should be *something* else here.

Her partner reached up and grabbed the shelving unit, giving it a pull. But instead of the unit coming away from the wall, the *entire wall* moved, revealing an opening into a hidden hallway beyond.

"What the hell..." Nat muttered.

Lights strung along the hallway illuminated the passageway and wooden beams supported the ceiling. It looked like it had been dug out almost by hand, though that would have taken forever.

"Do we call in backup now?" Nat asked.

Her partner raised his weapon, pointing it down the hallway and made his way forward. Nat, cursing inwardly, followed along, her heart practically threatening to break out of her ribcage. This was some next-level shit and she wasn't sure she was ready for it.

At the end of the tunnel stood a wooden door, with light spilling from beyond. Her partner held up three fingers, meaning he would open the door on three, and she needed to be ready. She nodded, and unlatched the safety from her weapon.

Mike grabbed the handle, counted down, and opened the door.

Nat held her breath as she made her way inside, her gun raised to shoot anything that might move, but the room was empty.

Except for bloody footprints on the ground. Footprints the size of a child's. They came from a second, larger door. Nat rushed forward, her weapon still ready before Mike could stop her. She had to see what was beyond.

But when she opened that door, Nat's world changed forever.

Chapter One

"I don't think I realized finding that room would dictate how the rest of my life would go," Nat said, her elbows on her knees as she finished relating the story. "What started out as a normal night on patrol was the single biggest turning point for me. After that, it was always 'before' the cabin and... 'after'."

Ivy sat, listening. Not that she had much choice. After Nat had showed up in her apartment, and Ivy had refused to leave with her, Nat had gotten the best of her and drugged her into a stupor. After all that, time had lost some semblance of meaning. She never fully lost consciousness, it was more like a dream state while she was still awake. Ivy knew they had been in a vehicle, but she couldn't have said for how long or where it went. All she knew was when she finally started feeling better—more like herself—she was in a strange house out in the middle of nowhere and dawn was breaking over the horizon.

She'd also found all the doors and windows had been locked from the outside, though the refrigerator was stocked with food and Nat had left a small packet explaining the situation. She'd even outfitted Ivy with an ankle monitor.

None of which Ivy had agreed to.

Despite all of that, when Nat had returned from wherever she'd gone, Ivy had decided to at least hear her out. Fighting was obviously out of the question, since Nat seemed to have the upper hand, which she still didn't understand.

But ever since Nat had accused Ivy of killing her own family, Ivy had flat out rejected the idea. It wasn't possible—Nat was lying for some reason, maybe because *she* was the one responsible. And Ivy hated her for that. So when Nat had offered to explain, Ivy hadn't argued. But she hadn't agreed either. Instead she'd stayed on the only couch in the house, far enough away from Nat that if she made a move for Ivy she could at least try to counter it.

Because this place was a prison. It might look like something else from the outside, but it was clear Nat had been planning this for a while. She'd obviously modified this house so there was no way Ivy could leave without her direct say-so. And the "info packet" had made that clear. Despite it all, Ivy had tried breaking every window in the place, only to find they were made up of ballistic-grade materials, set into steel frames. The doors were much the same way, and didn't have handles on the inside. They operated on some kind of electronic lock.

Nat had engineered a prison for one, and now it finally held the person it had been designed for.

Nat looked up, catching Ivy's eye, but Ivy still refused to talk to the woman. If Nat wanted to spill her guts, that was her prerogative. But Ivy had nothing else to say until she could figure a way out of here and away from this woman.

"I guess you already know what we found in the cabin," Nat continued, seemingly unaffected by Ivy's silence. Whatever all this was, this *performance*, Ivy wasn't about to give it any encouragement. Nat could talk until she was blue in the face, Ivy would never believe she was the one who killed her own family.

"The three of them were there," Nat said. "Multiple stab wounds to each."

Ivy winced and looked away, trying not to let the images fill her mind.

"We even had the murder weapon." Ivy glanced back, her eyes wide, causing Nat to nod. "A knife with a ten-inch blade. It wasn't hard to match it to the wounds on the bodies. And there it was, just lying in the room beside them. There was blood everywhere, *except* on the handle of the knife. Mike... he had been in forensics before transferring over to detective. He pulled the prints. They had been left by a child."

No. That couldn't be possible.

"I had the hospital get a copy of your prints, saying that I needed them to help identify you given you still hadn't woken up and couldn't give us your name. And they were a perfect match."

Her heart was pounding in her ears. "That's a lie," Ivy finally said.

Nat shook her head. "I wish it were. Mike and I searched every inch of that cabin trying to find some evidence to refute it. But... there was nothing."

"Then why wasn't I thrown in jail?" Ivy spat.

Nat took a deep breath, pulling her wild red hair behind her and binding it with a tie. When she looked back up at Ivy, dark bags hung under her eyes. "Because you woke up."

Ivy narrowed her gaze.

"You probably don't remember, but I was there when you came back out of whatever... state you'd been in. And no matter which way I asked, you couldn't remember what happened. The last thing you remembered—"

"—was going to sleep at my house that night," Ivy finished for her.

Nat nodded. "Mike—God, he was a hard-ass. But he had a gentle soul underneath. See, you may not have told us who you were, but we already knew. He recognized your father when we found him—*them*. We knew you were Michael Stanford's daughter: Ivy. And as far as we could tell, you killed both your parents and your brother."

"You never called it in," Ivy said.

"As soon as we realized what it meant for you, I managed to convince him not to."

Ivy sat forward. "Why?"

Nat took a deep breath. "You don't know this, but I have —had a brother. He was about ten years older than me; life was tough for us growing up. He helped provide when my parents—well, anyway. He took care of me. Of course, he did it using illegal methods. He did what he had to do. But he got picked up on a couple of drug charges that landed him in juvie. And then prison." She sighed. "And then one day I got a call from the warden telling me how sorry he was to report that Jerry had been killed in his cell. Took me years of digging but I finally found out a rival gang had gotten word he'd smuggled in something to the prison that competed with their product and they didn't take too kindly to that."

Ivy watched the woman recount the story. She'd never known about a brother. Nat had never mentioned him before.

"That was two years before I started with the force. I knew what a life like that could do to someone. And you—you were only twelve years old. A triple homicide on a *child*."

"But…" Ivy said. "If you thought I did it…why…"

"Why pretend like it hadn't happened?" She leaned back, looked at the ceiling for a moment then turned her attention back to Ivy. "Because I convinced myself I could stop you if it ever came to that. I couldn't see a good reason to destroy four lives when you didn't even remember what you'd done. They would have hammered you in a trial, broken you. Your life… I just couldn't watch that happen to you. You reminded me too much of myself. Of what might have happened if my brother hadn't been there for me. I decided that you needed someone in your corner. And I promised myself that if you ever remembered what you did, or even showed the slightest tendency towards that kind of violence again, I would stop you. Because from what the doctors told me, your memory was essentially a black hole. You had blocked out what had happened to you and buried it so deep that there was a good chance you would never remember. *That* is what I was counting on."

"That's why you stayed close all those years," Ivy felt herself nodding along even though she hadn't meant to.

Nat nodded. "I instructed Mrs. Baker to inform me of any strange behavioral changes, but she said you were always just a quiet kid. That you never really said or spoke up much. And then when Carol adopted you, I thought I could loosen the reins a little."

"You stopped coming around as much," Ivy said.

"I wanted to make sure you could make it on your own. *Had* to make sure. I guess the one thing I underestimated was how determined you'd be to find out what happened to your family."

"Wait," Ivy said, standing. "Is that why you didn't want me to be a detective? Because you thought it might cause some kind of... I dunno, relapse?"

"That was it exactly," Nat said, her demeanor calm. "I thought if you figured out the truth, it would unlock those memories and you might snap."

"But you have no problem telling me now," Ivy argued.

"You're in a safe place," Nat said. "You can't hurt anyone here. Except me, I guess, but I've always been pretty good at defending myself. I don't *want* you to remember, Ivy. I just want you to understand I had no choice. I put this off as long as I could, but when you found out about the cabin, learned that I had lied to cover up what happened to your family... I knew it was only a matter of time. I just wish I'd gotten to you sooner."

"I didn't kill Jasmine Quinn," Ivy said. "I've already told you that. A man named Zimmerman did. I saw it happen."

Nat gave Ivy a quick nod. "I'm watching the investigation. But even if you didn't, I can't risk you relapsing. If you were to go back out there and have a psychotic break, that would be on me. I'd be putting the public at risk." She stood as well. "I'm sorry, Ivy. I tried to give you as much of a life on the outside as I could. But I guess I was only delaying the inevitable."

"You can't keep me here forever," Ivy replied.

"It's either this, or jail," Nat replied.

"No, it isn't. Because if you reveal what I allegedly did, you'd implicate yourself too. You covered up a murder. That's a felony, Nat. And not only that, according to you, you let the murderer herself go free."

Nat nodded. "I did."

"How did you ever get your partner to agree to that?"

"Mike wasn't convinced you were behind it all. But he knew they would railroad you anyway, given you were the only person who could possibly tell anyone what happened. And he had two daughters close to your age. He was willing to give it a shot, but he retired shortly after. Said the pressure of what we'd done was too much. Went into private security."

"He was the man I met on the road that night, wasn't he? The one you met with at the café."

Nat nodded. "And now he's probably in another country. He always knew we were on thin ice. And he always had an exit plan. You finding out about the cabin was the trigger for him to disappear forever."

Ivy couldn't believe this. Her whole life had been a lie. And despite Nat's insistence she was only trying to help, she had doomed Ivy before she'd even had a chance. If only she'd told her about the cabin sooner, Ivy might have been able to get to Jasmine Quinn in time to save her life. She could still see the poor girl every time she closed her eyes, her head separating from her body from that insane contraption Zimmerman had built.

"I still don't believe it," Ivy said as Nat headed for the door.

"You don't have to believe it," Nat replied. "The truth doesn't care whether you believe in it or not. It's still the truth."

"If what you say *is* true, then why am I not trying to kill you right now?" Ivy growled.

"Because you still don't remember what happened," Nat replied. "And honestly, that's probably for the best. But in the event you do, you'll be safe here. And everyone else will be safe from you." As she approached the door to the house, the electronic lock automatically unlatched. She had to be carrying some sort of proximity remote.

Ivy didn't care what anyone said. She wasn't staying here a second longer. And if she had to get into a fistfight with Nat to get her freedom, she would.

She dashed for the door fully intending to push Nat out of the way, but before she got within five feet of her, a surge of white-hot electricity ran up her leg and through her body, causing her to crumple on the floor in a shaking, shivering mess.

"Sorry, kid," Nat said. "That little thing on your ankle, it's not just a monitor. It's attuned to another one I wear." She raised up her pant leg to show a small black band around her ankle, a light flashing on top. "It's been modified so it sends small jolts from a taser into your system if you get too close to me."

Ivy gritted her teeth as residual jolts of electricity flowed through her. She'd been tased a few different times during simulations, but those had been expected. And even when they were, she'd had trouble staying on her feet. This was completely out of the blue.

"I really am sorry, Ivy," Nat said. "But you should have

everything you need here. I'll keep the fridge full, coming by every few days. And there's a couple of weights in one of the bedrooms if you want to workout. Other than that, you have books, puzzles, plenty to keep you busy. Just... no access to the internet or phones obviously."

"Obviously," Ivy muttered, her teeth chattering. "Like your own p-personal pet."

"I'll be back in a day or so," Nat said. And with that, she closed the door behind her, the locking mechanism automatically engaging.

Ivy lay there on the floor, trying to stop the tremors in her body. She didn't care what Nat said. She *hadn't* killed her family. And no matter what it took, she was going to prove it.

But first, she needed to find a way out of this place.

When Nat returned... she'd be more than ready.

Chapter Two

Jonathan White stared at the stack of case files on his desk, but his mind wasn't on the burglary reports or traffic violations that had accumulated over the past week. Instead, he kept thinking about Ivy Bishop and the way she'd looked the last time he'd seen her—exhausted, traumatized, and more isolated than ever. That had been three days ago, and he hadn't heard from her since.

He'd wanted to call. Hell, he'd picked up his phone at least a dozen times, started to dial her number, then set it back down. What was he supposed to say? That night in her apartment, when they'd had that deep conversation, the one that had felt like something... *more*—it was like something had shifted between them. But then everything with the cabin and Zimmerman had exploded, and now she was on administrative leave pending the inquiry board's decision.

The department felt different without her. Quieter, somehow. Jonathan realized how much he'd grown accustomed to her presence, her sharp observations, the way she'd challenge him to think differently about a case. Now he was stuck working solo assignments while Ayford decided whether to bring in a temporary partner.

His phone buzzed against the desk. A text from his mother:

> Called the hospital again. Marie's numbers are worse. When are you coming home?

Jonathan closed his eyes and rubbed his temples. The pressure from Portland had been relentless since the Zimmerman incident made local news. His mother had been calling daily, sometimes twice, insisting that his "dangerous job" in Oakhurst was going to get him killed and that his sister needed him now more than ever.

The guilt was eating him alive. Marie was sick—had been sick for years with some rare blood disorder that the doctors couldn't quite pin down. Every specialist his family's money could buy had examined her, run tests, prescribed treatments, but nothing seemed to work. And here he was, three hours away, chasing criminals and worrying about a partner who might not even want to see him.

But he couldn't leave. Not now. Not when Ivy was going through the worst experience of her career, possibly her life. Not when there were still too many unanswered questions about Zimmerman and what had really happened in that cabin.

Jonathan pulled up the incident reports from the Quinn case on his computer, scrolling through the timeline for what felt like the hundredth time. Something about Zimmerman's story didn't sit right with him. The man was too calm, too prepared, too willing to throw Ivy under the bus. In Jonathan's experience, genuine kidnappers didn't have such elaborate backup plans or such detailed knowledge of police procedures.

The rumors circulating through the department made his blood boil. Yesterday, he'd overheard Officers Kellerman and Price speculating about whether Ivy might have been working with Zimmerman all along. Price had suggested that maybe she'd helped plan the whole thing, that her "discovery" of the tunnel system was too convenient to be coincidental.

Jonathan had shut that down fast, his voice cold and professional as he reminded them that Detective Bishop had risked her life trying to save Jasmine Quinn and that speculation without evidence was both unprofessional and potentially libelous. But he knew the whispers would continue. Small-town police departments were notorious for gossip, and Ivy's suspension only added fuel to the fire.

His computer pinged with an email from the district attorney's office. Zimmerman's preliminary hearing had been moved up to Thursday—two days from now. Jonathan made a note in his calendar. He planned to be there, both to support the case and to get another read on the man who'd caused so much damage.

There was something about Zimmerman that reminded Jonathan of the white-collar criminals his father used to prosecute back in Portland. The same calculating intelligence, the same ability to manipulate situations to their advantage. These weren't crimes of passion or desperation—they were carefully planned operations designed to achieve specific goals. But what had Zimmerman's goal been? What had he wanted with Ivy?

Jonathan's phone rang, interrupting his thoughts. The caller ID showed Lieutenant Ayford's extension.

"White," he answered.

"My office. Now." Ayford's voice was clipped. That probably wasn't a good sign.

Jonathan saved his work and headed down the hallway to Ayford's office, noting the way conversations seemed to stop when he passed. The suspension had made everyone uncomfortable, uncertain about what they could or couldn't discuss. It was like Ivy had become radioactive, and anyone associated with her was potentially contaminated.

Ayford was standing behind his desk when Jonathan entered, his expression grim. "Close the door."

Jonathan complied, then took a seat across from his supervisor. Ayford was a good lieutenant—fair, experienced, not given to unnecessary drama. But the stress of the past week had clearly taken its toll. His usually neat appearance was slightly disheveled, and there were coffee stains on his shirt that suggested he'd been working long hours.

"I need to ask you about Bishop," Ayford said without preamble.

"What about her?"

"When's the last time you spoke with her?"

Jonathan thought back. "Sunday night. After the inquiry board meeting. Why?"

"She was supposed to report to Dr. Mallory yesterday for a psychological evaluation. Part of her suspension requirements. She never showed up."

A cold dread settled in Jonathan's stomach. "Maybe she forgot? Or got the time wrong?"

Ayford shook his head. "Mallory's office called her apartment, her cell phone, even tried reaching her aunt. No response from any of them. I sent Suarez by her place this morning to do a welfare check."

"And?"

"No answer at the door. Landlord let him in with a key." Ayford leaned forward, his elbows on the desk. "Place looked like there might have been some kind of struggle. Furniture knocked over, lamp broken. But no sign of Bishop."

Jonathan felt his heart rate spike. "You think someone took her?"

"I think she realized the inquiry board was going to recommend termination and decided to run before we could question her further about her relationship with Zimmerman. Maybe she decided to stage her escape."

"That's bullshit," Jonathan said, his voice sharper than

he'd intended. "Ivy wouldn't run. And she sure as hell wasn't working with Zimmerman."

Ayford held up a hand. "No matter what really happened, the optics are bad, White. A suspended detective disappears right before a mandatory psych eval? After being involved in a case where a child died and she was the only witness to what happened in that hellish place? Internal Affairs is breathing down my neck, the mayor's office is asking questions, and now I've got a missing officer who might be a flight risk."

"So what are you going to do?"

"I'm going to issue a BOLO. Have her brought in for questioning."

Jonathan stood up abruptly. "You're going to put out a warrant on Ivy? She's a victim here, not a suspect."

"Sit down, White." Ayford's voice carried the authority of command, and Jonathan reluctantly complied. "Look, I hope you're right about Bishop. I really do. She's a good detective, and this department needs good people. But I can't ignore the facts. She's missing, her apartment shows signs of a struggle, and she was already under investigation for her conduct in the Quinn case."

"What if someone took her? What if Zimmerman had accomplices we don't know about?"

"Then we'll find that out when we find her. But until we do, she's officially a person of interest in her own disappearance."

Jonathan clenched his fists in his lap. Everything about this felt wrong. Ivy was methodical, careful, rule-following to a fault. Even when she'd bent procedures during the Quinn investigation, it had been to save a child's life. She wouldn't just disappear, and she certainly wouldn't skip out on her responsibilities to the department.

"I want to investigate her apartment myself," Jonathan said.

"Suarez already processed it."

"With respect, sir, Suarez doesn't know Ivy like I do. He wouldn't know what to look for, what might be out of place."

Ayford studied him for a long moment. "Fine. But you go with backup, and you treat it like a crime scene. No shortcuts, no assumptions. If Bishop is in trouble, we need to find her. If she ran, we need evidence of that too."

"Understood."

"And White? I know you think Bishop got a raw deal with the suspension. Maybe you're right. But until we know what happened to her, we have to consider every possibility. Even the ones we don't like."

Twenty minutes later, Jonathan was standing outside Ivy's apartment building with Officer Martinez, waiting for the landlord to let them in. He'd worked with Martinez before—she was thorough, professional, and less likely to jump to conclusions than some of the other officers.

"You really think she just took off?" Martinez asked as they climbed the stairs to the second floor.

"No," Jonathan said firmly. "Ivy's not a runner. Something happened to her."

The landlord, a nervous middle-aged man named Herbert, fumbled with the keys as he let them into the apartment. "I told the other officer, I didn't hear anything unusual. But I don't live on site, so..."

Jonathan stepped into the apartment and immediately felt the wrongness of the scene. The coffee table was overturned; its contents scattered across the floor. A lamp lay broken near the couch, its shade crushed. The couch itself was askew, as if someone had pushed or knocked it out of the way. There had clearly been a struggle of some kind, or someone had done a damn good job of making it look like it. But he couldn't let his personal feelings interfere right now. He needed to look at this with clear eyes, unburdened by his last time in this apartment.

Martinez was examining the overturned furniture. "Looks like maybe someone surprised her. Or there was an argument that got physical."

Jonathan moved through the apartment methodically, noting what was present and what was missing. Ivy's badge was still in her purse, along with her wallet and credit cards. Her car keys were on the hook by the door. But her cell phone was nowhere to be found, and when he called the number, it went straight to voicemail.

In the bedroom, he found something else that made his stomach clench. The bed was unmade, but there were what looked like small drops of blood on the pillowcase. Not enough to suggest serious injury, but enough to indicate violence.

"Martinez," he called. "In here."

She joined him in the bedroom, following his pointing finger to the bloodstains. "Could be a nosebleed, or maybe she bit her tongue during a struggle."

"Or someone drugged her," Jonathan said grimly. "Hit her with something that caused bleeding, then waited for her to lose consciousness."

They spent an hour processing the scene, bagging potential evidence and photographing everything. Jonathan found himself looking for signs of Ivy's personality in the sparse apartment—books on forensics and psychology, a few photos of her with Aunt Carol, but few other pictures.

It struck him how little personal stuff she had. No mementos from childhood, no pictures of friends, no decorative items that might suggest hobbies or interests beyond work. The apartment felt more like a temporary stopping point than a home, which made him wonder if Ivy had ever really felt settled anywhere since her family's disappearance.

His phone buzzed with another text from his mother:

Doctors want to try a new experimental treatment. They need family consent forms signed. Please come home.

Jonathan stared at the message, feeling pulled in two directions by forces beyond his control. His sister needed him, his mother was counting on him, and his family's resources could provide Marie with medical care that most people could only dream of. But Ivy was missing, possibly kidnapped, and he might be the only person in the department who truly believed she was innocent.

As they finished up at the apartment, Jonathan made a decision. He would stay—attend Zimmerman's hearing on Thursday, but first he needed help from someone with resources the police department didn't have. Someone who knew Ivy well enough to understand what they were really dealing with.

He needed to talk to Oliver.

Chapter Three

THE SILENCE IN THE HOUSE WAS OPPRESSIVE.

Ivy had been awake for three hours, staring at the ceiling of what Nat had designated as "her" bedroom, watching dust motes drift through the morning light that filtered through the bulletproof windows. The electronic ankle monitor felt like a shackle around her leg—which, she supposed, was exactly what it was meant to be.

She'd spent most of the night testing the limits of her prison. The house was maybe twelve hundred square feet, with two bedrooms, a kitchen, a living area, and a single bathroom. Even though Nat had said as much, Ivy had to check anyway. And sure enough, every window was reinforced with steel casing that looked decorative from the outside but were clearly functional. The doors had no interior handles—they operated on some kind of proximity sensor that only responded to whatever device Nat carried.

The refrigerator was indeed well-stocked, as Nat had promised. Fresh produce, frozen meals, even some of Ivy's favorite foods that must have been observed over the years. The attention to detail was unsettling. How long had Nat been planning this?

Ivy turned over, the red numbers from the clock telling her it was a little past five in the morning. Even though the bed was comfortable, she wasn't sure she'd ever be able to sleep in a place like this.

She forced herself to get up and make coffee, needing the routine to anchor herself in reality. Because what Nat had told her couldn't be real. She couldn't have killed her own family. The idea was so fundamentally wrong that her mind rejected it completely.

But as she stood at the kitchen counter, waiting for the coffee to brew, fragments of that night fifteen years ago tried to surface. She'd been having more dreams lately—flashes of images that felt both familiar and foreign. The blood running down her arms. The smell of something metallic. Cold hands.

She pressed her palms against her temples, trying to force the memories to come. If she could just remember what really happened, she could prove Nat wrong. But the harder she tried, the more elusive the memories became, like trying to hold on to an echo.

The coffee finished brewing, and Ivy poured herself a cup, adding cream from the refrigerator. She sat at the small kitchen table and forced herself to think systematically about what Nat had told her.

The facts, as Nat had presented them: Ivy had been found covered in blood, wandering near the industrial district. Her family had been discovered murdered in a cabin in the woods. The murder weapon bore Ivy's fingerprints. She had no memory of the events.

But facts could be manipulated. Evidence could be planted. And there were other explanations for all of it.

Ivy pulled out a notepad she'd found in one of the kitchen drawers and began writing down everything she could remember about that night. Not the trauma—she still couldn't access that—but the mundane details. She'd gone to bed in her room at home. Her father had been reading in his chair, her mother cleaning up after dinner. She'd come up to tuck Ivy in. Her brother Danny had been playing video games in his room.

Normal. Everything had been completely normal.

She wrote down what she remembered about the days leading up to that night. School had been routine. No arguments with her parents, no unusual visitors, no signs that anything was wrong. If she'd been planning to kill her family—which was insane to even consider—wouldn't there have been warning signs? Behavioral changes? Some kind of escalation?

But even as she tried to build a case for her innocence, doubt crept in. She'd always known there was something wrong with her, hadn't she? The way she struggled to connect with people, the nightmares that had plagued her for years. Feeling like she was an outsider no matter what she did to fit in? That she just didn't belong here—not really. What if those weren't symptoms of trauma but signs of something darker?

No. She shook her head firmly, setting down her pen. That was Nat's voice in her head, not her own. Nat had spent fifteen years watching her, looking for signs of violence, expecting her to snap. Of course she'd interpret everything through that lens.

Ivy couldn't help but think about Jasmine Quinn, and guilt threatened to overwhelm her. She had been in much the same position. A normal life suddenly destroyed with no warning. The girl had died because Ivy hadn't been fast enough, smart enough, brave enough to save her. She could still see Jasmine's face in those final moments—terrified but trying to be brave, trusting Ivy to get her out of there.

If Ivy really was capable of the violence Nat accused her of, wouldn't she have been able to kill Zimmerman before he could hurt Jasmine? Wouldn't some primal, protective instinct have taken over?

Instead, she'd frozen. She'd watched in horror as that

contraption did its work, too shocked and traumatized to act. That wasn't the response of someone with murder in her blood—that was the response of someone who'd never seen real violence before.

Zimmerman. Everything came back to him. He was the key to all of this, and Nat was so focused on her fifteen-year-old theory that she couldn't see the real threat.

Ivy spent the rest of the morning going over everything she knew about Zimmerman, writing it all down in careful detail. His knowledge of the cabin. His familiarity with the tunnel system. The way he'd spoken to her at the hospital, like he knew her, like this was all part of some larger plan.

And then there was what he'd said: *"I know the fire that burns within you. The one that asks 'why me, why my family'."* As if Zimmerman knew about other deaths in Ivy's past.

By the time she heard the electronic lock disengaging, Ivy had filled six pages with notes and observations. She looked up to see Nat entering with several bags of groceries and what looked like clean clothes.

"How are you feeling?" Nat asked, setting the bags on the kitchen counter.

"Like a prisoner," Ivy replied flatly.

Nat's expression was carefully neutral as she began unpacking groceries. "I brought some books, too. I remember how much you like to read."

"I like the outside better," Ivy said.

"Sorry, can't do it. Maybe one day. But for now—"

"For now you're just going to hold me like a trapped rat."

The other woman shrugged. "Sorry. That's how it has to be."

"No, it doesn't. Because I didn't do anything."

Nat paused in her unpacking. "Ivy—"

"No, listen to me." Ivy stood up, her notepad in hand. "You're so convinced I killed my family that you're not seeing what's really happening here. Zimmerman isn't just some random kidnapper. He knows things. About me, about my past, about that cabin."

"Of course he knows about the cabin. He owns it."

"For how long?" Ivy challenged, careful to stay at least five feet away from Nat. She didn't want another shock sending her into convulsions. "When did he buy it? Was it before or after my family was killed there?"

Nat turned to face her fully. "What are you suggesting?"

"I'm suggesting that maybe—just maybe—you got it wrong fifteen years ago. Maybe the real killer got away while you were so busy trying to protect a twelve-year-old girl who was just as much a victim as the rest of her family."

Nat's jaw tightened. "The evidence—"

"The evidence was my fingerprints on a knife. But who says I put them there? Who says I wasn't forced to touch it, or that someone didn't plant them?" Ivy held up her notepad. "At the hospital, Zimmerman asked me something. He knew about what happened to my family. How could he have known that if he wasn't involved?"

"You're grasping at straws."

"Am I? Or are you so invested in your version of events that you can't consider alternatives?" Ivy's voice grew more intense. "Think about it, Nat. You've spent fifteen years of your life believing I was a killer. You've structured your entire career around watching me. You've sacrificed your marriage, your relationship with your daughter, all of it based on one interpretation of evidence that could have other explanations."

Nat flinched at the mention of her family, but her voice remained steady. "I know what I saw that night. You should be thanking me."

"You saw a traumatized child covered in her family's blood. That doesn't make her the killer." Ivy stepped closer, then stopped as she felt the ankle monitor begin to warm—a warning that she was approaching the boundary. "In the cabin, Zimmerman had this whole setup. The tunnel, the chamber, the mechanism he used to..." She swallowed hard. "He'd been planning this for a long time. Years, maybe. And he specifically targeted me. He knew my name, knew about my past. You think that's a coincidence?"

Nat finished unpacking the groceries in silence, her movements precise and controlled. When she finally spoke, her voice was quiet. "Even if you're right about Zimmerman being involved somehow, that doesn't change what happened that night. The physical evidence—"

"Could have been manipulated by someone who knew enough about forensics to make it look convincing." Ivy sat back down at the table, leaning forward earnestly. "I know this is hard to hear. I know you've built your whole life around protecting me from myself. But what if you've been protecting the wrong person? What if the real killer has been out there this whole time, and now he's coming after me to finish what he started?"

For a moment, something flickered in Nat's eyes—doubt, maybe, or fear. But then her expression hardened again. "I can't take that risk."

"What risk? The risk that I might be innocent?"

"The risk that you might remember what you did and do it again." Nat's voice was firm, but Ivy could hear the uncertainty underneath. "I saw you that night, Ivy. You weren't just traumatized—you were gone. Completely dissociated from reality. Whatever happened in that cabin broke something in your mind, and there's no guarantee it won't break again under stress."

Ivy felt a surge of frustration. "Then help me remember! Stop trying to protect me from the truth and help me figure out what really happened. If I did what you think I did, then at least I'll know. But if I didn't—if there's another explanation—then we're wasting time while a killer is still out there."

Nat was quiet for a long moment, her hands gripping the

edge of the counter. When she looked up, her eyes were bright with unshed tears. "Do you have any idea what this has cost me? What I've given up to keep you safe?"

"I never asked you to."

"You were twelve years old! You didn't have a choice in any of this." Nat's composure finally cracked. "I had a wife who loved me, a daughter who needed me, a career that meant everything to me. And it all fell apart because I wanted to save one broken little girl from a system that would have destroyed her."

The words hung in the air between them, raw and painful. Ivy felt a stab of guilt at the anguish in Nat's voice, but she pushed it aside. She wouldn't be held responsible for Nat's actions, not when she didn't have a say in them.

"Then help me now," Ivy said quietly. "Help me find the truth, whatever it is. Because this—" She gestured around the house, at the windows, at the ankle monitor that kept her prisoner. "This isn't living. For either of us."

Nat wiped her eyes with the back of her hand, her professional mask sliding back into place. "It's too risky. I can't..." She turned and headed for the door again.

"They're gonna come looking for me eventually," she called after her.

"No they won't," Nat replied. "Everyone thinks you ran. There's a BOLO out for you."

Anger flooded Ivy's veins. They wanted to *arrest* her? Was she being serious or was this a trick? "Jonathan won't believe it. Neither will Carol."

"I guess we'll see." She disappeared behind the door.

"Nat!"

But the woman was gone before Ivy could say another word, the door lock clicking into place as soon as it was closed.

A fucking BOLO? Really?

Ivy sighed and returned her attention to her notes. She could still see the terror in Jasmine Quinn's eyes, and she recalled how Zimmerman had looked at Ivy afterward—not with the satisfaction of a job well done, but with anticipation, as if this was just the beginning.

Fifteen years ago, a family had been destroyed and a little girl had been left broken and alone. Now another family was suffering because that same little girl—now a woman—hadn't been strong enough or fast enough to save an innocent child.

But if Ivy really was the monster Nat believed her to be, wouldn't Jasmine's death have triggered something? Wouldn't she have felt satisfaction, or at least indifference, rather than this crushing guilt that threatened to consume her?

She picked up her pen and added one more line to her notes: *Zimmerman isn't finished yet.*

Whatever the truth was about that night fifteen years ago, Ivy was going to find it. And then she was going to make sure no other families suffered the way hers had.

But first, she had to find a way out of this house.

Chapter Four

Jonathan drove through the winding roads that led to Oliver's property, his mind churning over what he'd found at Ivy's apartment. The blood on the pillowcase kept flashing through his thoughts—not enough to suggest life-threatening injury, but enough to confirm that violence had occurred. Someone had hurt her, and that someone had taken her against her will.

The radio crackled with routine dispatch calls, but Jonathan barely heard them. His phone had buzzed twice more during the drive with texts from his mother, each one more urgent than the last. *Please come home.* He'd glanced at the messages at red lights but hadn't responded. How could he explain that he couldn't leave now, not when Ivy was missing and possibly in danger?

Oliver's property came into view as Jonathan rounded the final curve. Even from a distance, he could see that something was different. There were additional security cameras mounted on trees that hadn't been there before, and what looked like motion sensors along the driveway. The house itself seemed to hunker down among the trees like a fortress preparing for siege.

Jonathan parked in front of the house, his senses on edge. This place always made him a little nervous and he couldn't explain why. There was just something about Oliver's obvious paranoia he didn't like.

He knocked on the front door, noting the new deadbolt that had been installed since his last visit. He glanced up at the camera trained on the front door, making sure it had a good view of his face. Finally he heard shuffling on the other side of the door.

"Ah Christ," Oliver said as he opened the door. "What do you want?"

Jonathan studied Oliver's appearance. He leaned on a crutch and looked like he hadn't slept in days. His usually precise movements were jerky, agitated, and his hands had a slight tremor. Dark circles shadowed his eyes, and he was dressed in a bathrobe and little else.

"Ivy's missing," Jonathan said without preamble. "I need your help."

Oliver's expression shifted, genuine concern replacing the guarded wariness. "What do you mean missing?"

"She didn't show up for a mandatory psychological evaluation yesterday. When we checked her apartment, there were clear signs of a struggle. Overturned furniture, broken lamp, blood on her pillowcase." Jonathan watched Oliver's face carefully. "Someone took her, and it wasn't voluntary."

Oliver stepped back, allowing Jonathan to enter. The interior of the house showed the same paranoid preparation as the exterior—electronics had been packed into boxes, and multiple computers were running what appeared to be data deletion programs.

"Going somewhere?" Jonathan observed.

"Just covering my bases." Oliver moved to one of the active computers, his fingers flying over the keyboard. "When did this happen?"

"Sometime Sunday night or early Monday morning. She

was supposed to report for evaluation Monday afternoon." Jonathan moved closer, noting the multiple screens displaying various security feeds and what looked like financial transactions. "The department thinks she ran to avoid termination."

"That's bullshit," Oliver said, typing. "Ivy wouldn't do that."

"I know. That's why I'm here." Jonathan pulled out his phone and showed Oliver the crime scene photos he'd taken. "This isn't someone packing in a hurry. This is evidence of a struggle."

Oliver studied the images, his technical mind automatically cataloging details. "The blood could be from a nosebleed. She gets those sometimes, with certain kinds of drugs."

"Drugs?" Jonathan asked.

"Yeah, like allergy meds. They dry out her sinuses and can knock her out. It's why she stays away from them usually." He continued typing. "Any signs of forced entry?"

"None. Which means either she knew her attacker or they had some way of getting in without breaking down the door." Jonathan pocketed his phone. "I think it's connected to Zimmerman."

"I thought Zimmerman was in custody."

"He is. Scheduled for a preliminary hearing Thursday. But after what happened at the cabin I'm not so sure he's working alone. Even if she was on suspension, Ivy should be there at the hearing." Jonathan noticed Oliver flinch at the mention of Thursday, but pressed on. "I think Zimmerman had help. Resources. The kind of resources that could make a suspended detective disappear without a trace."

Oliver's hands stilled on the keyboard. For a moment, something flickered across his face—recognition, maybe, or fear. "What kind of help?"

"That's what I'm hoping you can tell me. You can access systems the department would need a warrant for. And warrants take time. You can get into communications networks, or the surveillance footage from around her building." Jonathan leaned against the desk, his voice taking on the persuasive tone he'd learned during his Portland upbringing. "I know we don't always see eye to eye, but Ivy saved your life when she found you after the attack. She's risked her career multiple times to help you. Now she needs help, and you're the only person I know with the skills to find her."

Oliver was quiet for a long moment, his gaze moving between the computer screens and Jonathan's face. When he finally spoke, his voice was carefully controlled. "I can try to track her phone, but if she was taken by professionals, they would have disabled it immediately."

"Try anyway."

Oliver turned to his keyboard, opening multiple programs and databases with practiced efficiency. Jonathan watched him work, noting the skill with which he navigated various systems. Whatever Oliver's other activities might be, there was no question he was exceptionally talented at what he did.

"Her phone went dark around eleven-thirty Sunday night," Oliver said after several minutes. "Last ping was from her apartment building. After that, nothing."

"No GPS data? No cell tower triangulation?"

"If there was, it's been scrubbed clean." Oliver's frustration was evident in his voice. "Whoever did this knew what they were doing. They either destroyed the phone immediately or used some kind of signal jamming device."

Jonathan felt his first real stab of worry. If Oliver couldn't track Ivy electronically, their options were severely limited. "What about surveillance cameras in her neighborhood? Traffic cameras along possible escape routes?"

Oliver's fingers moved across the keyboard, accessing different systems. "Most of the cameras in that area are privately owned. I can get into some of them, but it'll take time." He paused, glancing at Jonathan. "And it's risky. The kind of searching you're asking me to do leaves traces."

"What kind of traces?"

"The kind that attracts attention from people I really don't want to notice me right now." Oliver's voice carried an edge of fear that Jonathan hadn't heard before. "I'm already walking a tightrope with some very dangerous people. If they think I'm working with law enforcement—"

"Then don't work with law enforcement. Work with me." Jonathan pulled out a chair and sat down, making it clear he wasn't leaving. "Look, I don't pretend to understand your business or the risks you face. But I know Ivy, and I know she wouldn't abandon you if the situation were reversed."

Oliver stared at him for a long moment, clearly weighing something in his mind. Finally, he returned to his computer and began a more intensive search. "This will take a while. The camera systems aren't centralized, and some of them are pretty well protected."

As Oliver worked, Jonathan noticed the tension in the man's shoulders, the way he kept glancing at his phone as if expecting bad news. "You're in trouble, aren't you? Real trouble."

"You're all heart, White, you know that?" Oliver's response was deflective, but Jonathan caught the underlying anxiety.

"Is it related to the attack on you? The people who hurt you?"

Oliver's typing paused. "I'm trying to make things right. But it's complicated, and the people I'm dealing with don't forgive mistakes easily, despite what they say." He turned to look at Jonathan directly. "That's why I need you to understand—I want to help Ivy, but I have limitations right now. I can't do anything that would make my situation worse."

Jonathan felt a surge of frustration. "Your situation? Ivy's been kidnapped and you're worried about your situation?"

"You don't understand—"

"Then explain it to me," Jonathan's voice rose, his professional composure slipping. "Because right now, it looks like you're more concerned about your own problems than helping someone who's always been there for you."

Oliver's face flushed with anger. "You think this is easy for me? You think I don't care what happens to her?" He gestured at the screens around them. "I've been working for eighteen hours straight trying to track down any lead I can find on this Zimmerman guy. But the people I'm involved with—they don't just hurt you when you cross them. They hurt everyone you care about."

The admission hung in the air between them. So that was it. He was trying to distance himself.

"I may have something," Oliver said, turning back to his screen. "Traffic camera picked up a van leaving her neighborhood around midnight Sunday. License plate is obscured, but I can track its route."

Jonathan moved closer to look at the screen. "Where did it go?"

Oliver's fingers flew over the keyboard, following the van's path through various camera feeds. "Industrial district. Same general area where Ivy was found as a child." His voice grew tighter as he continued tracking. "But here's the problem—the van enters the district, but it never leaves. At least not on any route covered by cameras."

"Which means?"

"Either it's still there, or they transferred her to another vehicle inside the district." Oliver pulled up a map of the area. "It's a maze of warehouses and abandoned buildings. Perfect place to hide someone."

Jonathan studied the map, noting the various access points and dead ends. "Can you narrow it down further?"

Oliver worked for another twenty minutes, cross-referencing the van's path with property records and surveillance feeds. When he finally leaned back from his computer, his expression was grim.

"I've got it down to about a six-block area, but that's as precise as I can get with the available data." He printed out a map with the area highlighted. "But... this feels wrong, doesn't it? Why take her to the same area where she was found before? It's too obvious, too connected."

Jonathan took the map, studying the highlighted section. "Maybe that's the point. Maybe whoever has her wants the connection to be obvious."

"I don't know. Seems... off." Oliver's voice was carefully controlled.

Jonathan's phone buzzed with another text from his mother, but he ignored it. Oliver was right—they'd been operating under assumptions that might be completely wrong. If Ivy's disappearance wasn't connected to the Quinn case, then they were looking at something much more complex and potentially much more dangerous.

"Can you get me a list of all the properties in the area?" Jonathan asked. "Every warehouse, every abandoned building, every place someone could hold a person without being noticed."

Oliver nodded and turned back to his computer. "Give me a minute. But just consider—whoever took her, they could have had this planned for a while. They knew her schedule, her apartment security, her psychological state after the suspension. That level of preparation suggests resources and patience."

"And access to information they shouldn't have had," Jonathan added grimly.

As Oliver compiled the property information, Jonathan found himself thinking about Ivy's past, about the fifteen-year-old case that had never been solved. What if her family's disappearance and her current kidnapping were connected not by Zimmerman, but by something else entirely? Something that had been waiting all these years for the right moment to finish what it started?

"Here," Oliver said, handing him several pages of printed data. "Everything I could find about that area."

Jonathan folded the papers and put them in his jacket pocket. "What are you going to do?"

Oliver's expression was carefully neutral. "I'm going to keep working on this from my end. But I need you to understand—there are people I have to answer to, obligations I can't ignore. If helping you puts me in an impossible position…"

"You'll choose yourself over Ivy."

"I'll choose survival over suicide," Oliver corrected. "And right now, the best way I can help her is by staying alive and keeping my access to these systems."

Jonathan headed for the door, his mind already working through the possibilities presented by Oliver's research. As he reached for the handle, Oliver called after him.

"White." He turned to see Oliver's expression had shifted to something more vulnerable. "If you find her… let me know."

Jonathan nodded and walked to his car, the weight of the investigation settling on his shoulders. Somewhere in the industrial district, Ivy could be being held by people who had proven they were willing to kill. People who might have been watching her for years, waiting for the right moment to strike.

He started his engine and headed toward the industrial district. He would find Ivy, but first he needed to figure out who he was really hunting—and why they wanted her badly enough to risk everything to take her.

Chapter Five

It had been exactly twenty-seven hours since Nat had left Ivy alone in what she'd started thinking of as her cage. Twenty-seven hours of pacing the same twelve hundred square feet, testing every possible weakness in Nat's carefully constructed prison. Twenty-seven hours of analyzing her situation with the methodical precision that had made her a good detective—before everything fell apart.

Ivy stood in the kitchen, coffee cup in hand, surveying the house with fresh eyes. She'd spent the first day wallowing in disbelief and anger. The second day had been devoted to denial, hoping Nat would come to her senses and release her. But now, approaching the end of her third day in captivity, Ivy had moved into a different phase entirely: cold, calculated determination.

She wasn't going to wait for Nat to decide her fate. She was going to create her own.

The ankle monitor had a range of approximately four feet from any exterior door or window before it delivered a painful warning shock. She'd tested that boundary multiple times, mapping out exactly where the invisible barriers lay. The device itself was surprisingly sophisticated—waterproof, tamper-resistant, and apparently equipped with sensors that detected any attempt to remove it.

But every system had vulnerabilities. Every prison had weak points. Ivy just had to find them.

She started with the air circulation system. The house had central heating and cooling, which meant ductwork running throughout the structure. If she could access the ducts, she might be able to find an exit point that wasn't covered by the ankle monitor's proximity sensors.

Using a butter knife from the kitchen drawer, Ivy carefully removed the screws from the vent cover in the living room. The metal grate came away easily, revealing a rectangular opening just large enough for a person to crawl through—if that person was significantly smaller than Ivy.

She peered into the darkness with a flashlight she'd found in the bedroom, following the ductwork as far as she could see. The main trunk line ran toward what she assumed was the furnace room, but there were several branch lines that headed in different directions. One appeared to lead toward the exterior wall.

Ivy retrieved a coat hanger from the bedroom closet and straightened it into a measuring device. By carefully probing the ductwork, she determined that the branch line did indeed lead to an external vent—but it was only about six inches in diameter. Even if she could somehow remove the ankle monitor, there was no way she could fit through such a small opening.

She moved on to the second vent, located in the master bedroom. This one was slightly larger, and when she removed the cover, she found something interesting: the ductwork here had been modified. Instead of the standard rectangular ducting, someone had installed what appeared to be a custom piece that was significantly narrower than it should have been.

Nat had anticipated this escape route and deliberately blocked it.

One Dark Night

Ivy sat back on her heels, considering this development. The fact that Nat had modified the ductwork meant she'd put serious thought into preventing escape attempts. But it also meant Nat was thinking like a jailer rather than like someone who truly believed she was protecting Ivy. Protective custody didn't typically require extensive anti-escape modifications.

That realization strengthened Ivy's resolve. If Nat was thinking like a jailer, then Ivy needed to think like an escapee.

She replaced the vent covers and moved on to her next target: the attic access. Most houses had some kind of entry point to the space above the ceiling, usually through a panel in a hallway or closet. It only took a few minutes of careful searching before she found it—a rectangular outline in the ceiling of the hallway between the two bedrooms.

The panel had been painted over, and when Ivy probed the edges with her knife, she discovered it had been sealed with what felt like silicone caulk. But unlike the ductwork modifications, this appeared to be a hasty job. The caulk was uneven, and in some places, it hadn't fully adhered to the ceiling tile.

Ivy returned to the kitchen and assembled her tools: the butter knife, a larger carving knife, a metal spatula, and a wooden spoon. Working carefully, she began chipping away at the caulk around the panel's perimeter.

It was tedious work. The silicone was stubborn, and she had to be careful not to damage the ceiling tile in a way that would be immediately obvious to Nat. But gradually, she worked her way around the entire panel, loosening the seal bit by bit.

After two hours of work, the panel was loose enough that she could lift one corner and peer into the space above. Nat had left an emergency flashlight in the bedroom, which Ivy used to survey the space. The flashlight revealed wooden joists, insulation, and what appeared to be a plywood floor extending across part of the attic space.

More importantly, she could see daylight filtering in from what had to be an external vent or window.

Ivy's pulse quickened. This might actually work. If she could get into the attic space and find a way to the exterior opening, she might be able to escape without triggering the ankle monitor. The device seemed to be calibrated for horizontal movement toward doors and windows, not vertical movement through the ceiling.

She carefully replaced the panel and cleaned up the caulk debris, then spent the rest of the afternoon planning her ascent. She would need something to stand on—the hallway ceiling was at least nine feet high. The kitchen chairs were sturdy enough to support her weight, but she'd need to stack them or find some other way to reach the opening.

As evening approached, Ivy made her decision. She would attempt the escape that night, when Nat was least likely to be monitoring whatever surveillance system she had in place. The woman had to sleep sometime, and Ivy's best chance was during those hours of reduced vigilance.

She prepared carefully, laying out her tools and planning her sequence of movements. She would use the kitchen table, pushed against the hallway wall, with a chair on top to give her the height she needed. Once in the attic, she would follow the light source to what she hoped was an external opening.

She tried to get a few hours' rest, and then just past two in the morning, Ivy put her plan into action.

Moving as quietly as possible, she dragged the kitchen table into the hallway and positioned it directly beneath the access panel. The furniture made some noise against the hardwood floor, but nothing that should be noticeable. She wasn't sure how far away Nat stayed but the house seemed relatively isolated out here. It wasn't as if she was going to wake up any neighbors; but that wasn't what concerned her. Instead she was more concerned about any monitoring devices Nat may have set up to detect anomalies in sound, like a glass-break sensor.

Because as well as Nat knew Ivy, the opposite was also true. Ivy had spent most of her life looking up to the woman, learning everything about her. And Nat wasn't stupid. If Ivy was going to do this, she had to take every precaution.

Next came the chair, carefully lifted onto the table and positioned for maximum stability. Ivy tested the setup with her weight, ensuring it could support her climb into the attic.

Working by feel more than sight, Ivy used her tools to completely remove the loose panel. Cool air flowed down from the opening, carrying the scent of wood and insulation.

She climbed onto the table, then onto the chair, stretching to reach the opening. Her fingertips found the edge of the attic floor, and she hauled herself up with the upper body strength she'd developed through years of police academy training and departmental fitness requirements.

The attic space was larger than she'd expected, with enough clearance for her to move in a crouch. Following the faint light source, she made her way across the joists toward what she hoped was freedom.

That's when the ankle monitor began to vibrate.

Not the sharp shock that indicated she'd crossed a boundary, but a steady, warning pulse that meant she was approaching one. Ivy froze, suddenly understanding the true sophistication of Nat's system. The monitor wasn't just calibrated for horizontal movement—it was tracking her three-dimensional position relative to the exterior walls of the house.

The vibration intensified as she moved toward the light source, becoming almost unbearable as she approached what she could now see was a small window set into the gable end of the house. She was perhaps six feet from potential freedom when the first shock hit.

The electrical pulse sent her tumbling backward, her

muscles seizing as the current coursed through her body. She managed to catch herself before falling through the access opening, but the message was clear: this escape route was also anticipated and blocked.

"Goddammit!" she shouted, her voice echoing in the confined space. She knew there had to be cameras, knew Nat was probably watching her right now. "You can't just keep me here like this!"

The ankle monitor delivered another shock, almost as if it were triggered by her raised voice and agitated movement.

"I deserve better than this!" Ivy yelled, her voice breaking with frustration and desperation. "I deserve the chance to prove my innocence!"

She made her way back to the access opening, lowering herself carefully onto the chair and then the table. The ankle monitor continued its warning vibrations until she was back on the ground floor, finally falling silent as she moved away from the hallway.

Ivy slumped against the living room wall, her body still trembling from the electrical shocks. But beneath the physical discomfort, her analytical mind was processing what she'd learned. Nat's system was more sophisticated than she'd initially realized, but it wasn't perfect. The fact that she'd been able to get as far as she had meant there were still possibilities.

She just needed to be smarter about finding them.

As she returned the furniture to its original positions and cleaned up any evidence of her escape attempt, Ivy's determination solidified into something harder and more focused.

Because if there was one thing her years as a detective had taught her, it was that every criminal, no matter how careful, eventually made a mistake. And when Nat made hers, Ivy would be ready.

Chapter Six

JONATHAN ADJUSTED HIS POSITION IN THE HARD WOODEN SEAT of the Clackamas County Courthouse, his notebook balanced on his knee as he studied the man who might hold answers about Ivy's disappearance. The fluorescent lighting overhead cast stark shadows across the gallery, emphasizing the tension that permeated the room like static electricity before a storm.

Jason Zimmerman sat at the defense table in standard orange county jail attire, his hands secured with belly chains that connected to ankle shackles. From Jonathan's vantage point in the third row, the defendant appeared unnaturally composed for someone facing serious felony charges. Most arrestees displayed some combination of anxiety, defiance, or resignation during their first court appearance. Zimmerman, for some reason, exhibited none of these typical responses.

Instead, he conducted what appeared to be a methodical survey of the courtroom, his eyes moving systematically across each face in the gallery with the precision of someone who seemed to be taking mental notes, cataloging people, things, routes. Jonathan thought maybe he was attempting to plan an escape route should the opportunity arise, but with his shackles, there was no chance of him going anywhere. So what was he doing?

When his gaze settled on Jonathan, it lingered with unmistakable recognition and something that resembled expectation, as if Zimmerman had been looking for him.

The man's gaze unsettled Jonathan more than he cared to admit. How did Zimmerman know who he was? Their only previous interaction had occurred in the chaos following Jasmine Quinn's death, when standard procedures kept witnesses and suspects separated. Yet Zimmerman's focused attention suggested some kind of uncanny familiarity.

Jonathan's investigation over the past forty-eight hours had yielded frustratingly limited results. Using Oliver's intelligence about the industrial district, he had diligently poured through every accessible warehouse and abandoned building within the six-block radius where the suspicious van had disappeared from camera coverage. It had taken a solid sixteen hours across two days—examining loading docks, checking for signs of recent occupancy, interviewing security guards and maintenance workers who might have observed unusual activity.

And what did he have to show for all that work? Nothing. He had discovered evidence of recent activity in several locations—discarded food containers with fresh dates, tire tracks in areas that should have been undisturbed, even what appeared to be a makeshift tent home in one abandoned office building. But nothing that pointed to Ivy or gave him a clue about her current location.

In the absence of anything solid from the search, he'd turned back to the original case files. But even that had felt inadequate for a case involving missing persons and a traumatized child found covered in blood. Standard investigative protocols would have generated extensive witness statements, detailed forensic analyses, comprehensive interviews with family friends and neighbors, school officials, medical personnel who had treated the child.

Instead, Jonathan had found sparse reporting that read more like administrative summaries than thorough criminal investigations. Key elements were missing entirely—no follow-up interviews with the child after her initial hospital treatment, no standardized canvass of the neighborhood where the family had lived, no apparent efforts to track the family's movements in the days preceding their disappearance.

When he had brought his concerns to Lieutenant Ayford yesterday morning, the response had been dismissive to the point of irritation. "That case has been cold for fifteen years, White. We've got current problems that require our attention. I need you focused on active investigations, not archaeological expeditions through old files."

Ayford hadn't been here back then. And Jonathan understood the pressure he was under. Still, he didn't think dismissing the original case file out of hand was the right move.

Why would experienced detectives do such a poor job of documenting a case involving a missing family and traumatized child? Wasn't that sort of thing a priority back then? All he could think was maybe Ivy had been right; Nat had to be involved somewhere. Nothing else could explain what he was seeing.

The bailiff's voice cut through his analysis. "All rise. The Honorable Judge Patricia Barnes presiding."

Jonathan stood with the rest of the gallery, noting how Zimmerman moved with fluid precision despite his restraints. Most defendants struggled with the ankle chains and belly shackles, but for Zimmerman it was like they weren't even there.

Judge Barnes took her seat with the efficient authority of someone who had presided over thousands of preliminary hearings. She was known throughout the county for running a tight courtroom and moving through procedural matters with minimal tolerance for unnecessary delay or dramatic flourishes.

"The matter before the court is People versus Jason David Zimmerman, case number 2024-CR-8847," Judge Barnes announced. "Defendant is charged with capital murder, kidnapping in the first degree, false imprisonment, and conspiracy to commit murder. Counsel, please state your appearances for the record."

The prosecuting attorney rose first.

"Deborah Rennard for the State of Oregon, Your Honor."

Zimmerman's defense attorney stood next, and Jonathan recognized him immediately. Jerry Macon represented some of Portland's most affluent defendants, charging fees that typically ran into six figures for serious felony cases. His involvement indicated Zimmerman had access to substantial financial resources or powerful connections willing to fund an expensive defense.

"Jerry Macon representing Mr. Zimmerman, Your Honor. May I note for the record that my client maintains his complete innocence of all charges and looks forward to vindicating himself through the judicial process."

Jonathan watched Macon carefully. High-end defense attorneys didn't typically appear at preliminary hearings unless they had been retained well in advance or unless the case involved clients with special considerations. Macon's presence suggested either Zimmerman had known this was coming down the pipeline *or* he had enough money that Macon could put all his other cases on hold. Neither one left a good feeling in Jonathan's gut.

As the hearing progressed through standard procedural openings, Jonathan became aware of movement in the gallery behind him. Turning discreetly, his spine went cold.

Jerry and Brooke Quinn sat a few rows back with their surviving son, Albie, pressed close between them. What were they doing here? Normally families of the victims didn't attend preliminary hearings, especially when the victim had been murdered. It was often too hard on the family.

As expected, the Quinns appeared composed, but beneath their demeanors was a quiet devastation bubbling under the surface. Jerry Quinn's face had the gaunt, hollow appearance of someone who hadn't been eating or sleeping properly for weeks. His hands shook slightly as he gripped the pew-style seating, and his eyes remained fixed on Zimmerman with an intensity that suggested he might launch himself at the man at any second.

Brooke Quinn clutched Albie's hand, her body positioned as if she was prepared to shield him from any threat that might emerge from the courtroom proceedings. Her free hand frequently moved to touch her son's shoulder or adjust his position, seeking constant physical reassurance that he remained safe beside her.

Jonathan forced himself to refocus on Zimmerman's behavior during the proceedings. The defendant's attention continued to drift toward the gallery, but now Jonathan realized he wasn't just observing the attendees—he was specifically tracking the Quinns' reactions and emotional state. When Brooke Quinn's quiet sobbing became audible during the reading of charges, something in Zimmerman's expression shifted. The man almost looked *satisfied* with himself.

The observation sent another chill through Jonathan. Zimmerman wasn't just monitoring the proceedings; he was feeding off the family's pain. How could anyone think Ivy was involved with this man?

The judge called a brief recess due to a procedural matter she had to deal with, which gave Jonathan a moment to grab a breath of fresh air. The atmosphere in the courtroom was stifling and he didn't like being so close to Zimmerman. There was something just… not right about that man.

"Detective White?"

Jonathan looked up to see Mr. Quinn approaching from one of the nearby doors. "I was hoping I could speak with you for a moment."

Jonathan straightened, trying to maintain his professional demeanor. "Of course, Mr. Quinn. How can I help you?"

Quinn glanced around the hallway, as if to make sure no one was eavesdropping. "I need to ask you about Detective Bishop. There are rumors circulating, and I need to understand what really happened that... night."

The question caught Jonathan off guard. He'd been aware of the whispers surrounding Ivy in the station, but he hadn't realized they had started to spread to the general public. That wasn't good.

"What kind of rumors, Mr. Quinn?"

"People are saying she might have been... working with that man," Quinn gestured toward the courtroom where Zimmerman waited. "That she could have prevented what happened to Jasmine if she had really wanted to. I need you to be straight with me, Detective. Was she a part of this? Did she..." He bit his lip as it began to tremble.

Jonathan felt a surge of anger that he carefully suppressed. Quinn was angry, that was understandable. But engaging in this kind of speculation wouldn't do anyone any good. He was looking for someone else to blame, to make Jasmine's death seem like less of a random incident and more like a carefully crafted plan. Because that way, it was easier to accept there wasn't anything else he or his wife could have done.

"Mr. Quinn, I can assure you that Detective Bishop did everything humanly possible to save your daughter. She risked her own life entering that tunnel system and sustained injuries during the rescue attempt. Any rumors you hear that she was involved in the conspiracy are completely unfounded."

Quinn studied Jonathan's face. "Then where is she now? Why isn't she here today? The department won't give us straight answers about her current status. One of my friends on the force told me there's a warrant out for her arrest."

Jonathan suppressed a knee-jerk reaction. That was supposed to be an internal matter only. The fact someone had shared it with a civilian was troubling at best.

"Detective Bishop is dealing with trauma from the incident," Jonathan explained. Quinn didn't need to know any more than he was willing to share. And he certainly didn't need to know Ivy was missing. "The department is handling her situation according to established protocols for officer wellness."

"You don't know where she is?" Quinn's voice was like a hard edge. He didn't bother waiting for Jonathan's confirmation or denial. "She's missing, isn't she? Just like my daughter was missing."

Jonathan didn't like thinking about the similarities between Ivy and Jasmine's disappearances. In both cases, innocent people had been taken against their will by individuals with apparent resources and sophisticated planning capabilities.

"I'm not at liberty to discuss Detective Bishop's current status in detail," Jonathan replied, falling back on the procedural language that was standard for this type of situation. He hated to do it, especially given everything the Quinns had already been through, but he felt like he had no choice. If he gave into an emotional outburst, it would only make things worse for everyone.

Quinn's expression hardened. "My daughter is dead, Detective. Someone needs to be held accountable for that. And if there are people out there who helped make it happen —whether through action or inaction—I want them found and prosecuted. All of them."

Before Jonathan could reply, the bailiff announced that the hearing was resuming. Quinn returned to his seat, but his words echoed in Jonathan's mind as they filed back into the courtroom.

Barnes ran through the procedure quickly before arriving on the matter of bail. Given Zimmerman had pleaded "not guilty," Macon was pushing for Zimmerman to be released on his own recognizance until a trial could be held.

Of course, Prosecutor Rennard argued against any form of pretrial release, presenting evidence of elaborate planning and sophisticated criminal apparatus that suggested both flight risk and continued danger to the community.

"Your Honor, the defendant's actions demonstrate extensive premeditation and access to resources that enabled the construction of elaborate criminal facilities," Rennard argued. "The bladed contraption discovered at the cabin required months or years of preparation. Mr. Zimmerman has shown both the means and the willingness to engage in extended criminal conspiracies that pose ongoing threats to public safety."

"Your Honor, as already stated, my client knew nothing about that equipment," Macon responded quickly. "He's as confused as the rest of us as to what it was doing down there."

"Okay, enough," Barnes said, holding up her hands. Jonathan shot a glance back at the Quinns. Mrs. Quinn was quietly crying while her husband's arm was around her shoulder. Albie only stared into space, his face completely blank. "Given the brutal nature of this crime, bail is denied at this time. I'm not about to let a potential killer out on the streets hoping he'll come back for his hearing."

"Your Honor—" Macon began.

"Save it," she said, slamming her gavel down. "The defendant will be remanded at Clackamas County Correctional until a trial date is set."

Surprisingly, Zimmerman's didn't seem upset. On the contrary, he appeared almost relieved by the decision.

Jonathan felt a small surge of relief himself. Whatever Zimmerman was planning, keeping him in custody eliminated at least one variable from an already complex situation. But the man's calm acceptance unnerved him.

More significantly, Zimmerman's attention returned repeatedly to the gallery during the bail discussion, his eyes moving across the faces in attendance with renewed intensity. When his gaze settled on Jonathan again, he made a subtle gesture—barely perceptible but clearly intentional. A slight nod that suggested acknowledgment and perhaps invitation. Jonathan narrowed his gaze. What was he playing at?

Jonathan gathered his notes and prepared to leave the courtroom, eager to get some fresh air. The courtroom was stifling, as if the weight of Zimmerman's crime acted like a dark smoke clouding up the atmosphere. What was worse, Zimmerman's behavior suggested confidence, bravado even. The man acted as if he was about to have a relaxing weekend at a posh country club, not be remanded for what could be years in a state correctional prison.

As the gallery emptied, Jonathan caught one final glimpse of the Quinn family. Brooke Quinn supported her husband as they moved toward the exit, while Albie walked close beside them, not leaving his mother's side. Given what they had all been through, Jonathan couldn't blame any of them. They had a right to be angry, to want answers. And to still be cautious.

Walking toward the courthouse exit, Jonathan made a tactical decision about his next steps. The preliminary hearing had given him an insight into Zimmerman—maybe there was something to be discovered there. And it was obvious he was interested in Jonathan. Maybe Jonathan could use that to pump the man for information about Ivy. But how to approach him? And in what capacity?

Nothing about this felt right. But Jonathan was running out of options. And the clock was ticking. There was no telling where Ivy could be or even if she was okay. As far as Jonathan was concerned, he didn't have a choice. He needed to speak to Zimmerman as soon as possible.

Jonathan started his engine and pulled out of the parking lot; his attention going back to the mess he'd found in Ivy's apartment. Somewhere in this complex web of criminal planning and official procedure, Ivy's safety hung in the balance.

The answers he needed might be locked inside Zimmerman's head, but what price would get them back out?

And could Jonathan even pay it?

Chapter Seven

Ivy pressed her fingertips against the ankle monitor, feeling the faint vibration that preceded each shock. Four days of captivity had taught her more about Nat's security system than she'd ever wanted to know, but knowledge was power. And right now, power was the only thing standing between her and a lifetime in this carefully constructed prison.

The device pulsed against her skin in a predictable pattern—thirty seconds of warning vibration before the first mild shock, then escalating voltage if she didn't retreat. But what Nat didn't know was that Ivy had been building up a tolerance. Not just to the electrical current, but to the familiar burning sensation that accompanied any unwanted touch.

Her phobia had always felt like electricity shooting through her nervous system whenever someone made unexpected contact. The ankle monitor's shocks triggered the same response, which meant her brain was treating them as just another version of the same stimulus she'd been fighting her whole adult life. And if there was one thing Ivy had learned over the years—especially recently, it was how to push through that particular kind of pain.

She'd spent the morning timing the monitoring system's

patterns. The cameras in each room operated on a rotation—forty-five seconds focused on one area before shifting to the next. During the transition, there was a three-second blind spot where the previous camera had moved but the next hadn't yet locked on target.

Three seconds wasn't much, but it was enough if she moved fast and stayed committed to her plan.

The attic escape had failed because she'd approached it like her first attempt—cautious, methodical, retreating at the first sign of resistance. Tonight would be different. Tonight she would push through the shocks and accept whatever pain came with freedom.

Ivy glanced at the kitchen clock: 2:47 AM. Nat's pattern suggested she monitored the feeds most actively during evening hours, probably reviewing recorded footage from the day. By three in the morning, surveillance became more automated, relying on motion sensors and alarm triggers rather than real-time observation.

What was the saying? Second time's a charm?

She'd prepared differently this time. Instead of furniture, she'd spent the afternoon creating a makeshift ladder from the wooden shelving in the bedroom closet. The shelves were sturdy enough to support her weight, and the modular design meant she could assemble them quickly and quietly beneath the attic access.

The ankle monitor began its warning vibration as she carried the first shelf into the hallway, but Ivy ignored it. The sensation was unpleasant but manageable—no worse than the burning she felt whenever Jonathan accidentally brushed her hand or Carol tried to hug her goodbye.

She assembled the makeshift ladder with practiced efficiency, muscle memory guiding her movements while her mind focused on the tactical elements of the escape. Camera rotation in seventeen seconds. Access panel still loosened from her previous work. Attic route to the gable window mapped and memorized.

The monitor's vibration intensified as she climbed, but Ivy gritted her teeth and continued upward. Her hands shook as she pushed the panel aside, but she didn't stop.

The first shock came as she hauled herself into the attic space, causing her teeth to chatter. Her vision blurred momentarily, but she forced herself to crawl forward across the joists toward the window she'd identified during her previous attempt.

By the second shock, Ivy's muscles were screaming in protest, but something else was happening too. The electrical sensation was starting to feel less foreign, more like an extension of the touch sensitivity she'd been managing for years. She was right, she *could* adapt. She just had to be willing to push through. She just had to accept the pain, and make it part of herself. Like she always did.

She reached the gable window as the third and fourth shocks hit, this one strong enough to cause her hands to tremble. But instead of retreating, she wrapped her fingers around the window frame and pulled. The old wood groaned in protest, paint flaking away as she worked the window open inch by stubborn inch.

Cool night air rushed through the opening, carrying the scent of pine trees and freedom. Ivy looked down at the drop—maybe twelve feet to the ground, with thick undergrowth that would cushion her landing. Survivable, if she was careful.

The ankle monitor delivered its strongest shock yet, powerful enough to make her whole leg go numb. But Ivy was already committed. She'd come too far to turn back now.

She squeezed through the window opening, her shoulders scraping against the frame as she worked her body outside. For a terrifying moment she was suspended between the house and the drop, held only by her grip on the window sill. Then she let go.

The landing knocked the wind out of her, but the thick moss and fallen leaves absorbed most of the impact. Ivy lay still for a moment, listening for any sign that her escape had triggered additional alarms. The ankle monitor had gone silent—apparently its range didn't extend beyond the house's central system.

She was free.

Ivy pushed herself to her feet and oriented herself in the darkness. Dense forest surrounded the house on all sides, with no visible roads or structures. Nat had chosen her location well—isolated enough that screaming wouldn't bring help, remote enough that escape on foot would be challenging even for someone in good physical condition.

But years of hiking in the Willamette National Forest had taught her basic woodcraft and navigation. Her police training included wilderness survival techniques. And most importantly, now that she was out, there was no way she was going back, no matter how difficult the terrain became.

She chose a direction based on the position of the North Star and began walking, moving as quietly as possible through the underbrush. Every few minutes she paused to listen, but heard only the normal sounds of a forest at night—wind through trees, small animals moving through the undergrowth, the distant call of an owl.

After what felt like hours but was probably only thirty minutes, Ivy saw lights through the trees ahead. She approached carefully, staying low and using the forest cover to conceal her movement. The lights belonged to a small cabin, but not like the one where her family had died. This was clearly a vacation rental or weekend retreat—well-maintained, with a late-model SUV parked in the gravel driveway.

More importantly, she caught sight of a satellite dish on

the roof. A dish that meant the cabin had access to the outside world. A way to call for help.

Ivy was considering how to approach the cabin's occupants when she heard the unmistakable sound of a vehicle approaching through the forest behind her. Headlights swept through the trees, moving fast and getting closer.

Nat had discovered her escape.

Ivy abandoned stealth and ran toward the cabin. She pounded on the front door with both fists, not caring how crazy she might appear to whoever was inside.

"Help! Please, I need help! Someone kidnapped me and—"

The door opened to reveal a middle-aged man in pajamas, his wife peering nervously over his shoulder. Their expressions shifted from annoyance to alarm as they took in Ivy's appearance—torn clothes, scratched arms, the electronic device still attached to her ankle.

"Ma'am, what—" the man began.

"Please, I'm a police detective. Someone kidnapped me and I just escaped. I need to use your phone to call for help." Ivy spoke rapidly, aware that Nat's vehicle was getting closer. "The person who took me is following me. We're all in danger if she finds me here."

The woman gasped and stepped back, but the man remained in the doorway, clearly torn between helping and protecting his family. "Do you have identification?"

Ivy almost laughed at the absurdity of the question. "My kidnapper didn't let me pack a bag. Please, just let me call 911 and I'll wait outside for the police. I won't put you in danger, but I need help."

The vehicle sounds were much closer now. Through the trees, Ivy could see headlights approaching the cabin's driveway.

"She's here," Ivy said, backing away from the door. "Lock

your doors and don't let her in. Tell the police Detective Ivy Bishop needs immediate assistance."

The man started to protest, but Ivy was already moving away from the cabin, leading Nat away from the innocent family who'd had the misfortune of being in the wrong place at the wrong time.

Nat's SUV pulled into the driveway just as Ivy reached the tree line on the opposite side of the clearing. She heard a car door slam, then Nat's voice calling her name with the tone of someone trying to coax a frightened animal.

"Ivy! Come back here. You're going to hurt yourself running around in the dark like this."

Ivy kept moving through the trees, but she was getting tired. The adrenaline of escape was wearing off, replaced by the reality that she was mentally exhausted, and lost in unfamiliar wilderness. Behind her, she could hear Nat talking to the cabin's occupants, probably spinning the version of events so they wouldn't make that call.

She needed a different strategy. Running blindly through the forest would only delay the inevitable—Nat knew these woods better than she did, had probably planned for this exact scenario.

Ivy circled back toward the cabin, moving carefully to avoid detection. Through the windows, she could see Nat inside, talking earnestly with the couple while gesturing toward the forest. Whatever story she was telling, it seemed to be working. The man was nodding sympathetically while his wife wrung her hands and glanced nervously toward where Ivy had disappeared.

Taking a deep breath, Ivy stepped out of the tree line and walked openly toward the cabin's front door. If Nat wanted to convince people that Ivy was dangerous, let her try to do it while Ivy demonstrated exactly the opposite.

"Nat," she called out, her voice carrying clearly across the yard. "I know you can hear me. Come outside. I give up."

The conversation inside the cabin stopped abruptly. A moment later, Nat appeared in the doorway, her expression carefully controlled but her body language tense.

"Ivy, thank God. You scared me to death." Nat's voice carried just the right note of relief and concern for the benefit of their audience. "Come back to the car. We'll get you somewhere safe and figure this out."

"I am safe," Ivy replied, staying well outside the ankle monitor's range. She might be out of the house, but she couldn't risk getting into a physical altercation with Nat that might compromise everything she'd achieved. "Or I was, until you dragged me away from my life and locked me in that house like a prisoner."

"Look. We've talked about this. You've been under tremendous stress since the Quinn case, and—"

"I'm fine." Ivy turned toward the cabin, addressing the couple who were watching from their window. "Now either let me go, or we're going to have a serious problem."

"You just gave yourself up," Nat said.

"I'm not going back to that place," Ivy replied. "I need you to believe in me."

Nat stepped further onto the porch, her hands on her hips.

"You see?" Nat called to the couple. "She's having paranoid delusions. Detective Bishop has been struggling with PTSD since a recent traumatic incident. I'm just trying to get her the help she needs."

It was well-played, Ivy had to admit. Nat's badge would carry more weight with civilians than Ivy's torn clothes and wild story. They had no way of knowing Nat had been suspended. But there was one thing Nat hadn't considered.

"If I'm so dangerous," Ivy said loudly enough for the couple to hear, "then why aren't you calling for backup? Why isn't there an ambulance here, or other officers to help restrain me safely?"

She saw doubt flicker across the woman's face inside the cabin.

"And if I'm really crazy," Ivy continued, "then why am I standing here talking instead of attacking you? Or them? If I were really the violent killer you believe I am, wouldn't I have acted by now?"

Nat's composure cracked slightly. "Ivy, please. You don't understand what you're dealing with. The memories—"

"The memories of being twelve years old and watching my family die? Those memories?" Ivy's voice carried genuine anguish now, but also steel. "I may not remember everything that happened that night, but I remember enough to know I didn't kill them. And the fact that I'm standing here, begging you to let me prove my innocence instead of trying to hurt you, should tell you everything you need to know about who I really am."

The couple watched from their window, clearly torn between competing stories but uncertain how to proceed. The man held a cell phone, but hesitated to use it. If what Nat said was really true and Oakhurst had put out a BOLO on Ivy, then she would be arrested as soon as the couple notified the authorities. But it had to be better than going back to that prison Nat called a house.

Nat watched Ivy carefully, her hand hovering near her weapon but not drawing it. The standoff stretched between them—two women who had once trusted each other completely, now separated by fifteen years of secrets and assumptions.

"I'm not who you think I am," Ivy pleaded. "You've known me longer than anyone. Please."

Something shifted in Nat's expression—doubt, maybe, or the first crack in her certainty.

"If what you say is true, I should have cracked the second I met Kieran Woodward. Or when I found that room beneath the cabin. But I'm still here. I just want to find the truth."

Nat's shoulders sagged slightly. "Ivy—"

"I know you've built your entire career around protecting me from myself. I know what it cost." Ivy's voice softened. "But what if you were wrong? What if the real killer has been out there this whole time while you've been watching an innocent woman?"

"The evidence—"

"Could have been planted. You said it yourself—the knife was just lying there, no blood on the handle despite being used to kill three people. My fingerprints were perfect, undisturbed, like someone had carefully placed them there." Ivy stepped closer, careful to stay outside the ankle monitor's range. "How many crime scenes have you processed, Nat? How many murders? Have you ever seen a killer leave evidence that clean and convenient?"

Nat was quiet for a long moment, her professional mind clearly wrestling with the implications. When she finally spoke, her voice was barely audible. "If you're right... if I've been wrong all this time..."

"Then we prove who really killed my family, and we stop him before he hurts anyone else." Ivy's voice carried conviction. "But first, I need you to trust me. The same way I trusted you back when you were the only person who seemed to care what happened to me."

The couple inside the cabin had retreated deeper into their home, apparently deciding to let the two officers work out their differences without civilian involvement. In the silence that followed, Ivy could only hear the wind through the trees.

Finally, Nat spoke. "Where do you want to start?"

"I want you to take me back home," Ivy said immediately. "Let me look into this on my own. If what you say is true, then I think I deserve at least that much."

Nat nodded slowly. "Only if I can keep you under twenty-four hour surveillance."

"Fine." Anything was better than going back to that house.

Nat glanced toward the cabin, where the couple was undoubtedly still watching from their windows. "What about them?"

"What about them? Tell them Oakhurst PD appreciates their cooperation in a helpless victim training exercise. Or we're two police officers having a professional disagreement that we've resolved through discussion. Happens all the time." Ivy managed a slight smile. "Besides, they've got a good story to tell their friends about two cops showing up at their door in the middle of the night."

For the first time since this nightmare began, something resembling the old Nat flickered in her expression—dry humor mixed with resignation. "You always were too smart for your own good."

"Smart enough to know that running away won't solve anything." Ivy gestured toward the SUV. "So what do you say, Lieutenant? Ready to find out what really happened that night?"

Nat studied her for another moment, then pulled out a key fob and deactivated the ankle monitor with a soft beep. The device fell away from Ivy's leg, leaving only a red mark where it had been attached.

"Get in the car," Nat said quietly. "But Ivy...if you're wrong about this, if you really are what I think you are..."

"Then you'll do whatever you have to do to protect innocent people. I know. It's one of the reasons I always looked up to you." Ivy walked toward the passenger side of the SUV. "But you're wrong about me. You're wrong about what happened that night."

As they drove away from the cabin and deeper into the forest, Ivy felt something she hadn't experienced in days: hope. Not just for her own freedom, but for the possibility that the truth might finally come to light.

And maybe, just maybe, she could find justice for the family she'd lost so long ago.

Chapter Eight

Jonathan signed the transport request form with his usual precise signature, ignoring Lieutenant Ayford's skeptical expression across the desk. The fluorescent lights in the lieutenant's office cast harsh shadows that emphasized the stress lines around Ayford's eyes—lines that had deepened considerably since Ivy's disappearance more than four days ago.

"This is highly irregular, White," Ayford said, reviewing the paperwork with the eye of someone looking for reasons to deny the request. "Prisoner transports aren't investigative opportunities. They're security operations with specific protocols."

"I understand the protocols, sir." Jonathan kept his voice level, professional. "But Zimmerman knows more than he's letting on. He wouldn't talk with his lawyer around during the interrogation, but maybe once I get him alone he'll change his tune. If there's even a chance he has information on Detective Bishop, I need to pursue that lead."

Ayford leaned back in his chair, the leather creaking under his weight. Through the office window, Jonathan could see the department's usual afternoon bustle—officers processing reports, phones ringing with citizen complaints, the mundane machinery of law enforcement that continued regardless of personal crises.

"The man's a manipulator," Ayford pointed out. "Everything he says is calculated to serve his own interests. What makes you think he'll suddenly develop a conscience during a twenty-minute ride to county lockup?"

Jonathan had considered the same question ever since the hearing. Zimmerman's psychological profile suggested sophisticated manipulation tactics and long-term strategic thinking. The man didn't do anything without multiple layers of purpose.

"Because he wants something from me," Jonathan replied. "His behavior in the courtroom was too deliberate, too focused. He's been trying to get my attention specifically, not just any police officer. That suggests he has information he believes only I can act on."

"Or he's playing mind games to delay his processing and create opportunities for appeal." Ayford signed the form with obvious reluctance. "Fine. But you go armed, you follow transport protocols to the letter, and you document everything he says. The last thing this department needs is accusations that we violated a prisoner's rights during questioning."

Jonathan accepted the signed paperwork, already running through the tactical considerations of the assignment. The transport vehicle would be a standard prisoner van with a secured compartment separating the driver's area from the prisoner section. He would ride in the back with Zimmerman, while Officers Suarez and Stevens handled driving and security protocols.

"One more thing," Ayford called as Jonathan reached the door. "Whatever Zimmerman tells you about Bishop, remember that he's already demonstrated a willingness to kill innocent people to achieve his goals. Don't let him manipulate you into compromising this investigation or putting yourself at risk."

Thirty minutes later, Jonathan found himself in the back of the transport van, watching as corrections officers transferred Zimmerman from county holding to the vehicle. The prisoner moved with the same lazy nonchalance Jonathan had observed in the courtroom—no wasted motion, no apparent anxiety about his changing circumstances.

The van's interior was spartanly functional: steel mesh barriers, reinforced glass, communication equipment that allowed contact with the driver compartment. Zimmerman's restraints included leg shackles connected to a belly chain, standard for high-risk prisoner transports. But as the van pulled away from the courthouse, Jonathan noticed the man's relaxed demeanor suggested the restraints were merely inconvenient rather than limiting.

"Detective White," Zimmerman said once they were underway, his voice carrying the conversational tone of someone settling in for a pleasant chat. "I was wondering when we'd have a chance to talk privately."

Jonathan activated the recording device clipped to his vest, following department protocols for prisoner interviews. "You seemed determined to get my attention at your hearing. Considering how tight-lipped you were during your interrogation; I figured perhaps one-on-one might be better."

"Direct. I appreciate that quality in law enforcement." Zimmerman's eyes held an intelligence that made Jonathan's skin crawl. "Though I'm curious—why isn't Detective Bishop here with you? Or did her actions at the cabin perpetuate some kind of… suspension?"

The question contained assumptions that immediately put Jonathan on guard. Zimmerman was fishing for information, trying to determine how much the department knew about Ivy's current status. But his phrasing also suggested knowledge about the circumstances of her disappearance that he shouldn't possess if he was locked up when it happened.

"What recent actions are you referring to?" Jonathan asked.

"Her unauthorized investigation into matters that were better left undisturbed. Her insistence on connecting current events to cases that were resolved years ago." Zimmerman shifted in his restraints. "Detective Bishop has always been too curious for her own good. It's a trait that tends to attract the wrong kind of attention."

Jonathan felt the familiar surge of anger that accompanied any criticism of Ivy, but he forced himself to maintain professional detachment. Zimmerman was trying to provoke an emotional response that would compromise the interview. The manipulation was sophisticated but recognizable.

"What kind of attention?" Jonathan pressed.

"The kind that comes from powerful people who prefer their privacy." Zimmerman's voice carried a note of what sounded like genuine concern. "Detective Bishop is like a rabid dog. She doesn't know when to let go."

The van hit a pothole, jolting both passengers, but Zimmerman continued without missing a beat. "Tell me, Detective White, do you know where she is right now? Have you been in contact with her since she missed her psychological evaluation?"

Jonathan studied Zimmerman's expression, looking for signs of deception or hidden knowledge. How did he know about her psych eval? Or was he just fishing for information, knowing full well Ivy couldn't attend if he had people holding her?

"If you're asking because you're concerned about her welfare," Jonathan said carefully, "then you should know the department is taking the utmost care for her physical and mental state." He wasn't about to give anything away to Zimmerman, not unless the man gave him something first.

Zimmerman sat back, glancing out the window slit as if he were on a Sunday drive. "You know... I always have enjoyed a nice ride in the country, haven't you? We forget the little things in our busy day-to-day lives." He shot Jonathan a mischievous grin. "Tell me about yourself, Detective. How is that sister of yours doing?"

It was as if a flash bang had gone off in front of him—he couldn't see anything but white for a brief second. How did Zimmerman know about Marie? Was he threatening her? Was he threatening his entire family?

"Last I heard, her condition has worsened," Zimmerman said, toying with the words coming out of his mouth.

"My family isn't your concern," Jonathan said through barely gritted teeth.

The man only smiled in return. "It was only an innocent question."

Before Jonathan could say anything else, he heard the distinctive whine of high-performance engines approaching from multiple directions. Through the van's rear window, he saw three black SUVs moving with military precision to surround their vehicle. The lead SUV pulled alongside the driver's compartment while the other two took positions behind and ahead of the transport van.

"Well, well, looks like you'll have to defend your prisoner," Zimmerman observed with the calm satisfaction of someone whose expectations were being met perfectly. "Better get your weapon ready."

Jonathan keyed his radio to warn Suarez and Stevens, but the transmission was met with static. Some kind of jamming equipment was blocking their communications. Through the partition, Jonathan could see Suarez fighting with the steering wheel as the lead SUV forced them toward the shoulder. Suarez's voice crackled through the intercom, tense but professional: "Unknown vehicles attempting vehicular interdiction. Requesting immediate backup at mile marker forty-seven on Highway 26."

But the radio response was nothing but static. The attackers were jamming their communications.

Suarez tried to accelerate past the blocking vehicles, demonstrating the defensive driving techniques they'd all learned at the academy. For a moment, Jonathan thought they might break free of the coordinated attack. But the SUV drivers displayed professional-level tactical driving skills, boxing in the transport van with precision that spoke of military or specialized law enforcement training.

The van was forced to a complete stop on a section of highway bordered by dense forest on both sides. Jonathan's heart was in his throat as he drew his weapon, making sure a round was chambered and the safety was off. Had Zimmerman orchestrated this entire thing? It would explain why he was so calm during his hearing.

Armed figures emerged from the SUVs with coordinated efficiency. Jonathan counted six operatives, all wearing tactical gear and carrying military-grade weapons. Their movements were too exact to be common criminals. These were professionals—probably ex-military or private security contractors with specialized training.

Jonathan positioned himself to defend against entry through the van's rear doors. But his tactical options were severely limited by the confined space and Zimmerman's presence. Any firefight in the confined space would likely result in either him or Zimmerman getting shot. And right now, he needed the man alive.

"On second thought, I wouldn't recommend resistance, Detective," Zimmerman said calmly. "These people look like they are very good at what they do, and they might not like it when others don't cooperate."

The rear doors exploded inward in a shower of metal and glass. Flash-bang grenades followed immediately, filling the confined space with overwhelming light and sound that left Jonathan temporarily blinded and disoriented. Through the ringing in his ears, he heard the distinctive sounds of suppressed gunfire from the driver's compartment.

Strong hands grabbed him, wrenching the weapon from his hand and pulling his arm behind his back so far that he swore they popped it out of the socket. A series of punches and jabs connected with his face and ribs before he was thrown from the vehicle onto the dirt beside the road.

This was it. This was how he was going to die. He felt a boot on his back and the muzzle of a weapon pressed up against the back of his head, most likely from a high-powered automatic weapon of some sort. Jonathan squeezed his eyes closed, waiting for the inevitable.

But it didn't come.

Instead, he caught words in a language he didn't understand, along with the sounds of chains rattling and falling to the metal floor of the van. Footsteps shuffled all around him, moving quickly and methodically.

"Okay," Zimmerman said from behind him. A hand grabbed his wrenched shoulder, sending a wave of pain through Jonathan as he was flipped on his back, staring up at Zimmerman who wore a smile on his face.

"Deliver a message to Detective Bishop for me," Zimmerman said, his voice calm and clear. "Tell her that we're not done yet. And I'll be coming."

Jonathan opened his mouth to speak, only to find the muzzle against the side of his head again.

"And Detective White?" Zimmerman leaned closer, his voice dropping to a whisper. "A little word of advice. Don't bite off more than you can chew. You never know who might get caught up in the crossfire."

The man's message was clear.

Marie.

Zimmerman offered him a wan smile and stood back up, motioning for the rest of the operatives to follow him. Jonathan moved to get up, only to receive a swift kick in the midsection that knocked all the air out of his lungs. Apparently he'd missed the last guy standing behind him. Jonathan doubled over, struggling for breath as the operatives and Zimmerman loaded into the SUVs and drove off, leaving him there by the side of the road.

Through his blurred vision and the van's shattered rear doors, Jonathan could see Suarez and Stevens motionless in the driver's compartment, dark stains spreading across their uniforms. Zimmerman had wanted him there so he could send a message. That was the only reason Jonathan was still alive.

As air finally returned to Jonathan's lungs and he managed to get on his knees, he tried processing the implications of what Zimmerman had revealed. If the man was telling the truth—and the sophisticated nature of his extraction suggested he was—then Zimmerman *didn't* know where Ivy was either. Which meant she was being held by someone else. Or, as Ayford suggested, had gone willingly.

And as much as he wanted to pursue that thread, he knew he needed medical attention, and fast. Thankfully, with the SUVs gone, the radio was again clear, which he used to call for emergency response, his voice hoarse. *Officer down. Multiple casualties. Prisoner escaped with professional assistance. Request immediate backup and medical response.*

As he waited for help to arrive, he realized everything they'd assumed about Ivy's disappearance had been wrong. Zimmerman didn't have her—he'd been looking for her just as desperately as Jonathan was.

The medical team found Jonathan conscious but shaken, sitting beside the transport van with the thousand-yard stare of someone who'd witnessed more than his mind could easily process. As they loaded him into the ambulance for medical evaluation, his thoughts remained focused on a single, terrifying question:

If Zimmerman didn't take Ivy, then who was holding her?

And what did they really want from a detective whose only crime had been asking too many questions about a fifteen-year-old case that was supposedly closed?

As the sedatives from the emergency personnel coursed through his system, causing him to drift off, he could only think of one other person who might be responsible.

The woman who had once been his boss.

Wild red hair and all.

Chapter Nine

Throughout the entire drive, Ivy could practically feel the tension in the air between them. They'd forged an uneasy alliance, but Nat was still acting standoffish, though she had at least given Ivy a large coat and a cap to obscure her given the BOLO was still in effect.

Honestly, if anyone had a reason to be upset here, it was Ivy. After all, she had been the one who was imprisoned, the one who was practically tortured by that ankle device, not to mention having been stolen away from her life without a moment's notice.

But she hadn't wanted to get back into it with Nat on the drive. She just wanted to go home already, to get back to her own place, let Carol and Jonathan and Oliver know she was okay. And hopefully smooth things over with Ayford. Once all that was done, *then* she could start looking into Nat's theories, though she already knew for herself none of it was true. She also wanted to get back to Zimmerman. She needed to talk to him again, find out what he really knew.

She could feel Nat's eyes on her the whole way, the subtle glances every now and again, even as the sun broke over the horizon, lighting up the morning sky. As they entered the city limits, Ivy noticed Nat was taking a very *indirect* route back to her apartment.

"Umm... where are we going?" she asked.

"Back to your place," Nat replied.

"Then why didn't you take Folston Road?" Ivy asked. "You just added an extra twenty minutes to the trip."

"We need to make a quick stop first."

Ivy's stomach bottomed out. "You never were going to take me back home, were you?"

"No, I am," Nat replied. "I stand by my word. But you need to see something first."

"Nat—"

"If you want me to trust you, this is non-negotiable."

"I should have just kicked your ass the second you unlocked that ankle monitor." Ivy crossed her arms. "Stolen your Jeep and came back all on my own."

"This won't take but a few minutes," Nat replied. "Also, give me a little credit here. This is a big step for me."

"Why? Afraid I'm going to go all *crazy* and murder you while you drive?"

"The thought did cross my mind."

Ivy scoffed and sank down in the seat further. "I can't believe after all this time—after everything we've been through, you'd believe that about me. It's like you don't even know me at all."

"I know you well enough," she said. "I flinched every time that temper of yours got the better of you. Or when you would go off by yourself and not report in for a few days. I always wondered what you could be out there doing, if it was taking hold of you."

"*Taking hold of me?*" Ivy shook her head. "You make it sound like I'm possessed."

"The kind of trauma you experienced at a young age could have very well fractured your psyche. I spoke to more than a few specialists about it." Ivy's eyes went wide but Nat shook her head. "I never used your name or details. Just 'hypothetical' scenarios. But more than one told me that your mind could have fractured so badly that you didn't even know what you were doing. That it was a completely different person who killed your family, then left you to pick up the pieces. They never managed to explain why you went into a coma that night after I found you. My theory was it was your brain trying to bury or destroy your other persona. Which is why you can't remember anything."

"That's ludicrous." They passed Grove Street. "I am not schizophrenic. And I don't have multiple personalities."

"You know who says that? Schizophrenics."

"Yeah, are you one then?"

"I guess I wouldn't know unless someone else told me I was."

"That's a convenient bit of circular logic," Ivy muttered under her breath. "So then you think this other person—this killer emerged and killed Jasmine Quinn. Even when I've already told you what happened and I seem to have a perfect memory of that event. There's no blank spot, no missing time. I saw it happen. I *still* see it. I see it every time I close my eyes, every time I fucking *blink!*" She glared at Nat with a burning rage.

Her former boss and friend tightened her features, but didn't look at her.

"Make it make sense, Nat," Ivy said. "Either I'm a cold-blooded killer. Or I'm not. Decide."

"We're here," Nat said, pulling the car to the side of the road.

Ivy looked around. They were in an industrial area of town.

"Know where we are?"

Above them, the street signs indicated they were at the intersection of Braswell and Sixteenth streets. Ivy's hands felt clammy as she surveyed the area before them.

"Right down there, about a hundred feet or so, was where I first found you," Nat said. "The night everything happened." She opened the door and stepped out into the wet morning air. Ivy reached for the handle of the car, her hand beginning to shake slightly. She grabbed the handle and opened the door, following Nat.

"Did you ever come here?" Nat asked, walking around to the back of the Jeep and opening the tool chest in the back. She pulled out a small, brown package.

"Of course," Ivy said. But the truth was she hadn't been in this exact spot since that night, because she hadn't remembered it. And every time she went to ask Nat about it, they were either at odds or not even speaking. Plus, what good would coming out here do? The real location had been the cabin. That's where everything had happened.

Nat took the package and walked down the street, stopping just under a street light. "I was down there." She pointed back towards Ivy. "Patrolling the area. Middle of the night. About two-thirty. Raining like a motherfucker. And all of a sudden, out of the corner of my eye, I see something moving in the rain." She walked out into the middle of the street as Ivy cautiously approached her.

"So I pulled over just about where I've parked now and got out of the car. I called to you at first. Do you remember that?"

Ivy didn't reply.

"You were kind of shuffling along, your clothes stained with blood. At first I thought you'd been in an accident or something, but I couldn't find a scratch on you. *Anywhere.*" She walked back over to the cracked and decaying sidewalk.

"C'mon Nat, what are you trying to prove out here?" Ivy asked, holding her shoulders. Even though the morning was warm, she couldn't get the chill out of her bones. Maybe because she'd had to run through the woods in the middle of the night.

Or maybe it was something else.

Nat reached into the bag, and removed a long knife with a ten-inch blade inside of an evidence bag. The edge of the blade was darkened with a blackish material and it had a solid wooden handle.

Ivy's heart bottomed out. "Is that…"

Nat paused, then nodded.

"You kept it."

"I *should* have thrown it away," she replied. "I wish I could have. But I guess there is just too much cop in me. I couldn't destroy evidence. Not after everything else I'd done."

"Where did you keep it?" Ivy asked.

Nat furrowed her brow. "I buried it. With your family. When you found out about the cabin I thought… I wanted to be prepared."

"You dug it up."

She nodded again.

Ivy took a few tentative steps forward. She knew she should be familiar with the knife, but if someone had asked her, she couldn't say she'd ever seen it before. Other than the fact it looked like a standard kitchen knife, there was a symbol carved into the back of the handle.

"What's that symbol?"

Nat sighed. "It's the manufacturer's mark. *Dolphin Kitchenware*."

Ivy swallowed. "I know you think I should know all about this, but Nat, I swear to you I've never seen that before in my life."

"Yeah. I guess you haven't," the other woman replied, putting it back into the bag.

Ivy arched an eyebrow, though she stayed where she was. Nat was acting very strangely. There was no telling what she might do. "I haven't," she repeated, making sure she heard what she thought she heard.

"I've been a cop for a long time. Lost count of how many

suspects I've interviewed. I've watched people make up shit about the dumbest things. And I've watched criminals smarter than me get off scot-free. I know when someone is lying to me. And you're not lying."

Ivy didn't know what to say.

Nat took a few steps closer. "I thought... I thought bringing you here might trigger something in you. Showing you the murder weapon might bring out that other side. But I think I already knew it wouldn't work. Because you're right. You went back in that cabin and you watched that poor girl get killed."

"Oh, so *now* you believe me." She had to stop herself from mentally lashing out. But she couldn't keep the words from coming.

"I pulled the report last night, *before* your little escape attempt," she said. "The prosecution believes Zimmerman acted alone, *despite* what the rumor mill has churned up."

Ivy furrowed her brow. "The rumor mill?"

"The point is, I think I may have made a serious mistake," Nat said. "One that stretches back fifteen years."

Ivy took another tentative step forward. "What about all that schizophrenic talk? Couldn't there be another personality just waiting to jump out and start murdering at random?"

Nat cast her gaze at the ground. "To be honest, I don't know if that was ever a realistic possibility. Everyone I spoke with said the odds of that were astronomical and even if it were the case, the personality would have emerged again at some point in the past fifteen years, even if only for a few minutes." She sighed and sat on the edge of the curb just as a large dump truck went rumbling by. "You know how when you tell a lie, you have to keep lying in order for the story to make sense?" She was staring across the street, but in reality she wasn't looking at anything, at least as far as Ivy could tell.

Ivy took a seat beside her. Closer than they'd been in the car.

"I think that's what I did. I was just so determined to see that you wouldn't face the kind of life my brother had—that you would actually have a future, I kept making the 'evidence' fit my narrative. I broke the first rule of detective work. I let my personal biases determine the course of the case." She turned to Ivy. "And I may have ruined both our lives in the process."

"You thought you were doing the right thing," Ivy said. "You were willing to give someone a chance who—in your mind—had no chances left. You put everything on the line for me. I just didn't realize until now what that meant."

"Sam… Audrey," Nat said. "My whole career… all down the drain."

"You can't beat yourself up for this," Ivy said. "What's done is done. You made a decision based on the information you had at the time."

She shook her head. "I should have talked to you sooner. I should have…fuck, I dunno."

"You thought it would only make things worse," Ivy said, finding it strange that she was trying to comfort the same person who held her prisoner not more than twelve hours ago. "Nat. You did the best you could."

When the older woman turned to her, her eyes had begun to shimmer. "What am I going to do?"

"You're going to help me get to the bottom of this," Ivy said. "Zimmerman is obviously connected to all this in some way. I don't know if he was behind what happened to my family or not, but I'll be damned if I'm not about to find out. We need to go back to Ayford and Armstrong, explain the situation. I want a go at Zimmerman. Assuming I'm not going to be charged with manslaughter, that is."

"There's just one small problem with that plan," Nat said. "Zimmerman escaped custody. He's MIA."

Chapter Ten

The hospital room smelled like disinfectant and bad coffee, a combination that made Jonathan's already-queasy stomach churn as he shifted against the pillows propped behind his back. His left shoulder was immobilized in a sling, the torn ligament a constant reminder of yesterday's disaster. The pain medication made everything feel slightly fuzzy around the edges, but his mind was sharp enough to replay the attack over and over, looking for clues he might have missed.

Suarez and Stevens were dead. Two good officers who'd had families waiting for them at home. Jonathan stared at the ceiling tiles, counting the holes in the acoustic panels to keep himself from thinking about their final moments. The medical examiner had confirmed what Jonathan already knew—both men had been shot execution-style after the initial flash-bang assault. Professional job.

His phone buzzed against the hospital bed's side rail. Another text from his mother: *Marie had a bad night. Doctors are concerned.*

Jonathan closed his eyes and tried to push down the guilt that threatened to overwhelm him. Every night was a bad night according to his mother. Every day she acted like Marie was on her deathbed, when in reality she was living her best life, dealing with her illness on a daily basis. Was she the picture of heath? No. But she also wasn't some walking corpse, minutes from death.

But of course, thinking of his sister only brought back Zimmerman's words to him.

Don't bite off more than you can chew. You never know who might get caught up in the crossfire. The threat to Marie had been clear enough, but how did Zimmerman even know about her? That had been a message all on its own, one that stayed in the forefront of his mind.

He pulled up his laptop from the bedside table, wincing as the movement sent fresh pain through his shoulder. If Zimmerman had access to information about Jonathan's personal life, then the man had resources far beyond what they'd initially suspected. He had to figure out exactly who they were dealing with.

The basic biographical information came up easily enough. Jason David Zimmerman, fifty-three years old, licensed psychologist with a practice in Portland. Graduate degree from Oregon Health & Science University, internship at a private psychiatric facility in California, clean criminal record until the Quinn case. On the surface, he looked like exactly what he claimed to be—a respected mental health professional who'd somehow gone off the rails.

But Jonathan knew to look deeper than surface appearances. He pulled up property records, financial filings, professional licensing databases. The cabin where Jasmine Quinn had died was registered to Zimmerman, purchased fifteen years ago for cash. No mortgage, no financing. Just a straight cash transaction for a quarter million dollars.

Where did a graduate psychology student get that kind of money?

Jonathan tried to dig deeper into Zimmerman's financial

history, wishing he had the kind of access Oliver touted. But it was frustratingly impossible to get any useful information and stay within the bounds of the law. He wasn't a hacker—he couldn't just go out and scrape whatever information from the web he wanted. Not to mention any information gained from illegal searches couldn't be used when they did find Zimmerman again.

His eyes began to go fuzzy and he had to close them and lean his head back to keep his head from spinning. Whatever they'd given him was messing with his concentration and giving him vertigo. And he couldn't keep his mind from drifting back to the attack again, to seeing Suarez and Stevens hunched over in their seats, blood splattered all around them.

That could have been him. If not for Zimmerman's insistence that he deliver a message. And Jonathan had put himself in that position without even realizing the risks.

A simple prisoner transport. That was all it had been meant to be.

His phone rang, snapping him awake again. Lieutenant Ayford's name appeared on the caller ID.

"How are you feeling, White?" Ayford's voice carried the strained politeness of someone dealing with too many crises at once.

"Like I got hit by a truck," Jonathan replied, trying to clear his throat. It felt sore and scratchy. "But I'll live. Any word on Zimmerman?"

"Nothing concrete. We've got every agency from here to Canada looking for him, but these guys knew what they were doing. No trace of the extraction vehicles, no witnesses other than you who can provide useful descriptions. It's like they vanished into thin air."

Jonathan wasn't surprised. The operation had been too smooth, too professional to leave obvious traces. "Sir, I've been thinking about Zimmerman's background. This wasn't some spontaneous escape. He has to be in league with some serious players."

"If that's true, there's no record of it," Ayford replied. "I've got half a dozen officers working on it down here."

"The FBI?" Jonathan asked.

"They've been notified. They're staying out of it for right now, but I wouldn't be surprised if they showed up at my door any minute."

"We can handle this," Jonathan said, though he winced as he did, pain shooting through his shoulder.

"That's right, *we* can," Ayford replied. "While you get some rest. I only called to check up on you. And to ask you a question."

"Sure, go ahead," Jonathan said, the pain beginning to subside.

Ayford was quiet for a moment. When he spoke again, his voice was carefully controlled. "White, I need you to give me a straight answer. Did he say anything about Bishop's whereabouts?"

The question contained implications that made Jonathan's chest tighten. "No, sir. He didn't seem to know anything about her, other than she wasn't where she's supposed to be."

"What does that mean?" Ayford asked.

"I don't know. It was as if he was looking for her as well. Which tells me he wasn't behind her disappearance."

"Or he's trying to throw you off the trail," Ayford said.

Jonathan shook his head. "He had a gun to my head. He could have told me anything he wanted. I'm—*we're* not a threat to him."

"Then where is she?" Ayford pressed. "Why did she miss her psychological evaluation? Why does her apartment look like a crime scene? I'm trying to give her the benefit of the doubt here, but I need answers."

Jonathan chose his words carefully. "I think someone else

took her. But I don't think it was the same people who funded Zimmerman."

"Who?"

"I'm not sure yet," Jonathan said. It wasn't technically a lie, because he *wasn't* sure. But he had very good reason to believe that his old boss Natasha Buckley hadn't disappeared as completely from the world as she'd made it seem.

Ayford sighed heavily. "The task force is already out hunting for Zimmerman. We're going to find him and bring him back to face justice for what happened to Suarez and Stevens. *And* the Quinn girl."

"Good." But even as Jonathan said it, he knew Zimmerman wouldn't be found unless he wanted to be. The man had planned every aspect of his capture and escape with surgical precision. He was probably already on his way out of the country, or holed up in some safe house that his criminal associates had prepared years in advance.

"I want you to take some time off," Ayford continued. "Get that shoulder healed, spend some time with your family. Let the task force handle this."

"With respect, sir, I can't do that. Not while Ivy is still missing."

"White—"

"She's my partner. She's saved my life more than once, and I'm not abandoning her now." Jonathan's voice carried a finality that he hoped would end the discussion. "I'll follow doctor's orders about my shoulder, but I'm staying on this case."

"I know you mean well, White, but you're officially on leave until further notice. I'll be in touch."

After Ayford hung up, promising to keep Jonathan informed about the task force's progress, Jonathan set his laptop to the side, feeling deflated. If he couldn't even work the case, what good was he? How could he help Ivy if he wasn't even a cop anymore?

"You look like hell."

Jonathan glanced up to see Alice Blair standing in the doorway, her expression carrying the particular brand of sarcasm that had once been endearing but now felt more like a defense mechanism. She looked tired, which, for Alice, meant her makeup was only slightly smudged and her lipstick wasn't as bold as normal.

"Alice." He tried sitting up higher in the bed. "How's your mother doing?"

Something flickered across Alice's face—pain, maybe, or exhaustion. "She had a good week, then took a turn for the worse yesterday. Doctors are talking about… adjusting expectations." She moved into the room but stayed near the door, as if keeping her escape route open. "Thanks for asking." She looked him up and down. "You look like death rolled over."

"Just stopped by to bust my balls, huh?"

"As much fun as that would be, no." Alice pulled out her phone and scrolled through what looked like a series of photos. "I've been monitoring those surveillance cameras you had me set up in the industrial district. The ones you were too polite to mention you'd installed without proper warrants when you asked for my help in procuring them."

Jonathan felt a flush of embarrassment. After coming up empty in his search, he'd figured whoever took Ivy might return to the same area eventually. But the only way to monitor such a large area was to set up cameras, strategically placed at certain intersections in the industrial district. And he'd contacted Alice for her help in buying and setting them up, since she had so many contacts in the industry. That… and he trusted her not to say anything to anyone. It wasn't as if what he was doing was exactly legal. But he'd been desperate. "Alice, I can explain—"

"Save it. I kind of like this new, rule-breaking Detective White. But you should have been straight with me. I figured someone needed to keep an eye on what you were doing before you got yourself arrested for illegal surveillance." She found what she was looking for on her phone and held it up for him to see. "Lucky for you I did."

The image was grainy, clearly taken from a distance, but Jonathan's heart nearly stopped when he recognized the figures it showed. Ivy stood next to another woman with red hair, both of them apparently engaged in serious conversation next to a Jeep parked on a street he recognized as being in the industrial district. Was that *Nat*? Where had she come from?

"When was this taken?" he asked, his voice barely above a whisper.

"This morning. About six-thirty." Alice swiped to the next image, which showed Ivy and the red-haired woman walking together, examining something the other woman was holding. "Your missing detective isn't as missing as everyone thinks."

Jonathan studied the photos, relief flooding through him so intensely that his hands started shaking. Ivy was alive. She was free. She was moving around under her own power, not bound or restrained or obviously under duress. Did that mean she'd gone with Nat willingly? If so, why the mess at her apartment?

But the implications were complicated. If Ivy was free, why hadn't she contacted the department? Why hadn't she returned to her apartment or reached out to let people know she was safe? Why hadn't she called him?

"That's Lieutenant Buckley, isn't it?" Alice asked.

Jonathan nodded.

"They're in this together. Whatever 'this' is."

"I'm not sure about that yet," Jonathan replied, pulling the covers off. "I need to get out of here." He moved toward the edge of the bed.

"Whoa, hold up there, hero." Alice stepped forward, throwing the covers back over him. "You've got a torn ligament and enough painkillers in your system to drop a rhino. Where exactly do you think you're going?"

"To find Ivy before something happens to her."

"And how do you plan to do that? Drive around the city with one arm hoping to spot her on street corners?" Alice shook her head. "Use your brain, dummy. If she's with Buckley, there's probably a reason. Maybe she's finally getting answers about her family. Maybe she's exactly where she needs to be."

Jonathan wanted to argue, but Alice was right about his physical condition. The painkillers were making it difficult to think clearly, and his shoulder would be useless for at least another week. Any attempt at active investigation would be hampered by his injuries.

But he couldn't just lie here while Ivy was out there, possibly in danger from someone she trusted.

"What do you suggest?" he asked.

Alice pulled out a chair and sat down, her expression shifting to something more businesslike. "I suggest we use what we're both good at. You're good at police work, analyzing evidence, following leads. I'm good at finding information, asking the right questions, getting people to talk." She gestured toward his laptop. "Let me start investigating this Zimmerman asshole while I start asking my resources about Bishop. You lay there like a soft potato and heal. Then you and I can figure out our next steps, *together*."

It wasn't the kind of partnership Jonathan would have chosen under normal circumstances, but normal circumstances had gone out the window the moment Ivy disappeared. And Alice had already proven herself capable of finding information that official channels had missed.

"Why?" he asked. "Why are you willing to help with this?"

Alice was quiet for a moment, her gaze drifting toward the window. "Because my mother is dying in a room three floors up, and I know what it feels like to lose someone important to you. Because fifteen years ago, a twelve-year-old girl lost her entire family and never got real answers about what happened to them." She looked back at Jonathan. "And because I think you're right about Ivy. She's innocent, and she deserves better than what she's gotten from your department."

Jonathan nodded, feeling something that might have been gratitude mixed with respect for the woman who'd once been the most important person in his life. Their romantic relationship had ended badly, but that didn't mean they couldn't work together to help someone who needed it.

"Okay," he said. "Partners. For now."

Alice smiled, and for a moment, Jonathan caught a glimpse of the woman he'd once loved. "Don't get any ideas, hot shot. This is strictly professional."

"Wouldn't dream of it."

But as Alice left him to his work, Jonathan found himself hoping that when this was all over, he'd be able to tell Ivy that she'd been right to trust people despite everything she'd been through. That sometimes, when it really mattered, people came through for each other.

He just hoped they wouldn't be too late.

Chapter Eleven

THE NEWS ABOUT ZIMMERMAN'S ESCAPE HAD FLOORED IVY. She gripped the edge of the Jeep's passenger seat as Nat pulled away from the curb, her mind racing through the implications. The man who had built an elaborate torture chamber, who had murdered Jasmine Quinn in front of her face, was now free to continue whatever sick game he'd been playing.

"How did he get out?" Ivy asked, her voice tighter than she'd intended.

"From what I can tell, he was banking on the prisoner transport. It got hit by some professional extractors," Nat replied, her knuckles white on the steering wheel. "That's all I know. Multiple vehicles, coordinated attack. Two officers died in the attack."

"He's not working alone," Ivy said, realizing this was bigger than she had originally thought.

Nat's jaw tightened. "No, and whoever he's working with, they have serious resources."

The familiar burn of guilt spread through Ivy's chest. More people died because she hadn't been fast enough, smart enough to stop this from the beginning. If she'd figured out

Zimmerman's connection to her family sooner, if she'd pushed harder during their conversation at the hospital…

Stop. She forced herself to think like a detective instead of a victim. Zimmerman's escape meant he still had unfinished business. The question was what—and with who else.

"I can't let this happen again," Ivy said, staring out the window.

"What?"

"I can't let him take another victim like Jasmine. I failed once. But not again."

"Ivy, you're exhausted," Nat said. "We both are. You need a good night's sleep in your own bed."

She scoffed. "*Now* you want me to get some rest."

"I always wanted you to get rest," Nat argued. "I was just… misguided about where you should get it." She turned down the next street, heading for Ivy's apartment.

"It's my fault he's still out there," Ivy said. "I should have nailed him to the wall in that damn cabin. I should have stopped him for good. If I'd just…" She trailed off.

"What?"

"I could have taken him down. I had a clear shot."

"You couldn't do that," Nat replied. "You said he was unarmed."

"He might not have had a weapon pointed at me, but he had his hand on the trigger of that damn machine. If I'd realized what was about to happen I could have stopped all of it. I should have just killed him right there."

Nat was silent beside her. Ivy knew she would have been violating her oath as an officer of the law, that there were certain rules they had to follow. But she couldn't see a downside to killing Zimmerman before he had the chance to harm Jasmine. Ivy certainly wouldn't be any worse off. She still would have been suspended or even arrested. And Jasmine would be alive. "We need to find him."

"Ivy, there is a full task force out looking for him. Every department from here to Kansas has him on their watch list."

"They won't find him," she replied, going over everything in her head. Had he gotten arrested on *purpose*? If so, why? He obviously hadn't been worried about getting out if Nat was telling the truth about his extraction.

"Then what makes you think you can?"

"Because I think he wants to find *me*," Ivy said, recalling their discussion in the hospital. Zimmerman had seemed oddly preoccupied with her. In the cabin too. Whatever was going on, Ivy was certain it involved her in some capacity. "We need to go back to the cabin. Find a way to figure out where he's hiding."

"How are we supposed to do that?" Nat asked.

Ivy turned in her seat to face Nat fully. "There's something you don't know about that night with Jasmine. Zimmerman used a chemical compound called Vapoxil to incapacitate the Quinn family before taking them. It's a gaseous sedative that can be administered through HVAC systems."

"You think he used the same method on your family?"

"That's what I went there to check. Because Jonathan and I found a connection between him and an order for the stuff fifteen years ago." The words came out in a rush as the pieces clicked together in Ivy's mind. "He's had all this time to perfect his methods, to plan his next move. He could have spent years preparing for this. I don't know what finally set him off, but whatever it was, everything is in motion now."

Nat pulled into a gas station parking lot and turned off the engine. "Why didn't you mention this before?"

Ivy struggled to explain the fragmented way the realization had come to her. "During the Quinn investigation, Oliver found traces of Vapoxil at their house. It was how Zimmerman got past their security system, how he was able to take both kids without any sign of struggle. But I didn't connect it to my family until…"

Until she'd smelled something in her old house that triggered a memory she couldn't quite grasp. The scent of something chemical and wrong mixed with the terror of waking up somewhere dark and cold.

"Until when?" Nat pressed.

"Until I realized Zimmerman knew too much about me. About my past. He's been studying this case for years." Ivy rubbed her temples, fighting off the headache threatening to break through. "We need to check the cabin's HVAC system. If there are traces of Vapoxil there, even after all this time, it proves he was using the same MO fifteen years ago."

Nat grimaced. "And then what? After fifteen years and multiple crime scenes—"

"It's all we've got." Ivy's voice carried a determination that surprised even her. "Zimmerman is out there, probably planning his next move. If we can establish his pattern, maybe we can figure out his next move."

After a quick stop by Ivy's apartment so she could shower and change into clean clothes, as well as give Nat shit about the state she'd left her apartment in, they headed back out to the cabin. Ivy had only been here twice—once when she'd found Jasmine, and once with Alice when they'd first learned about the place. Both times, adrenaline and crisis had dominated her thoughts. Now, approaching in daylight with Nat beside her, she felt the building's oppressive atmosphere settling around her like a heavy fog.

The cabin looked smaller than she remembered, more ordinary. Crime scene tape still fluttered from the trees, and the front door bore an official seal, but otherwise it could have been any weekend retreat tucked away in the Oregon wilderness. Except for the knowledge of what lay beneath.

"I'll take care of the door," Nat said, producing a lockpick set from her middle console. "Technically, it's still an active crime scene."

"Already a pro with that?" Ivy asked, thinking about how Nat got into her own apartment.

Nat didn't reply, only kept her gaze off Ivy.

They entered through the main door, and Ivy was immediately struck by how normal everything looked now that she knew what lay below. The furniture was basic but comfortable, the kitchen clean and functional. Nothing suggested the horror beneath their feet.

But as they moved through the rooms, Ivy began to notice details that hadn't registered during her previous visits. Family photos on the mantle—but not of Zimmerman's family. The faces were unfamiliar, generic stock photos that came with picture frames. Books on the shelves with uncracked spines, as if they'd been placed for decoration rather than reading.

"This place was staged," she said, running her finger along a dustless shelf. "It's meant to look lived-in, but nobody actually lived here."

Nat opened several kitchen drawers, finding them stocked with new utensils and gadgets still in their packaging. "A front. Question is, a front for what?"

Ivy moved to the HVAC register in the living room and knelt beside it. Using her fingernail, she unscrewed the vent cover and peered inside. The ductwork looked standard, but when Nat shined her phone's flashlight into the system, Ivy saw something that made her pulse quicken.

"I think that's it."

Additional tubing had been installed alongside the main ductwork—thin lines that shouldn't have been there. They connected to what appeared to be a small reservoir system hidden behind the main unit.

"That's not standard HVAC," Nat observed, crouching beside her.

"It's a delivery system. You could introduce anything into

the air circulation—gas, aerosols, chemical compounds." She sat back on her heels. "Vapoxil would disperse through the entire house within minutes."

They checked the other vents throughout the cabin, finding the same modifications in each room. Whoever had installed this system had planned for comprehensive coverage of the entire structure.

As they worked, Ivy found herself fighting waves of disorientation. The cabin's layout felt familiar in a way that went beyond her recent visits. The angle of light through the kitchen window, the creak of floorboards in the hallway—sensory details that triggered recognition without conscious memory.

It was the same familiar sensation that had led her to the tunnel in the first place. The same one that had caused her to leave Alice here to investigate the cabin alone. The one that told her to *get out* and never come back.

Ivy kept her thoughts to herself. Nat was finally accepting her innocence; she didn't need to introduce new complications by admitting to recovered memories that might suggest otherwise.

"We need to check the basement," Ivy said, though the thought made her stomach clench.

The hidden door behind the wall panel was still open, revealing the tunnel system that led to Zimmerman's chamber. But instead of heading directly to the torture room, Ivy examined the tunnel walls more carefully.

The excavation was extensive—far more than could have been accomplished in a few months or even a year. Support beams showed weathering and age that suggested construction had taken place over an extended period. Electrical lines powered LED strips along the walls, and she noticed junction boxes that indicated the system had been expanded multiple times.

"This is a decade's worth of work," she said, running her hand along the wooden supports. "Maybe more."

Nat studied the engineering with a professional eye. "Had to be done gradually, probably during winter months when the property was less likely to be visited. Dirt would need to be removed bit by bit to avoid detection."

"Jesus," Ivy said. "How long was he working on this?"

They reached the chamber where Jasmine had died, and Ivy forced herself to examine it with clinical detachment. The elaborate mechanical system that had killed the girl was gone —removed as evidence—but the mounting points and pulley systems remained. What struck her now was the precision of the construction. Every element had been carefully planned and engineered.

"This wasn't built for Jasmine specifically," Ivy said. "It was built for someone else. She just happened to be the victim who triggered its use. Why were there three seats?"

"Okay, if not for her…who?"

Ivy studied the dimensions of the chamber, the height of the mounting points, the spacing of the restraints. "I don't know." Though she had a sinking thought that made her skin crawl. "Maybe for me. He'd been planning this for years… maybe he thought I'd have a family by now. Other people he could…" She let the thought die in her throat.

Nat examined the measurements and slowly nodded. "But that would mean—"

"That Zimmerman has been planning this for fifteen years. That taking Jasmine was just… practice. Or bait. He hadn't planned for me to get away that night. To get the best of him." Ivy backed away from the chamber, suddenly needing distance from the space that had could have been designed for her own death.

They climbed back through the tunnel system in silence. When they emerged into the cabin's main room, Ivy felt like she could breathe again.

"So what's his endgame?" Nat asked as they secured the property and prepared to leave. "If this was all designed around you, what does he want?"

Ivy considered the question as they walked back to the Jeep. Zimmerman's behavior during their hospital conversation, his knowledge of her past, his willingness to kill Jasmine just to get her attention—it all pointed to an obsession that went far beyond simple revenge.

"I think he wants to finish what he started," she said finally. "Whatever happened to my family that night, I think I was supposed to die with them. The fact that I survived, that I escaped—it left his work incomplete."

"But why? What's his connection to your family? Did you know him before that night?"

Ivy searched her memories—both the clear recollections and the fragmentary flashes that came and went like half-remembered dreams. "I don't remember ever meeting him. My parents never mentioned anyone named Zimmerman. As far as I know, we had no connection to him at all."

That was what made this so terrifying. If Zimmerman's obsession was random, if her family had been chosen arbitrarily, then there was no way to predict his next move. But if there was a connection, something that linked him to her past…

"We need to look at the original case files," Ivy said as they drove away from the cabin. "But this time, I want you looking at them with me. Maybe you'll remember something from back then you *forgot* to include."

Nat nodded grimly. "I can do that. I… admit I probably wasn't as thorough as I should have been. Mike and I were busy trying to… take care of things."

Ivy winced. "What about Mike? Can you get in contact with him? He might remember something too."

Nat shook her head. "No, he's gone. I don't have any way of contacting him again; I've already tried. He's a ghost."

"Then I guess we'll just have to rely on your memory," Ivy replied.

Nat took a deep breath. "The problem now will be how to access the files. With the department looking to arrest you and the fact that I've been placed on suspension for leaving my position means we can't just walk into the precinct and requisition old case files."

"Jonathan can," Ivy said. A pain shot through her as soon as she thought about him. He probably thought she was AWOL like the rest of the department, that she had shirked her responsibility and ran. She only hoped she could convince him that hadn't been the case at all.

"White? There's no way. He's too by the book," Nat countered.

"You don't know him like I do," Ivy said, heading back to the Jeep. "He's changed a lot; he just doesn't show it."

"I guess it's worth a shot," Nat replied. "Are you sure you're ready for this? Once we open that box, once we start down this path, there's no going back."

Ivy thought about Jasmine Quinn's final moments, about Zimmerman somewhere out there planning his next move. Whatever truths waited in those files, whatever pain they might bring, it couldn't be worse than allowing this cycle of sadistic violence to continue.

"I'm ready," she said. "I'll call Jonathan on the way."

Maybe, if they were lucky, they'd find something that would help them stop Zimmerman before he could finish what he'd started fifteen years ago.

Chapter Twelve

ALICE BLAIR NAVIGATED THE STERILE HOSPITAL CORRIDORS with the practiced efficiency of someone who'd spent too many hours in similar places over the past few weeks. The fluorescent lighting cast everything in that particular shade of institutional beige that made even healthy people look sickly. She checked her phone as she walked—two missed calls from the station, three texts from various contacts, and nothing from Jonathan since she'd left him that morning with promises to find information about Ivy's whereabouts.

The cardiac intensive care unit occupied the entire fourth floor, a maze of monitoring equipment and hushed conversations that had become Alice's second home since her mother's condition had deteriorated. She found Room 612 and peered through the glass partition, taking in the sight that had become both familiar and devastating over the past week.

Her mother lay connected to a ventilator, the rhythmic wheeze of the machine marking time in a way that made Alice's chest tight. The doctors had been cautiously optimistic after the surgery, talking about recovery timelines and rehabilitation plans. But optimism had given way to concern, then concern to the kind of careful language medical professionals used when they were preparing families for the worst.

"She had another episode during the night," Dr. Beltran said, appearing beside Alice with the quiet authority of someone who delivered difficult news for a living. "We've stabilized her, but her heart is showing significant strain."

Alice nodded, not trusting herself to speak. The rational part of her mind understood that her mother's condition wasn't anyone's fault—a lifetime of poor health choices and genetic predisposition had created a situation where recovery was always going to be uncertain. But the guilty part, the part that had been secretly relieved when the ambulance took her mother away from her house and back to the hospital, whispered that she was somehow responsible.

"Can I see her?" Alice asked.

"Of course. But she's sedated, so don't expect much response."

Alice entered the room and took the chair beside the bed, studying her mother's face in the harsh medical lighting. Even unconscious, Margie Blair looked tired—the kind of bone-deep exhaustion that came from fighting battles you were never going to win. The woman who had raised Alice to be independent and cynical, who had taught her that journalism was about finding truth in a world full of people trying to hide it, had been reduced to monitoring equipment and IV drips.

Alice found she couldn't even suppress the disgust she felt with herself. For more than four months, she'd been her mother's primary caregiver, managing medications and doctor's appointments, helping with basic daily activities that she could no longer handle alone. It had been exhausting and frustrating and emotionally draining in ways Alice hadn't anticipated. But it had also been necessary, a duty she'd accepted because it was what family did for each other.

What she hadn't expected was the relief. When the paramedics had loaded her mother into the ambulance five days ago, Alice's first emotion hadn't been worry or fear—it had been the shameful realization that she could go back to a quiet home, one without the constant pestering and commentary that accompanied her mother wherever she went.

She was a terrible daughter. A terrible person. And the fact that she was sitting here now, using her mother's hospitalization as an excuse to work on a story that had nothing to do with family obligations, only made it worse.

Alice pulled out her laptop and opened the files she'd been compiling about Zimmerman. If she was going to be here anyway, if she was going to feel guilty regardless of what she did, she might as well be productive about it.

The basic biographical information about Jason Zimmerman had been easy enough to obtain through standard journalistic channels. But Alice specialized in finding information that people preferred to keep hidden, and Zimmerman's financial connections had required more creative approaches.

She'd started with property records and business filings, tracing the network of shell companies and holding corporations that seemed to orbit around Zimmerman's legitimate psychology practice. The pattern was subtle but consistent—money flowing in from sources that were deliberately obscured, payments to contractors and suppliers that didn't quite match up with the services they claimed to provide.

But it was the phone call to Conrad Scott that had really opened doors. Conrad was a financial investigative reporter at the Portland Tribune who owed Alice several favors from stories she'd helped him develop over the years. He had access to financial databases that were officially off-limits to someone like Alice, but unofficially available to journalists who knew how to ask the right questions.

"Your boy Zimmerman is connected to some seriously heavy players," Conrad had told her during their conversation that morning. "Shell companies that trace back to international money laundering operations. Payments from organizations that the FBI has been trying to map for years."

He'd sent her a list of names and corporate entities, some of which Alice recognized from other investigative pieces about organized crime on the West Coast. But it was the international connections that made her skin crawl—payments from companies with ties to human trafficking networks, money flowing through accounts linked to the kind of people who made witnesses disappear permanently.

"This isn't just some psychologist who snapped," Conrad had continued. "This is someone who's been funded by serious criminal organizations for years. The kind of people who can arrange professional prison breaks are not people you want noticing you. Do you understand, Alice? This information didn't come from me. We're square."

She couldn't blame him for being paranoid. In all her years as a journalist and reporter, she'd never seen an extraction like the one that had taken Zimmerman. That was like something out of the movies. Not to mention the brutality with which they worked. Jonathan was lucky to be alive after that fiasco.

Alice studied the financial documents on her laptop screen, trying to piece together a timeline that made sense. The payments to Zimmerman dated back more than fifteen years, starting small but gradually increasing as his usefulness to the organization apparently grew. Whatever services he'd been providing, they'd been valuable enough to justify significant ongoing investment.

Her phone buzzed with a text from one of her other sources, a private investigator named Darcie Pratt who specialized in corporate background checks. Alice had reached out to her the previous day, asking for anything unusual about the companies on Conrad's list.

> Found something interesting about Pacific Research Associates. They've been hiring freelance contractors for "specialized psychological consultation" for years. Contract amounts suggest they're not talking about standard therapy sessions.

Alice made notes on her laptop, cross-referencing the information with what she already knew about Zimmerman's escape. The level of coordination required for the prison transport attack suggested resources and connections far beyond what a single individual could access. But if Zimmerman had been working with international criminal organizations for years, if he'd been providing specialized services that made him valuable enough to extract from custody...

"Visiting hours are almost over," a nurse said from the doorway, interrupting Alice's thoughts.

Alice glanced at her mother's motionless form, then back at her laptop screen. "Can I have a few more minutes?"

The nurse nodded sympathetically and moved on to the next room. Alice returned to her research, but found herself distracted by the sound of the ventilator and the periodic beeping of monitoring equipment. Her mother was dying, and here she was, working on a story about criminal networks and missing detectives instead of holding her hand or reading to her or doing whatever it was that good daughters did in situations like this.

The truth was, Alice didn't know how to be a good daughter. She'd spent most of her adult life maintaining careful distance from family obligations, building a career that required objectivity and emotional detachment. She was good at finding other people's truths, but terrible at confronting her own.

Her phone rang, Jonathan's name appearing on the caller

ID. Alice glanced at her mother one more time, then answered.

"Please tell me you found something," Jonathan's voice carried the strained quality of someone fighting pain medication and exhaustion.

"I found plenty," Alice replied, gathering her materials. "But not what you're hoping for. No sign of Ivy or Buckley beyond those photos I showed you this morning."

"Damnit."

Alice could hear the disappointment in his voice, and felt an unexpected surge of empathy. Jonathan was dealing with his own family obligations—a sick sister in Portland who needed him, parents who expected him to abandon his career and return home. At least Alice's situation had a clear endpoint, even if it wasn't the one she wanted.

"I did find some interesting information about Zimmerman's connections," she said, taking one last look at her mother before walking toward the hospital exit. "I'll be down there in a few." She hung up, her gaze lingering on her mother. Even though no one wanted to say it, the woman was already gone, the machines just keeping her shell alive. Her brain activity was minimal and it was unlikely she'd ever regain consciousness. The woman who'd raised her, who'd loved her every day of her life wasn't here anymore. So what point was there in sticking around?

Five minutes later, Alice was back in Jonathan's hospital room, spreading documents across his bedside table while he struggled to maintain focus through the haze of pain medication. His shoulder was immobilized in a sling, and dark bruises covered the left side of his face from the prison transport attack.

"Why do you look worse than when I left?" she asked.

He smiled. "Guess that's just my charm. But these painkillers are making it hard to think straight." Jonathan picked up one of the financial documents, squinting at the small print. "Walk me through it."

Alice arranged the papers in chronological order, building the narrative like she would for any investigative piece. "Zimmerman has been receiving payments from criminal organizations for more than fifteen years. Not small amounts either—we're talking about hundreds of thousands of dollars annually for unspecified services."

She pointed to specific entries in the financial records. "Pacific Research Associates, Northstar Consulting, Global Development Solutions. All shell companies with ties to international trafficking networks and money laundering operations."

Jonathan studied the documents, his expression growing more troubled as he processed the implications. "What kind of services would a psychologist provide to organizations like these?"

"That's the million-dollar question. But given his escape yesterday, I'm thinking it wasn't standard therapy sessions." Alice pulled out another document. "My source says Pacific Research Associates has been hiring freelance contractors for 'specialized psychological consultation' for years. The contract amounts suggest they're paying for something well beyond normal professional services."

"I don't guess you have any idea what that might be?"

"I can't do *all* your work for you," Alice said, smiling and pulling out her phone. "But there's something else. I managed to get a few more security shots from a few locations around the industrial district where I spotted Ivy and Buckley this morning. They're not hiding exactly, but they're being careful about where they go and when."

Jonathan examined the photos, relief evident on his face despite the circumstances. "She looks okay. Not under duress."

"No, but she's not exactly following standard procedure either. Whatever she and Buckley are doing, they're doing it off the books." Alice hesitated, then decided to voice the concern that had been bothering her all day. "Jonathan, what if they're right to stay hidden? What if there are people in the department who can't be trusted?"

"What do you mean?"

"Think about it. Zimmerman knew details about your personal life during the transport. He knew about your sister's condition, about your family situation. That information had to come from somewhere." Alice leaned forward. "What if he had help from inside the department? What if that's why Ivy and Buckley are staying off the grid?"

Jonathan was quiet for a long moment, clearly struggling with the implications. Alice could see him fighting against the natural law enforcement tendency to trust colleagues and follow established procedures.

"Even if that's true," he said finally, "we can't help them if we don't know where they are or what they're planning."

Alice was about to respond when she noticed Jonathan's attention had shifted to something on her laptop screen. He was staring at one of the corporate documents with an expression she couldn't quite read.

"What is it?" she asked.

"This company," Jonathan said, pointing to one of the shell corporation names. "Regional Holdings, LLC. I've seen that name before."

"Where?"

Jonathan's expression grew troubled as he worked through the memory. "Oliver's place. When I was there asking for help tracking Ivy's disappearance. He had some financial documents visible on his computer screen, and I remember seeing that name."

Alice felt the familiar tingle that came when pieces of a story started falling into place in unexpected ways. "You're sure?"

"Positive. It was on some kind of banking interface, like he was managing accounts or transferring money." Jonathan tried to sit up straighter, wincing as the movement aggravated his shoulder injury. "Fuck me. What if Oliver isn't just a victim in all this? What if he's connected to the same people who broke Zimmerman out of prison?"

Alice stilled. Jonathan rarely cursed, if ever. Between the drugs and what they'd uncovered, she was seeing a whole new side of him. One that wasn't entirely offensive to her.

Alice had met Oliver O'Toole only briefly during the investigation into Ivy's family, but she knew he was important to Ivy, someone she trusted implicitly. If he was working with the criminal organizations that had been funding Zimmerman...

"That would explain how Zimmerman knew so much about department procedures," Alice said. "If Oliver has been feeding information to these people, if he's been monitoring Ivy for years..."

Jonathan was already moving, swinging his legs over the side of the hospital bed despite the obvious pain the movement caused. "I need to get out of here."

"Wait, where are you going?"

"To confront that son of a bitch. To get some answers." Jonathan reached for his clothes, his movements hampered by the sling but determined. "I'm done with half-truths and manipulation. If he's been playing Ivy this whole time, if he's been working with the people who killed her family, I'm not letting him get away with it."

Alice watched him struggle with his shirt, noting the way his face paled with the effort. "You're not exactly in fighting condition right now."

"I don't care. Ivy trusts him completely. He could be the mole in this whole thing." Jonathan's voice carried a cold anger that Alice hadn't heard from him before. "I'm not letting him hurt her again."

Alice felt something that might have been jealousy mixed

with respect. Jonathan's dedication to Ivy was absolute, the kind of loyalty that made someone willing to ignore their own pain and safety. In fact, it went beyond loyalty. She'd seen him this way only once before. Back when they had been together. He was in love with Ivy.

"Let me come with you," she said.

"Alice, this isn't your fight."

"Like hell it isn't. I've been working on this story for months. I've put pieces together that your department missed. And right now, I'm the only backup you've got." She gestured toward his immobilized shoulder. "Besides, you're not exactly intimidating anyone in your current condition."

Jonathan started to argue, but his phone began ringing from the bedside table. He glanced at the caller ID, and Alice saw his expression shift from determination to something approaching shock.

"It's... the Lieutenant... Nat," he said, staring at the illuminated screen.

Alice felt her pulse quicken. After hours of searching, after all the speculation about Ivy's whereabouts and motivations, they were calling Jonathan directly. Whatever she and Ivy had been planning, whatever information they'd discovered, they were apparently ready to share it.

"Answer it," Alice said, her hand gripping the end of the bed.

He hesitated a moment longer before snatching the phone and pressing it to his ear.

Chapter Thirteen

Ivy stood pacing back and forth across the pavement while Nat leaned up against the railing behind her, her arms crossed. She wore shades despite the fact the sun had disappeared behind the overcast clouds, making her look like a character out of an '80s music video.

Ivy shouldn't have been nervous. But since talking with Jonathan on the phone and learning that he'd been part of the convoy guarding Zimmerman, and had almost died at the man's hands, she was anxious to get eyes on him, even though she knew he was okay. For some reason her mind wouldn't let her accept that fact until he was standing here, right in front of her.

"They should be here by now," Nat said, checking her watch for the third time in as many minutes. "How long does it take to get discharged from a hospital?"

"Depends on how convincing he is," Ivy said. During their brief conversation, Jonathan had mentioned the attack during prisoner transport, but he'd been deliberately vague about the specifics. Apparently he had been the only one to survive the attack—something not even Nat had known. Still, the fact it had happened at all made her want to throw up.

She'd spent the past four days focused on her own captivity, her own struggle to prove her innocence to Nat. But while she'd been locked away in that modified house, the investigation had continued without her; events had unfolded that she was only beginning to understand. Jonathan had been hurt because she hadn't been there, while he was trying to get answers from a man who'd proven himself capable of orchestrated brutality.

More collateral damage from her past. More people hurt because she'd been too slow to piece together Zimmerman's obsession before it claimed additional victims.

Finally, Alice's car pulled up to the parking lot and Ivy's heart jumped upon seeing Jonathan in the passenger's seat. He wore a sling across one arm and was a little bruised, but otherwise looked unharmed, other than he could use a good night's sleep.

Ivy made her way over and opened the door for him as Alice got out of the driver's side.

"Ivy," she said.

"Hey, Alice." She turned to Jonathan as he got out of the car with some effort. Before she knew what came over her, she wrapped him in a hug.

He stiffened, as if unsure how to respond. Ivy could feel the telltale "shock" that normally came with this kind of physical contact, but for some reason, it didn't bother her as much. It neither hurt nor caused her to recoil.

"Ivy…" Nat said from behind her.

Ivy let go quickly. "I'm just glad you're okay."

Jonathan stared at her a second, pure shock across his features before they finally relaxed. "Yeah. Me too."

"Looks like you went toe-to-toe with a truck."

A genuine smile spread across his face. "I'm glad to see you're not hurt."

"Me?" she asked. "I'm fine. You're the one in a sling."

"Let's take this inside," Nat said from behind her. "I don't like being this exposed."

Jonathan looked over Ivy's shoulder. "Lieutenant."

Nat nodded back.

"Well, this is fun and awkward," Alice said, hauling Jonathan's effects out of the back of the car. "But I agree with Stoneface over there."

Jonathan led the way up to his apartment with Ivy behind him, ready to catch him if he stumbled. Of course he didn't, but for some reason she felt like he might at any second and she didn't know why.

Once they were inside, Alice deposited his stuff on the kitchen counter while he made his way into the living room, Ivy practically forcing him to sit down and taking a seat beside him.

"I need some answers," Jonathan finally said. "First and foremost, where have you been?" He glanced at Nat hovering precariously near the door. "And where did she come from?"

Ivy debated telling him the truth. After all, she was still on shaky ground with Nat and didn't want to do anything that would reverse all the progress they'd made. At the same time, she didn't want to lie to him. It seemed very important that she not do that.

"I..."

"It was my fault," Nat said, finally removing her sunglasses. "I made some... assumptions that may not have been... accurate." She let out a long breath. "Assumptions that wasted time."

"Just what the hell does that mean?" Alice asked.

"Nat... *confronted* me at my apartment," Ivy said. "We had a disagreement."

"We found blood," Jonathan said. "I thought you'd been kidnapped."

Ivy's shoulders slumped. "I had been." His eyes went wide

with concern. "But we worked it out," she said quickly. "It's all okay now."

Jonathan turned to his old boss, his eyes questioning her.

"I thought... I *believed* Ivy had been involved with her family's murder fifteen years ago," Nat admitted. "It caused me to make some questionable choices."

"Wait," Alice said. "You thought Ivy killed her family?"

Nat nodded.

"For how long?" Jonathan asked.

"Ever since I found her that night."

"I don't—"

"Here," Ivy said, standing back up. "There's a lot to go over. Do you have some coffee or something?"

"I got it," Alice said, opening the cabinets and pulling out four mugs along with some individual coffee pods. As she made the brew, Ivy studied the bruises on Jonathan's face. It was worse than she'd imagined, likely from the blunt trauma impact he sustained during Zimmerman's escape.

"You know," Alice said as the third mug began brewing. "I really should be recording this. It's going to make one hell of a story. Disgraced police lieutenant attacks and kidnaps one of her own subordinates—the same subordinate whom she saved fifteen years ago. I mean... that's at least a five-part podcast."

Nat shot her a look that could melt steel, but Alice only grinned, bringing her mug to her lips.

"Listen, it's not that simple," Ivy said as she handed Jonathan a mug. "There are a lot of details here that you need to understand."

"Then explain it to us," Alice replied. "Cause I can't wait to hear this."

Ivy took a deep breath, sat back down across from Jonathan, and began relating everything that had happened since the night she'd found Nat in her apartment. Along with everything they'd discovered since then.

"So you have the original murder weapon with Ivy's prints on it?" Jonathan asked once Ivy had finished.

Nat nodded. "It's in my vehicle."

"But what we really need are the case files from back then," Ivy said. "We need to start from scratch, figure out what Nat missed fifteen years ago and how it connects to Zimmerman. I think that's the key to finding out the reason behind this whole thing."

Jonathan shot a quick glance at Alice, who only raised her eyebrows before turning away.

"What?" Ivy asked.

"This isn't part of the official report," he began. "But I didn't just survive that attack by luck. Zimmerman spared me. Because he wanted me to deliver a message… to you."

Ivy leaned back, on alert. "What kind of message?"

"He said to tell you that he's not done with you yet. And that he's coming."

"Jesus," Nat said under her breath. "Fucking psycho. That settles it. We need to put Ivy in protective custody."

"Absolutely not," Ivy replied. "I am not going into some bunker until this is resolved." She turned back to Jonathan. "Did he say anything else?"

"He knew about my sister," Jonathan replied. "I don't know how. But he more or less threatened me to stay out of his way."

"He's got connections," Alice replied. "He's been receiving payments from international criminal organizations for more than fifteen years. Hundreds of thousands of dollars for unspecified services." She opened her laptop and turned the screen for the three of them to see. "Pacific Research Associates, Northstar Consulting, Global Development Solutions—all shell companies with less than stellar reputations."

Ivy studied the corporate names, noting the professional appearance of the documents. Whatever services Zimmerman had been providing to these organizations, they'd been valuable enough to justify substantial ongoing investment.

"What kind of services would a psychologist provide to people like that?" she asked.

"That's what we need to figure out," Alice replied. "But given the sophistication of his escape yesterday, I'm pretty sure he isn't just the on-call therapist."

"What are you suggesting?" Nat asked.

"I don't know for certain," Alice replied. "But maybe Ivy not being able to remember what happened that night wasn't an accident. Maybe it was on purpose."

The realization sent a chill down Ivy's spine. "You think he did something to me to make me forget?"

"Maybe. His profession deals with traumatic memories all the time. Maybe he wanted you to suppress yours. And maybe he found a way to force you to do that."

Ivy stood abruptly, needing movement to process what she was hearing. The apartment suddenly felt too small, too confining. She walked to the window, staring out at the street while her mind worked through the connections being drawn around her past.

"So my family was collateral damage," she said quietly. "They died because I was the real target."

"We don't know that for certain," Nat replied, but her voice lacked conviction.

Ivy turned back to face the group. "Think about it—a twelve-year-old girl from a middle-class family, no obvious connection to criminal organizations or high-value targets. But a child that age would be perfect for testing psychological manipulation techniques. Young enough to be vulnerable, old enough to provide meaningful data about memory suppression and trauma response."

"If that's true," Jonathan said, "then Zimmerman's current obsession with you makes perfect sense. You were his greatest success and his greatest failure simultaneously."

"How so?"

"He successfully suppressed your memories of what he did to you, but he failed to complete the experiment. You survived when you were supposed to die, you recovered enough to build a life for yourself, and eventually you became a threat to his operation." Ivy could see Jonathan's mind working through the psychological profile. "From his perspective, you represent unfinished business."

Ivy returned to her seat, her legs suddenly feeling unsteady. "So what does he want now? To finish what he started?"

"Or to study how his techniques held up over time," Alice suggested. "Fifteen years is a significant test period for psychological conditioning. Your current mental state would provide valuable data about the long-term effectiveness of his methods. Methods that he may be wanting to deploy at a larger scale."

The idea that she'd been walking around for fifteen years as a living experiment made Ivy's skin crawl. Every struggle with memory, every nightmare that had plagued her sleep, every difficulty she'd had forming close relationships—all of it potentially the result of deliberate psychological manipulation designed to serve criminal enterprises.

But there was something else, a detail that had been bothering her since their visit to the cabin earlier that day.

"The chamber where Jasmine died," she said. "The restraints, the measurements—everything was calibrated for more than one person. Zimmerman didn't build that for her specifically. He built it for something—someone else."

"Who?" Jonathan asked.

"We don't know," Nat replied. "Ivy thinks it was for the family she never had."

"You think he was planning some kind of retribution?"

"It makes sense, doesn't it?" Ivy asked. "He kills my

parents and my brother, but misses me. Then he spends years developing a way to do it again."

"But that would mean he hasn't been watching you closely," Alice said. "Otherwise he'd know you didn't have any other relatives."

"Look, we can't begin to psychoanalyze a sociopath's motives," Nat said. "The point is we need to find him before he goes after Ivy."

Ivy thought about Zimmerman's calm demeanor during their hospital conversation, the way he'd seemed to know exactly what was going to happen during each stage of their interaction. Even in custody, even facing serious charges, he'd projected the confidence of someone following a carefully rehearsed script.

"It won't be easy. He's prepared for anything."

Nat turned to Jonathan. "How soon can you get us those files?"

Alice nearly spit back into her mug with laughter, causing all of them to turn their attention to her. "Sorry, but he's not doing anything. He's been put on leave."

"I can still—"

"No, *I* will go get the files," Alice said. "I still have a few favors in the department. Plus, I know that place like the back of my hand."

"You're sure?" Ivy asked. "You know what to look for?"

She shrugged with the nonchalance of someone who didn't seem bothered by the lack of confidence. "Give me a couple of hours. It's better than going back to the hospital and sitting with my dying mother."

"Your mother..." Ivy said. "She's..."

Alice shrugged again. "It's not a big deal." She took a last big gulp from her mug before heading for the door. "I'll be back."

"Alice," Jonathan called after her, but she was already gone.

"I… had no idea," Ivy said.

"Neither did I, until she showed up in the hospital," Jonathan replied.

Ivy now realized that was probably why she had been there waiting for Ivy that night after she'd confronted Zimmerman too. Ivy couldn't imagine losing—

"Oh my God," Ivy said. "Carol. I need to call her, she's—"

"I've been keeping in touch with her," Jonathan said. "I told her not to worry, that I would find out what happened."

"Still," Ivy said. "She needs to hear from me. She's got to be worried sick. Can I use your phone?" She asked Jonathan as she glanced at Nat. "Someone destroyed mine."

"I already apologized for that," Nat replied. "I didn't want your hacker buddy to track you."

But instead of handing her his phone, all the color drained from Jonathan's face.

"Hey," Ivy said. "Are you okay? Do you need some water or something?"

"What? No, I'm fine. Why do you ask?"

"Because you look like you just saw a ghost or something," Ivy said.

"It's probably just the meds. I *was* almost killed." There was a playfulness in his voice, but also something else. Ivy couldn't tell exactly what… but she was tired herself. Maybe she was seeing something that wasn't there.

"Here," he said, handing over his phone. "She's probably expecting me to call anyway."

Ivy held his gaze a moment as she took the phone. "You're sure you're okay?"

He nodded. "Fine. Don't worry about me."

But as Ivy headed to the bedroom to make the call, she couldn't help but think he wasn't telling her something. Jonathan wasn't the kind of person to keep secrets because he wasn't very good at it.

She shrugged it off. If he had something to tell her, he would do it when he was ready. Right now, she needed to let Carol know everything was okay. As she dialed, she tried to catch Jonathan's eye through the open doorway, only to find him looking anywhere but at her.

Chapter Fourteen

"Jonathan?" Aunt Carol's worried voice said on the other end after half a ring. "Any news?"

"It's me," Ivy said.

"Oh, thank God," her aunt's voice carried relief and worry in equal measure. "Ivy, where have you been? I've been worried sick. Jonathan said you were safe, but—"

"I'm fine," Ivy interrupted gently. "I'm sorry I couldn't call sooner. There were some complications with the case, but everything's under control now."

"Complications?" Carol's voice sharpened with the instincts of someone who'd raised a traumatized teenager and learned to read between the lines. "What kind of complications?"

Ivy closed her eyes, trying to find words that would reassure without lying outright. Carol had been through enough worry over the years; she didn't need to know about Nat's misguided protection or the larger conspiracy that seemed to surround Ivy's past.

"Some misunderstandings about my role in the Quinn investigation," she said carefully. "But Nat and I have worked things out. I should be able to come home soon."

"Nat?" The surprise in Carol's voice was unmistakable. "I thought she was missing."

"It's a long story. But I need you to promise me something. You still have that shotgun in the hall closet?"

"Of course."

"Keep it handy."

The silence on the other end stretched long enough that Ivy wondered if the call had dropped. When Carol finally spoke, her voice carried the steel that had helped her raise a damaged child into a functioning adult.

"Ivy Katherine Stanford-Bishop, you tell me right now what's really going on."

The use of both her birth and adopted names—something Carol only did when she was truly worried—made Ivy's chest tight with guilt. She'd put this woman through so much over the years, and now she was doing it again.

"I think we may have found who took my family," Ivy said, choosing her words carefully. "We're going to stop him, but until we do, I need to know you're safe."

"Are *you* safe?"

Ivy glanced through the kitchen doorway at Jonathan, noting the way he winced as he shifted position in his chair. At Nat, who'd spent fifteen years carrying the weight of a secret that had cost her everything. At the empty space where Alice had been, off breaking laws to obtain information that might help them understand a conspiracy that stretched back decades.

"I'm with people who care about me," she said, which was true even if it wasn't a complete answer. "And I'm going to end this. Whatever it takes."

"You keep me in the loop," Carol replied, worry still tinting her voice. "I don't want to turn on the news and find out you've been shot in an alley somewhere. I mean it, Ivy."

"I will," Ivy replied. "And I'll be coming by soon."

After hanging up, Ivy returned to the living room to find

Nat studying her with the expression she remembered from her teenage years—the look that meant she was being scrutinized. Knowing now that she was waiting for Ivy to break and start stabbing people put a whole new perspective on things.

"How much did you tell her?" Nat asked.

"Enough to keep her safe. Not enough to make her panic." Ivy reclaimed her seat across from Jonathan, noting that some color had returned to his face. "She's stronger than people give her credit for."

"She had to be, to raise you," Nat said, and there was something that might have been affection in her voice.

Jonathan lolled his head back, struggling to keep his eyes open.

"You need sleep," Ivy said.

"I'm good."

"She's right," Nat said. "You're no good to us if you can't stay awake. Just take a nap until Alice returns."

"If you insist," he said, struggling to get up. In an instant Ivy was by his side, allowing him to push on her hand while Nat got the other side. Nat shot Ivy a look but didn't say anything as they led Jonathan to the bedroom.

Once they had him down and he had passed out—probably from the drugs he was still taking—Ivy and Nat returned to the living room.

"Is it just me, or did something change since we last spoke?" Nat asked.

"What do you mean?"

"I *mean*, you're touching White and as far as I can tell, it isn't affecting you."

"Oh," Ivy said, trying to play dumb. It had been impossible not to notice, but at the same time she didn't have an explanation. Sure, her phobia hadn't been as bad with Jonathan as it had with other people, but that didn't really tell her *why*. "Maybe getting the shit shocked out of me from that damn ankle monitor has something to do with it."

Nat grabbed hold of Ivy's arm and instantly Ivy felt the surge of electricity through her, though she gritted her teeth until Nat released it a second later. "Nope, that's not it."

Ivy rubbed her arm. "Then what?"

Nat glanced back at the door to the bedroom. "I don't know."

Four hours later Alice returned, her arms full of manila folders and her expression carrying the satisfied look of someone who'd accomplished something difficult and possibly illegal.

"Don't ask how I got these," Alice said, dumping the files onto Jonathan's coffee table. "And don't ask what rules I broke in the process. Let's just say my infamy knows no bounds."

It hadn't been an easy wait. Now that she was out of her "prison", Ivy's mind had begun to wander. And just like before, it kept coming back to Jasmine Quinn, seeing her brutally murdered over and over in her mind.

But it hadn't stopped there. Ivy started to imagine other people in that chair, and she didn't know why. But when she closed her eyes she'd see Carol there, or Oliver. Or even Jonathan. And it had taken willpower she hadn't realized she'd had to keep herself from raiding Jonathan's medicine cabinet for some of those high-grade painkillers.

Ivy stared at the folders, recognizing the case numbers and evidence labels that represented the official investigation into her family's disappearance. Fifteen years of wondering what the police had found, what leads they'd followed, what conclusions they'd drawn—all of it contained in manila folders that looked disappointingly thin for such a life-altering case.

"I should probably mention," Alice continued, settling into the remaining chair, "that obtaining these files may have raised some eyebrows. So if anyone comes asking where you got them, my name is Astrid and this conversation never happened."

Nat moved toward the coffee table, her expression grim. "So much for staying under the radar."

"What can I say? People have a hard time not noticing me."

Ivy watched Nat open the first folder, noting the way her former mentor's hands trembled slightly as she revealed documents she'd helped create fifteen years ago.

"Nat," Ivy said gently. "Before we start—I need to know you're ready for this. If there are things in those files that you're not proud of, things you did or didn't do because of your assumptions about me…"

"I know what's in here," Nat replied, her voice sharp despite the obvious emotional cost. "Or rather, I know what's not in here. The interviews I didn't conduct, the leads I didn't follow, the evidence I didn't properly document because I was so focused on protecting you from the truth." She looked up at Ivy. "You don't need to rub it in."

"I wasn't," Ivy replied. "I'm just making sure you're okay."

"I'm fine," she replied. "It's my mess. And I'll fix it." Nat began laying out documents in chronological order: crime scene photographs, witness statements, forensic reports, and investigative notes. The visual representation of the official investigation was sparse, professional, and completely inadequate for a case involving three murders and a missing child.

"Where's Jonathan?" Alice asked, looking around the room.

"Meds knocked him out," Nat replied. "We should let him sleep."

Alice scoffed. "He won't like that."

"He's injured. He's not going to be of much use."

"I guess you're right," Alice said. "Let the man take a break. He's got enough on his mind as it is."

Ivy furrowed her brow. "What do you mean?"

Alice winced, like she shouldn't have said anything. "His sister is getting worse. His mother keeps pestering him to go back to Portland."

"How bad is it?" Ivy asked.

"I don't know. But he refused to go anywhere until he found you," Alice replied.

Ivy glanced back at the door again. If Marie was getting worse... he really should go be with his family. "Has he told them about the accident?"

"Not to my knowledge. Constance White is not the most... nurturing person," Alice replied.

"Okay," Nat said, her attention on the files. "Going back, we did some basic interviews, just enough to satisfy my boss. But Mike and I knew the more questions we asked the more attention we'd draw to the story, so we kept things brief."

"No neighborhood canvass reports?" Ivy asked. "Where are the interviews with my parents' friends, their coworkers, people who might have known if they were being stalked or threatened?"

Nat's expression grew more troubled as she searched through the folders. "Here. Three witness statements from neighbors who were closest with your family at the time."

She handed Ivy a thin file containing photocopied reports that looked hastily written and inadequately detailed. The first was from Mrs. Crane, who lived two houses down from Ivy's childhood home. Her statement mentioned seeing a dark sedan parked across from the Stanford house that night, but she didn't know if someone was inside. At the time it was ruled coincidental.

The second report came from Ruben Lane, who delivered mail to the neighborhood. He'd noticed that the Stanford family's mail was being collected irregularly, sometimes by family members he didn't recognize. When he'd asked Michael Stanford about it, he'd been told they were expecting important documents and had asked some friends to help watch for deliveries.

The third statement was the most disturbing. Sarah Kelly, a family friend who'd occasionally babysat Ivy and her brother, reported that Rebecca Stanford had seemed increasingly anxious in the weeks before the disappearance. She'd mentioned feeling uneasy, but could never (or refused) to explain why. While interesting, it hadn't been enough to merit pursuit.

"None of these were followed up," Ivy said, her voice tight.

Nat nodded miserably. "I was so convinced you were responsible that I didn't want to find evidence of outside threats. I thought if I could prove the case was contained to family dynamics, it would be easier to protect you from prosecution."

"And instead you protected my family's killer," Ivy said, the words coming out harsher than she'd intended.

Nat didn't bother defending herself. "You're right. That's exactly what I did."

The door to Jonathan's bedroom opened and he emerged, shuffling along. "You were supposed to wake me when Alice got back."

"Sorry, chief," Alice replied. "But you needed your beauty sleep."

He shot her a look and made his way over, slumping into one of the stools in the kitchen. "What do you have?"

"A whole lot of nothing," Ivy replied, glaring at Nat. "I would have been fired if I'd turned in work like this."

"Ivy, I'm going to fix this," Nat replied. "I promise."

Jonathan glanced over the documentation on the table. "This could indicate a pattern of predatory behavior," he said. "You'll need more, but this could be the basis for Zimmerman keeping an eye on the family."

"It could just as easily have been a bunch of coincidences that don't mean anything," Alice said.

Nat grabbed her things. "I'll take care of this. You three sit tight," she said with renewed determination.

"Not by yourself you're not," Ivy said.

Jonathan looked up, "If you're planning on interviews, it's been fifteen years. Some of these people might not still be alive."

"Then we find the ones who are," she replied. "And we get the information that I should have gathered the first time around."

Alice checked her watch. "It's getting late, but we might be able to reach a few people before evening. I can start with public records, find current addresses and contact information."

"Great. Text me what you find. Ivy and I will conduct the interviews," Nat said. "Hopefully that will give us a direction to follow."

Ivy looked at Jonathan, noting the way he was fighting to stay alert despite his obvious exhaustion. "Will you be okay here? You should rest."

"I'll keep an eye on him," Alice offered. "Make sure he doesn't do anything stupid like get into vans with strange men again."

"I'm sitting right here," Jonathan protested, but his voice lacked its usual strength.

Ivy found herself wanting to reach for him, to offer the kind of comfort that came naturally to people who didn't carry fifteen years of trauma around physical contact. The impulse was so normal, so automatic, that it took her by surprise.

"We'll be back soon," she said instead.

"Good hunting," Jonathan called after them as they headed out the door.

Chapter Fifteen

NAT DIDN'T SAY A WORD AS THEY MADE THEIR WAY BACK TO Ivy's old neighborhood, despite the pings coming through from Alice, updating them on information she'd uncovered on the witnesses. It was a silence Ivy had become used to working with the woman for so many years, but this also felt different. Charged with a new kind of energy from Nat, a frustration that was almost as thick as the air between them. The more they dove into this case, the angrier she was becoming.

But Ivy knew Nat wasn't angry at her or anyone else; it was all self-directed. Because Ivy would have done the exact same thing if she were in the other woman's shoes.

It was funny: she'd dreamed of this moment more times than she could count—working a case with Nat, being treated as an equal rather than someone who needed protection. It was ironic that it had taken fifteen years and a kidnapping for them to finally reach this point.

"You know," Ivy said, breaking the silence, "I used to fantasize about us working together like this. Back when I was first starting out, when you still came around sometimes."

Nat's hands tightened on the steering wheel. "Ivy—"

"I'm not trying to make you feel worse than you already

do," Ivy continued. "I just think it's comical that this is what it took. Me being accused of murder, you kidnapping me, Zimmerman escaping prison." She let out a bitter laugh. "Not exactly how I pictured things."

"Life never really works out how we plan," Nat said. "No matter how hard we try."

Ten minutes later they pulled into the driveway of a modest two-story house that showed signs of recent maintenance—new paint, well-tended garden, fresh mulch around the flower beds. It looked nothing like the neglected property Ivy remembered from her childhood, when Mrs. Crane had been an elderly widow who rarely left her house.

"I'm going out on a limb and saying Mrs. Crane doesn't live here anymore," Ivy said.

"Unlikely," Nat replied, scanning her texts. "According to Alice the house is registered to a *B. Crane*, so maybe we'll get lucky."

They approached the front door together, and Ivy felt a strange mixture of nervousness and determination. These people had been part of her life fifteen years ago, had witnessed the events leading up to her family's disappearance. The fact that their testimony had been dismissed or inadequately investigated filled her with an fury she was struggling to keep in check.

Nat rang the doorbell, and after a few moments, a man in his early forties answered. He was tall and thin, with the kind of pale complexion that suggested he spent most of his time indoors. His expression shifted from mild annoyance to curiosity as he took in their appearance.

"B. Crane?" Nat asked, showing her badge. "I'm Lieutenant Buckley; this is Detective Bishop. We'd like to ask you some questions about your mother's statement from fifteen years ago regarding the Stanford family disappearance."

"My... *what?*" the man asked, bewildered.

"Fifteen years ago your mother was a witness in the disappearance of the Stanford family that lived at 4610, two doors down."

"Oh," he said. "Okay. My mom's dead."

Nat nodded. "I'm sorry for your loss. Do you happen to remember if she ever said anything about what happened that night?"

Ivy caught the man staring at her, almost like he was examining her. "You're Ivy Stanford, aren't you?"

Ivy nodded. "I changed my name after... what happened."

"I remember you," he replied. "I used to see you and your brother out in your backyard all the time. Bobby... remember?"

"*You* saw them?" Nat asked.

"I was living here," the man replied. "In the basement. Easier than renting a place."

Ivy had forgotten that the neighbors would have known her, would have watched her grow from a child into the woman standing before them now. But that was another life, one she didn't see as hers any longer. She'd changed so much since then, she didn't even feel like the same person.

"Then I'll ask you," Nat said. "Do *you* remember anything from that night?"

"That night? No," he said. "We just woke up and heard about it on the news. Mom was pretty distraught. She made me get new locks for all the doors."

"Your mother mentioned seeing a dark sedan parked across from the Stanford house the night they disappeared," Nat said, pulling out a notebook. "Do you remember anything about that?"

"Oh, shit, you know what? Yeah, I do. That bastard kept parking in my spot on the street. Did it for a few weeks in fact. But after—" He glanced at Ivy. "—um, after that day it was gone."

"Do you happen to remember the make and model of the car?"

"Nah man, that was like forever ago," he said. "Just that it was dark in color. Maybe maroon?"

"Is there anything else you might remember?" Ivy asked.

Bobby shook his head. "I was pretty absorbed in my own world back then. World of Warcraft had just come out, and I was spending most of my time online." He looked embarrassed by the admission. "I wish I could be more helpful, but I honestly didn't pay attention to what was happening in the neighborhood."

Ivy felt her disappointment settle like a stone in her stomach. Their first lead was already a dead end, just like so many other aspects of this case had been.

They thanked Bobby and returned to the Jeep, neither of them speaking. Ivy was lost in the memories of those days, of playing with Danny in the backyard. She hadn't thought about those days in years. But the yearn to experience them again produced an ache in her chest so profound she thought it might cripple her.

Instead, they headed to their next destination. Alice was making short work of finding Nat's original witnesses, sending over screen shots of social media accounts and an address for their next target.

The Sunset Manor Retirement Community was a sprawling complex of low buildings surrounded by carefully maintained gardens.

"At least this one's still alive," Nat muttered as they parked.

They found Ruben Lane on one of the outdoor courts, engaged in what appeared to be an intensely competitive game of pickleball with three other residents. Despite being in his eighties, he moved with surprising agility, his competitive spirit evident in the way he celebrated successful shots and cursed missed opportunities.

"Mr. Lane?" Ivy called during a break between games.

Ruben turned toward them, squinting in the afternoon sun. When his eyes focused on Ivy, his entire demeanor changed. The competitive player became a gentle old man whose face lit up with recognition and genuine warmth.

"Well, I'll be damned," he said, setting down his paddle. "Ivy Stanford. Look at you—all grown up." He glanced at Nat. "I remember you. You're the detective who was working her case back then."

"Yes, sir. May we have a moment of your time?"

They found a quiet bench in the shade of an oak tree, away from the continuing pickleball games. Ruben's memory was sharp despite his age, and he seemed eager to help in any way he could.

"I've thought about your family so many times over the years," he told Ivy. "Wondered what happened to that sweet little girl who used to wave at me from her bedroom window when I delivered the mail."

Ivy's throat tightened. She'd forgotten about waving to the mailman, but now she could picture herself as a child, watching for his arrival as part of her daily routine. This excursion was dredging up a whole host of memories she'd tucked away.

"Thank you for speaking with us," Nat said. "Your original statement mentioned some irregularities with the mail delivery in the weeks before the disappearance. I don't know how much you remember, but can you tell us more about that?"

Ruben nodded, his expression growing more serious as he turned to Ivy. "It isn't something you forget easily. You know what they say about trauma making our memories sharper? I can't tell you what I ate last week for breakfast, but I *can* remember just about every piece of mail I delivered in the weeks leading up to your family's disappearance."

"Your father started acting strange about the mail. Real anxious, like he was expecting something important or dreading it. He'd intercept me before I got to the mailbox, asking if there was anything for the family." He paused, clearly working through the memory. "But here's the thing— there was an increase in personalized mail for your mother. Hand-addressed letters, which was unusual back then. Even more unusual now."

"What kind of letters?" Ivy asked, leaning forward.

"Always addressed to Mrs. Rebecca Stanford. Neat handwriting, like someone had taken their time with it. They came maybe once a week at first, then more frequently as time went on. By the end, there were sometimes two or three in a single delivery."

Ivy exchanged glances with Nat. This was the first concrete evidence they'd found of ongoing contact between an unknown person and her family before the disappearance.

"Did you ever see who was sending them?" Nat asked. "Any return addresses?"

"No return addresses that I ever noticed," Ruben replied. "And I never saw your mother receive them directly. Your father was always there first, like he was screening the mail." He scratched his head thoughtfully. "I asked him once if everything was okay, and he said they were just waiting for some important documents. But he looked worried when he said it."

"How worried?" Ivy pressed.

"Like a man who wasn't sleeping well. Like someone carrying a weight around his neck." Ruben's eyes were kind but troubled. "I delivered mail for thirty-seven years, honey. You learn to read people's faces when you see them every day. Your father was scared."

The revelation hit Ivy harder than she'd expected. Her father—the strong, capable man who'd been her hero and protector—had been afraid. Someone had been threatening her family, and she'd been too young to understand the signs.

"Did you ever mention this to the police?" Nat asked, her voice carefully controlled.

"To you, actually," Ruben replied, looking at Nat directly. "But you seemed more interested in other aspects of the case. I got the impression that you already had a theory about what happened and weren't looking for information that might contradict it."

Nat's face flushed with shame, but she maintained her professional composure. "What else do you remember from that time period?"

"Just that your mother seemed more withdrawn in those final weeks. She used to garden in the front yard, always had a smile and a wave for me. But toward the end, I rarely saw her outside. When I did catch glimpses of her through the windows, she looked… worried."

They spent another twenty minutes with Ruben, but he'd told them everything he could remember.

Back in the Jeep, Ivy stared out the window as Nat started the engine.

"You okay?" she asked.

"Fine," Ivy replied.

"If you want to take a break—"

"No, let's just get this over with," Ivy replied. "Where to next?"

"I know what you're thinking," Nat said suddenly.

"Do you?"

"You're thinking that if I'd done my job properly fifteen years ago, we might have caught Zimmerman before he could hurt anyone else. Before Jasmine Quinn died."

Ivy turned to look at her. Nat's profile was rigid with self-recrimination, her knuckles white on the steering wheel.

"I am thinking that," Ivy admitted. "But I'm also thinking that beating yourself up about it now won't help us catch him."

"How can you be so calm about this? I destroyed the

investigation into your family's murder because I was too stubborn and too convinced of my own theory to follow the evidence."

"Because being angry won't bring them back," Ivy said quietly. "And because you thought you were protecting a traumatized child. Your intentions were good, even if your execution was flawed."

Nat swallowed hard, but continued to stare straight ahead.

Their final stop was a small apartment complex on the east side of town. Sarah Kelly had aged well, her silver hair styled elegantly and her posture still straight despite being in her seventies. But when she opened the door and saw Nat, her expression hardened with remembered frustration.

"Lieutenant Buckley," she said coldly. "I wondered if I'd ever see you again."

Nat's jaw tightened, but she kept her voice level. "Mrs. Kelly, I believe you know Detective Bishop. We'd like to talk to you about Rebecca Stanford."

Sarah's expression softened immediately when she looked at Ivy. "Oh, my dear child. You look so much like your mother."

"Hi, Mrs. Kelly," Ivy said, suddenly feeling like she was five again.

"You can call me Rebecca," she said, approaching Ivy and wrapping her in a gentle hug. Ivy winced at the surge of electricity moving through her body, but bore it until the woman released her. "Please, come in."

The apartment was small but comfortable, filled with photographs and mementos from a life well-lived. Sarah directed them to a couch while she prepared tea, her movements efficient despite her age.

"I tried to tell the police what was happening," Sarah said, settling into her chair with a cup of tea balanced on her lap. "But nobody wanted to listen. They kept sending me back to you," she said, looking at Nat, "and you acted like I was wasting your time."

"We're listening now," Ivy said before Nat could respond. "Tell me what you tried to tell them."

Sarah's eyes filled with tears as she looked at Ivy. "Your mother thought she was being stalked. She was receiving threatening letters, strange phone calls at odd hours. The whole family was on edge, but they didn't want you children to know what was happening."

Ivy's heart began to race. "From whom?"

"She didn't know. But whoever they were, they knew a lot about your family. Mostly about her, though. About her past. Things she hadn't told *anyone*. She confided in me that she was terrified." Sarah wiped her eyes with a tissue. "She wanted to move away, but your father said they couldn't afford to start over somewhere else."

"Did they contact the police?" Nat asked, her voice barely above a whisper.

"Multiple times. Rebecca filed reports, but since they couldn't identify the sender, there wasn't much the police could do. One officer came to the house once, but he said until something actually happened, their hands were tied."

Ivy felt sick. Her family had reached out for help, had followed proper channels, and the system had failed them. They'd been left to face their stalker alone, with no protection and no recourse. It reminded her of the Quinn family, trying to do the right thing and still suffering the consequences in the end.

"She never had an idea about who it could have been?" Ivy asked.

"The letters weren't signed. But Rebecca was convinced it was someone from her past. Someone who had reason to hold a grudge." Sarah paused. "She mentioned once that she thought it might be connected to something that happened before you were born. Something she'd tried to put behind her."

"What kind of something?"

"I don't know, dear. Your mother was very private about certain aspects of her past. But whatever it was, it had her convinced that this person wasn't going to stop until they got what they wanted."

"Mrs. Kelly, does the name Jason Zimmerman mean anything to you?"

"That man who escaped police custody?" she asked.

"Did my mother ever mention him?" Ivy asked.

"Not that I recall," she said. "I'm sorry."

They spent another hour with Sarah, but she'd told them everything she could remember. As they prepared to leave, she caught Ivy's arm, sending another jolt through Ivy that nearly caused her to cry out. But the touch had been gentle, not meant to harm.

"Your mother loved you so much," she said. "Whatever happened that night, whatever you might have seen or experienced, know that she died trying to protect you."

In the Jeep afterward, Ivy and Nat sat in silence for several minutes, both processing what they'd learned. The picture that was emerging was clear and devastating: Ivy's family had been systematically terrorized by someone with detailed knowledge of their lives and access to their personal information. Someone who had ultimately followed through on his threats in the most brutal way possible.

"It was never about me," Ivy said finally. "It started with her. Something from her past."

"But it became about you," Nat replied. "Whatever connection Zimmerman had to your mother, you became his primary focus after that night."

Ivy thought about the chamber beneath the cabin. About Zimmerman's obsession with her memory of that night.

About fifteen years of watching and waiting for the right moment to reclaim his unfinished experiment.

"I need to know what happened in my mother's past," she said. "What connection she had to Zimmerman that made him target our family."

Nat started the engine, her expression grim but determined. "Maybe Alice can help us find those original police reports your parents filed."

As they drove back toward Jonathan's apartment, Ivy felt the weight of fifteen years of unanswered questions pressing down on her. But for the first time since this nightmare began, she also felt hope.

She and Nat were finally pursuing the truth instead of running from it. And she wouldn't stop until she uncovered everything.

Chapter Sixteen

JONATHAN'S PHONE BUZZED FOR THE SIXTH TIME IN THE PAST hour, his mother's name flashing insistently on the screen. He stared at it from where he lay on the couch, his shoulder still throbbing despite the pain medication and grimaced.

"You're not going to get that?" Alice asked from the kitchen, where she was scrolling on her phone, watching over him like a vulture waiting for its meal to finally die.

"No," Jonathan said, and was surprised by how easy the word came out. "I'm not."

Alice paused, arching an eyebrow. "Wanna talk about it?"

"Not particularly." Jonathan took a sip of cold coffee. "You don't have to hover over there. You can sit in the living room you know. I'm not contagious with anything."

"Old habits," she replied. "Remember I used to spend my mornings working from this counter." She headed into the living room. "Also I don't do well with just... *sitting*."

"I remember."

The phone buzzed again. This time, Jonathan reached over and turned it face down without looking at the caller ID.

"You know," Alice said, "when we were together, I used to think your mother was just overprotective. Controlling, sure, but in that wealthy helicopter parent way." She looked up at him. "But watching you now, seeing how you react when she calls... you gotta put a stop to that. It's eating you up."

Jonathan shifted uncomfortably. Alice had always been perceptive, able to see through the polite facades that his family had perfected over generations. It was one of the things that had attracted him to her initially, and one of the reasons their relationship had ultimately failed—she'd seen too much, asked too many questions about things he wasn't ready to examine.

"She has very specific expectations," he said carefully.

"And we all know what happens when we don't live up to our parents' expectations." She shot him a knowing grin.

"She withdraws her approval," he said finally. "Makes it clear that I've disappointed her. Usually involves threatening to cut me out of the will or telling me I'm abandoning my sister."

Alice nodded like she'd been expecting that answer. "How often do you talk to your sister without your mother as the go-between?"

"Not often enough," he admitted. Marie's illness had been... it had been tough for the whole family. It was hard to move forward with your life when you didn't know exactly what was wrong. And sure, she had bad days, but she was amazingly adept and had proved she could handle her own care.

Yet, Constance White had made it her mission from God to watch over her daughter, as if her vigilance could somehow cure whatever was inside her.

"You're right," he finally said. "I need to be better about that." He reached for his phone as Alice cocked an intrigued expression at him.

He scrolled past the seventeen missed calls and four voicemails from his mother and found Marie's number. She answered on the second ring.

"Hey there." Her voice was weak but genuinely pleased. "Calling to see if I was dead yet?"

Jonathan smiled. "The way she makes it sound I wasn't sure."

His sister laughed on the other end. "I'm fine. Just had a rough few days, that's all. I'm on the mend."

In the background, Jonathan could hear his mother's voice rising in indignation, something about ungrateful children and family obligations. Marie must have moved away from her because the volume dropped significantly.

"Well, she knows you called, at least," Marie said. "She's going to give herself an aneurysm if she's not careful. How are you doing? We heard some big criminal escaped down there or something."

Jonathan's throat tightened. "Yeah… uh, I was in the truck with him."

"*What?*"

"I'm fine, I'm okay," he said before she could alert their mother with nothing more than the tone of her voice. "I was banged up; my shoulder is sprained and I'm a little bruised. But that's it. *Don't* tell her."

Marie's voice dropped to a whisper. "Are you sure you're okay?"

"Just need some rest, but I'm already home," he said. "Mainly I just wanted to make sure *you* were okay. Even though I know she's exaggerating, I worry."

"You shouldn't," his sister replied. "It's going to take a lot more than this to keep me down. Did she tell you I was seeing one of the nurses? Big hunky guy with biceps as big as my neck."

"Oh really?" Jonathan asked.

"His name's Sean. He wants to be a pediatrician one day."

"I'm sure Mom loves that."

"She doesn't approve. Thinks I'm too fragile for a relationship. So we've been keeping it on the down low."

Jonathan shook his head, knowing exactly what she meant. "Smart move."

"*You tell him to come home right this instant! I won't have any more of this insubordination!*" Constance screeched from somewhere on the other end of the line.

"Mom says hi," Marie added before dropping her voice again. "You're fine. Stay there. I'll call if things truly get bad."

"I'll be up as soon as this case is over," Jonthan said. "But we're dealing with something of a time crunch."

"Okay. Love you, dummy. Oh, and stay out of the hospital, for my sake at least. Our family's had enough medical drama for one year."

Jonathan scoffed. "Deal. Love you back."

After he hung up, Alice was quiet for a moment. "She sounds strong."

"She's probably the strongest person in the whole family." Jonathan felt something loosening in his chest, a tension he'd been carrying for so long he'd forgotten what it felt like to breathe without it. "Mom just needs to let her live her own life."

Alice smiled, the first genuine one he'd seen from her since she'd picked him up from the hospital. "It's funny. Your mother putting on this front of an elegant society matron who just wants the best for her children. When in reality she's—"

"Emotionally manipulative?"

"I was going to say toxic, but sure."

Jonathan's phone buzzed again. This time, he didn't even glance at it.

"You know what's ironic?" Alice continued. "I've been dreading losing my mother for weeks now, even though she drives me absolutely crazy. We fight constantly—about my job, my choices, my refusal to settle down and give her grandchildren. But despite all of that, I'm going to miss those fights. I'm going to miss her caring enough to have opinions about my life."

She paused, looking out the window toward the street where Ivy and Nat had disappeared an hour earlier.

"But you... you're finally getting to live out from under your mother's thumb. And the timing is so weird because when Ivy hugged you after getting out of my car, I saw your face. You looked like someone who'd never experienced unconditional affection before."

Jonathan felt heat rise in his cheeks. "I don't know what you're talking about."

"Jonathan." Alice's voice was gentle but firm. "You're in love with her."

He swallowed, *hard*. Alice never had been one to mince words. He thought about the relief he'd felt when Ivy had called yesterday, the way his entire body had relaxed when he'd seen she was safe. He thought about the protective fury that had overwhelmed him when he'd learned Oliver might be involved in her family's murder, the desperate need to shield her from any additional pain.

"I guess I've never been great about disguising my feelings," he said.

"No, you haven't." Alice's expression was thoughtful rather than hurt. "She's good for you, you know. I've watched her challenge you, push you to be better, make you laugh in ways I never could. And more importantly, she doesn't try to control you." She hesitated. "But if you two are ever going to be something, you have to be honest with her."

He glanced up.

"I'm guessing you haven't told her about Oliver yet."

He sighed. "How could I? They're... they have this connection. She trusts him. I thought maybe I could handle it myself, but—"

"It's not your place to do that. It's hers," Alice said.

He nodded. "You're right."

"That's what happens when you're smart. You're usually right."

They drank their coffee in comfortable silence; both lost in their own thoughts. Now that he'd been confronted with it, it wasn't as if he could hide it any longer. He would need to have a private talk with Ivy about his feelings, about their partnership, about the possibility of something more than professional collaboration. But more importantly, he needed to tell her what he knew so she could make the decision on her own. Only after that would it be appropriate to talk about… *them*.

But he couldn't keep the burning question from invading his thoughts: did she feel the same as he did?

Alice's phone rang, interrupting his thoughts. She glanced at the caller ID and her expression grew serious.

"It's the hospital," she said, answering immediately. "Hello? Yes, this is Alice Blair… I see… How long?… Okay, I'll be right there."

She hung up and looked at Jonathan with a mixture of sadness and relief. "I gotta go."

"Do you want—"

Alice held up a hand, already reaching for her purse and keys. "No, you stay here. You need your rest. I can handle this. You need anything before I go?"

"I'll be fine. Alice… I'm sorry."

"Thanks. Rest up. Tell Ivy I hope she finds what she needs."

After Alice left, Jonathan settled back against the couch cushions and allowed himself to think about what came next. They still had to deal with Oliver, still had to figure out how Zimmerman fit into the larger conspiracy Alice had uncovered. They had to find him before he could hurt anyone else.

But for the first time since this investigation began, Jonathan felt like they had a real chance. They had information, they had a team, and he had clarity about what mattered most to him.

When his phone eventually buzzed with an incoming call from Ivy, Jonathan answered immediately.

"Hey," he said, unable to keep the relief out of his voice at hearing from her. "How did it go with the witnesses?"

"We got some good information," Ivy's voice came through clearly, though she sounded tired. "My mom was definitely being stalked. Her friend remembers her getting threatening letters, and my parents even filed police reports that got buried. Nat's… not handling it well."

"That gives us a pattern leading up to their disappearance. And it supports the theory that your mother was the primary target."

"Yeah." She paused. "Nat and I are going to call it a day. It's been… a lot. We'll pick this up tomorrow."

"That's probably smart. You both need rest. Alice got a call from the hospital. I think her mother is dying."

"Oh," Ivy said. "Is she okay?"

"She's tough. But I imagine she's going to be busy for a while."

"Are you okay there by yourself?"

Jonathan felt a warmth spread through his chest at her concern. "I'm fine here. Actually, I'm better than fine."

Another pause. "You sound different."

"I'm fine. Let's… regroup tomorrow. Are you staying back at your apartment?"

"Actually, we're going to Carol's. She has more bedrooms and I need to see her. If for no other reason than to apologize. We'll be over first thing in the morning."

Jonathan hesitated. He needed to tell Ivy about Oliver, but after the day she'd had, maybe now wasn't the time.

"You still there?" she asked.

"Yep, just… my meds. You know. Sleep well. We'll talk tomorrow."

"Okay. You too."

After they hung up, Jonathan settled back against the

couch, frustration with himself boiling under the surface. Alice was right. Ivy deserved to know the truth.

As he struggled to get up from the couch, he made himself a pledge. He'd tell her tomorrow and whatever she decided to do, he would support.

After all... it was her life. And she deserved to decide what to do with it.

Chapter Seventeen

"Are you sure about this?" Nat asked as they pulled into the driveway.

Ivy didn't answer, only got out of the Jeep and headed to the front door that was already open, where Carol stood wearing an oversize sweater. Ivy remembered thinking while she'd been stuck in that prison of a house that eventually Carol would realize she was missing. That she would have alerted someone. But now, seeing her face, Ivy realized she hadn't wanted that to happen at all. She didn't want Carol to know what she'd gone through because Carol was a protector at heart... and she might see it as her own fault. It would be easier just to never tell her the truth... but Ivy couldn't do that. She owed the woman an explanation. Given Ivy was technically now a fugitive of the law *and* she had been missing for four days *and* Jonathan had almost been killed, she imagined the woman was going out of her mind.

"Ivy," Carol said as she approached. "What—"

Ivy glanced over her shoulder at Nat following behind.

"Hi," Ivy said. "A lot's happened. Can we come in?"

"Can you—of course you can, sweet girl." She glanced at Nat again. "Are you okay?"

Ivy nodded. She wanted to reach out for Carol, that same sensation that had pulled her to Jonathan now pulling her to her foster mother. But she hesitated, only giving her a weak smile.

Carol remained immovable for a moment before letting the women in, staring Nat down as she did. Nat, for her part, avoided the older woman's gaze and kept her head down as she followed Ivy into the house. At their feet Hero jumped about, clearly thrilled to have someone else in the house.

"Hey, buddy," Ivy said reaching down to rub his head. The little dog immediately ran off to grab a toy, returning with it in his mouth and pushing it into Ivy's leg so she'd try to take it from him.

"Cute dog," Nat said.

"He belongs to Oliver," Carol said, passing them on the way to the kitchen. "I'm just keeping an eye on him temporarily."

"Can I get you some tea?" Carol asked, seemingly unsure what to do with Nat there. As far as Ivy could recall, Nat hadn't been in this house in a good eight years. Maybe ten. Ever since she stopped coming around after Ivy turned eighteen.

"Honestly, I could use something stronger," Nat said.

Carol gave the woman a terse smile. "Ivy?"

"We… should sit down," she said. "There's a lot to tell you."

"Ivy—" Nat began.

"No, she needs to know the truth. All of it."

Ivy spent a solid hour going over everything that had transpired over the past five days. From what happened in the cabin to her semi-interrogation of Zimmerman, to her capture and eventual truce with Nat. In between she sprinkled in what she'd learned about Zimmerman from both Jonathan and their research from Nat's old case files.

Carol sat and listened intently, nodding as she went along but making few other movements. Every now and again she would shoot a glance at Nat before turning her attention back to Ivy.

It was nearly ten P.M. by the time Ivy finished and Hero had fallen asleep on Carol's couch, one of his toys still in his mouth.

"Excuse me a moment," Carol said, standing and returning to the kitchen.

Ivy turned to Nat, only to find the woman staring off into space, her expression completely blank. It couldn't have been easy for Nat to hear it all again, but Ivy thought it was better this way. Better for them both to be here to explain things, rather than Ivy try to do it alone. That... and she wasn't sure what Nat would do if she left her alone. She'd been melancholy all day, which only seemed to be getting worse. Carol *had* poured her a whisky, but it sat untouched on the side table beside her.

Carol came back into the room with a refreshed cup of tea, taking a seat back beside Hero. "There's something I don't understand."

Ivy raised her eyebrows in response.

"You told Mrs. Baker to watch out for any strange tendencies with Ivy... anything that might indicate a... relapse... as you put it."

Nat's glassy eyes came back and she nodded. "Yes ma'am."

"Why didn't you tell me that? You knew I had a history in social work when I put in my application for Ivy."

Nat swallowed. "I didn't want to poison your relationship from the beginning," Nat admitted. "Mrs. Baker was a temporary situation. I knew Ivy wouldn't be there forever. Not to mention she never said anything that I deemed concerning or that might lead to a relapse. It had been nearly a year by that point, I figured if it was going to happen, it would have already."

"That means one of two things," Carol said calmly. "Either you were willing to put my life in danger, or you never really believed Ivy was behind it in the first place."

Nat clenched and unclenched her hands, the grimace on her face sharp enough to cut through granite. "No. I was sure."

"You couldn't have been," Carol replied. "Otherwise, you never would have let Ivy out of your sight."

"Look, what do you want me to say?" Nat replied. "I screwed up. We all know it. I sacrificed *everything* for this and I was *wrong*."

Carol set her cup of tea to the side and stood, taking a seat right beside Nat. She took the woman's hands in her own. "You made a judgement call. One based on faulty information and one that was probably biased. But take it from someone who has made a lot of mistakes in her time. You need to face this… move through it and then move on. Otherwise it will eat you from the inside out."

Nat pulled her hands away. "How can you say that, of all people? I *jailed* your daughter. I thought she was a killer. I've never been right about anything in my entire life."

"That, right there. That's what will consume you if you let it," Carol said. "You will use this mistake to redefine your whole life. To convince yourself that everything you do is wrong. And that really *will* destroy you. And I don't want that to happen."

"Why do you care so much?" Nat asked, her eyes beginning to shimmer.

"Because one time, you brought someone very special into my life. Someone I love very much." She gave Ivy a quick smile. "It's going to take you a long time to process this. To move past it. But I want your promise that you *will*, because I don't want to see you ruin your life over this."

"You should be furious with me," Nat said, her voice barely above a whisper. She turned to Ivy. "You too."

"We can't change what we've done," Carol said. "We can only decide to make better decisions. Don't let this define you." She pulled Nat to her, wrapping her arms around the woman who had only a few days ago, been keeping Ivy detained with a shock bracelet.

Ivy smiled. She knew Carol wouldn't judge Nat, that she could help her begin to process what had happened. Because despite everything, Ivy still loved Nat, deep down. She was the big sister she'd never had. Even when she was plotting behind Ivy's back, it didn't change anything. And if Nat was going to find a way out of this, she needed help.

"Now," Carol said, pulling away from Nat as the other woman wiped at her cheeks. "You two must be exhausted."

"I just want to sleep in a regular bed," Ivy said.

"Nat, I have another spare room if you want it," Carol said.

Nat nodded. "I appreciate that."

"And in the morning," Carol said as they stood. "I'll make sure both of you get a good breakfast."

Ivy awoke to sun streaming through her window. She grabbed for a phone that wasn't there before everything came back to her. As she turned to get up, she noted a certain stiffness in her joints —probably a result of not moving much during the night. She hadn't even remembered her head hitting the pillow. She'd been so exhausted and hadn't realized she'd been running on fumes.

The low murmur of conversation coming from the kitchen caught her ear. Ivy made it halfway down the hall before the smell of bacon and pancakes hit her nose. She'd barely had anything to eat yesterday and had purposefully not eaten much at the house Nat kept her in as a form of protest. But now she couldn't keep her mouth from watering.

"Morning," Carol said as she entered the kitchen. "Sleep well?"

"What time is it?" Ivy asked.

"A little past seven-thirty," Nat replied, a cup of coffee in front of her at the breakfast table. "Don't worry, I wasn't going to let you sleep past eight."

Ivy surveyed the room. Nat and Carol had been sitting across from each other at the breakfast table, while Hero laid in his little bed, chewing on a small bone. His tail wagged as soon as he saw Ivy. "What… um… what's going on?"

"Just catching up," Carol replied. "We haven't seen each other in quite a while. Can I get you a plate?"

"Yeah," Ivy said, still a little groggy. "That would be great. What are you catching up on?"

"I was just telling Carol about some of the cases you've been working since your promotion," Nat replied. "And about Sam… and Audrey."

"I can't believe she's already eighteen," Carol said, loading up a plate for Ivy full of scrambled eggs, bacon and three pancakes. She then topped the pancakes with whipped cream and an astonishing amount of syrup—something she hadn't done for Ivy in years.

Nat nodded. "And enrolled at UCLA. She got tired of the cold and the wet. Said she wanted to go to college where it was warm."

"What's her major?" Carol set Ivy's plate down at one of the empty spots and grabbed her a glass of juice, adding it to the setting.

"Right now, it's chemistry, but I'm sure that will change. She's headstrong, but she isn't much of a scientist. I figure she'll probably pivot to business or logistics or something."

"I didn't know she'd been accepted to UCLA," Ivy said. "When did that happen?"

"About three months ago," Nat said. "Early enrollment. I …never got the chance to tell you."

"Do you and Samantha still speak often?" Carol asked.

"Not really. Now that Audrey is eighteen there's no more custody agreement. I get most of my news about her from Audrey, actually. Plus… things have been a little hectic for me lately."

Ivy wasted no time digging into her breakfast. It was the most mouth-watering meal she'd ever eaten… the eggs and bacon cooked to perfection and the pancakes were practically manna from heaven. There was just nothing like a home-cooked meal. And Carol had the magic touch.

Ivy caught Carol smiling at her, but it didn't stop the intake of food into her mouth. "What?"

"Just happy to see you eating is all," Carol said.

Ivy turned to Nat, her mouth still full of pancakes. "Do you think Alice can get those old reports—"

"I already put a call in to one of my contacts first thing this morning," she said. "Apparently Alice left quite the impression yesterday. Ayford is scrambling to prevent another security breach. I'm not sure how much more she'll be able to do for us."

Ivy couldn't help but smile despite the setback. Classic Alice. Like a tornado through a cornfield.

"We'll find a way," Ivy said. "Somehow."

After breakfast Ivy took a quick shower and changed, feeling more like herself than she had in almost a week. As they prepared to head out, Ivy caught a look from Carol.

"You go ahead," she told Nat. "I'll be there in a minute."

Nat nodded. "Thank you, Carol. For breakfast, for the bed… for everything."

"You are welcome here anytime, Natasha." The woman stilled at the use of her full name, but smiled on the way out.

"I want you to know, I am very proud of you," Carol said as soon as Nat was outside. "You could have left her behind. But you didn't."

"It didn't seem right," Ivy said.

"What I told her last night goes for you too." Carol stilled Ivy with her gaze. "Do not let what happened with Jasmine Quinn define the rest of your life. Accept it. Learn from it. Move forward."

Ivy nodded, though she found it difficult.

"Be careful, okay? And let me know if there's anything I can do to help."

"Just don't let your guard down," Ivy said. "And keep that shotgun close. If Zimmerman really does know everything about me, I don't want you to be caught unaware."

"Don't worry about me," Carol said, reaching out for Ivy but pulling back as she always did. But this time, Ivy leaned forward and wrapped her arms around the woman. She could still feel the pulse of the electricity running through her, but it was as it had been with Jonathan. It didn't hurt like it once had. Or if it did, she'd become so used to it that it didn't matter anymore. Whatever the reason, she didn't care.

"Ivy," Carol whispered.

"Love you," Ivy said, pulling back. "I'll be in touch again soon." She headed for the Jeep, leaving Carol and Hero at the door, watching them.

But as they pulled away, she couldn't get the ominous feeling out of her gut that she'd never see them again.

"You okay?" Nat asked as they drove away from the house.

"Yeah," Ivy said. "Don't worry about me. I'm fine."

Chapter Eighteen

"Morning," Ivy said as she and Nat walked into the apartment. Jonathan was on the couch, but he'd apparently moved at some point, as he was in different clothes and his hair was slightly damp. "Did you take a shower?" Ivy asked.

"Just a quick one," he said. "I can't stand sitting in my own filth."

Ivy set two Tupperware containers on the counter. "Breakfast from Carol. She said to rest up. And this would do you some good."

Ivy had hoped he'd been more elated at a Carol Chamberlain breakfast being hand-delivered to him. But Jonathan's features were pulled into a concerned look.

"Is everything okay?" Ivy asked. "Is it Alice?"

"No, no, she's fine," Jonathan said. "But we need to talk."

Ivy exchanged glances with Nat. "Okay. About what?"

"You may want to come sit down," he replied.

What the hell could be wrong now? Didn't they have enough to worry about? And why was he trying to coddle her? Ivy felt like she could wade through molten lava right now if she had to. "Jonathan, just spit it out. What's going on?"

He took a deep breath. "Okay. When Alice was doing

some research on Zimmerman, she found he worked with a couple of companies, Regional Holdings, LLC and Pacific Research Associates."

"Yeah," Ivy said, remembering looking at the paperwork yesterday that had those names on it. "So?"

"I've seen those company names before. When you were missing, I went to visit Oliver, hoping he could maybe track your phone again like he did the last time."

"See?" Nat said. "Told you so."

Ivy waved her off. "I don't understand. What does this have to do with Oliver?"

"I saw the same names on his computer," Jonathan said.

"So? I had him looking into Zimmerman as well," Ivy said. "Maybe he found the same thing Alice did."

Jonathan shook his head. "No, this wasn't research. He was into their financials, moving money around for them. Ivy, I think he might work for them. I think they're one of his clients."

"That—" Ivy automatically wanted to argue, but as she opened her mouth, she realized how little she actually knew about Oliver's operations. She knew he worked for criminals sometimes, and given one of his clients had seen fit to break into his house and beat him within inches of his life, they weren't the kind of people you crossed. Given what they knew about Zimmerman, could it be possible Oliver had some of the same connections?

"Okay…but just because…that doesn't mean…" She was having a hard time forming words.

Ivy began pacing abruptly, needing movement to process what felt like another fundamental shift in everything she thought she understood. Oliver had been her anchor through some of the worst periods of her life—the one person who understood her past because he'd lived through similar experiences in the foster system. The idea that he might have been working with the people who'd destroyed her family was like trying to reconcile two incompatible realities.

"There has to be another explanation," she said, pacing toward the window. "Maybe he's trying to expose their operation."

"Maybe," Jonathan said gently. "But whatever he's into, it isn't good. If he's in league with these people—"

"No," she said again. "It's not possible."

"Ivy, *anything's* possible," Nat replied. "I was wrong about you. Maybe you're wrong about Oliver."

"He saved my life," she said, turning back to face Jonathan. "When I found him after the attack, he was barely conscious. He was hurt because he'd been helping me."

"Or because he'd outlived his usefulness to his employers," Nat suggested. "Criminal organizations aren't known for their loyalty to assets who become liabilities."

Okay, maybe he didn't always work within the confines of the law. That didn't make him an accessory to Zimmerman. Oliver was a good person at heart; she knew it.

"I need to talk to him," she said finally.

"Ivy, if he really is working with these people—" Jonathan started.

"Then I need to hear it from him. I need to understand why." The words came out sharper than she'd intended, but she couldn't help the anger that was building alongside the hurt. "I've spent my entire adult life trusting him. If that trust was misplaced, if he's been manipulating me all this time, then I deserve to know."

Nat moved away from the door, folding her arms across her chest. "If Oliver is connected to Zimmerman's network, confronting him directly could be dangerous. These people killed two transport officers to free one prisoner. They won't hesitate to eliminate threats."

"And alerting Oliver may inadvertently alert others to your location," Jonathan added.

Ivy ran her hands down her face, feeling like she was being pulled in three different directions. "So what then? Just ignore it? I can't do that."

"I'm just saying we need to be careful," Nat replied.

"I'm going to see him," Ivy said. "And clear all this up."

"But—"

"No," she replied. "He's going to explain himself. *Then* I'll decide what to do."

Oliver's modest one-story house sat behind an eight-foot chain-link fence topped with razor wire—a stark contrast to the suburban normalcy of the neighborhood around it. The security cameras mounted at the gate tracked their approach, and Ivy felt the familiar weight of being watched as she pressed the intercom button. The electronic lock disengaged with a harsh buzz, and they walked up the concrete path past motion sensors and flood lights that Oliver had installed after the incident that almost took his life.

"Jesus. You weren't kidding," Nat said as they approached the door.

Oliver opened the door before they could knock, relief flooding his features when he saw Ivy. The sight of him stopped her short—no crutch anymore, but the evidence of the attack lingered in the yellow-green bruises along his jaw, the careful way he held his left shoulder. For a moment, her anger wavered, replaced by the concern that had become second nature where he was concerned.

"Oh my God, Ivy." His voice carried exhaustion and something that might have been gratitude. "Why didn't Jonathan tell me you were okay? I've been going out of my mind."

The words hit her wrong, sparking the fury she'd been banking during the drive. "This isn't a social call," she said, pushing past him into the living room. The space felt different today—gone was the makeshift bed she'd set for him after bringing him home from the hospital. Replaced with file folders and computer equipment. "We need to talk."

That was when Oliver noticed Nat, and his entire demeanor shifted. The relief faded, replaced by wariness that bordered on alarm. Ivy watched his face cycle through recognition, confusion, and something that looked dangerously close to fear. He knew everything about her history with Nat—everything except the kidnapping, which felt like a lifetime ago now instead of just days.

"What's she doing here?" Oliver's voice carried an edge she'd rarely heard, the careful control he maintained slipping just enough to reveal the calculating mind beneath. "Ivy, what's going on?"

"Answer my questions first." The demand came out harder than she'd intended, but she didn't soften it. "Are you involved with Regional Holdings and Pacific Research Associates?"

The color drained from Oliver's face. It was answer enough, but Ivy needed to hear him say it. Needed to understand how deep this betrayal ran.

"Why are you asking me that?" He was stalling, she knew.

"Answer the question." Her voice rose, and she didn't care that Nat was watching this intimate confrontation unfold. She was getting the answers she needed *now*.

Oliver ran a hand through his hair, a gesture she recognized as his tell when he was about to admit something he'd rather keep hidden. "Those are two of the companies owned by my… clients."

Ivy felt something crack inside her chest—not her heart breaking, exactly, but the foundation of trust she'd built their relationship on shifting dangerously.

"Did you know?" The words came out like razors.

"Know?"

"About Zimmerman. Have you been playing me this whole time?"

"What? No! What are you talking about? What does Zimmerman have to do with anything? Ivy, what is going on here?"

"Alice discovered that Zimmerman has ties to both those organizations." The words came out in a rush, propelled by fury and betrayal and the desperate need to make him understand what he'd done. "Which means you've been supporting him this entire time. You've been helping fund the man who destroyed my family."

"That's not—" Oliver started.

"We have the data," Nat said, cutting him off. "There's no question."

"Okay, listen," Oliver said slowly. "I had no idea Zimmerman was connected to them. None."

"Right." Nat's voice was cool and skeptical, just like she was interrogating a suspect. "What a convenient coincidence that you just happen to work for the same people funding a sociopath who's been stalking your best friend for fifteen years."

Oliver rounded on her, his composure finally cracking completely. "You don't know what you're talking about. I've been trying to get away from them for months. That's why they attacked me—because I was stealing from them."

The admission hung in the air between them, heavy with implications. It had never been a secret that Oliver had always worked in the gray spaces between the law. He'd made no attempt to hide what he could do, and Ivy had even used that to her advantage on occasion. But this felt like something worse. Something much worse.

"Stealing how?" she asked, her voice barely above a whisper.

"Skimming from their accounts. Moving money around, creating delays in their operations." He looked older suddenly, worn down by secrets he'd been carrying. "I was trying to build up enough resources to disappear completely. To cut all ties with them so I could—" He stopped, glanced at Nat, then back to Ivy. "So I could have a clean slate."

"You were stealing from criminal organizations." Ivy said it slowly, testing the words. "Oliver, do you have any idea how dangerous that is?"

"Of course I do." His laugh was bitter, humorless. "I have the bruises to prove it. But I wasn't going to keep working for them forever. I couldn't."

Nat crossed her arms, skepticism written in every line of her body. "And you expect us to believe you had no idea these same people were funding Zimmerman? That's one hell of a coincidence."

"It's not a coincidence," Oliver said quietly. "It's how these networks operate. They fund dozens of different operations, keep their assets compartmentalized. I never knew what their money was going toward. Never wanted to know."

Ivy wanted to believe him. The desperation in his voice, the way his hands shook slightly as he spoke—it all felt genuine. But the evidence was damning, and she'd been wrong about people before. Catastrophically wrong.

"What exactly did you think you were doing for them?" she asked.

Oliver moved to his desk, wincing as the motion pulled at his injured shoulder. He unlocked a drawer, pulled out a thick folder. "They don't tell me. I'm not high enough on the pole. But I figured out they were using some of it to diversify. To support regular businesses while funneling funds to illegal ones and then back again. It's how they wash all the money."

He spread papers across his coffee table—contracts, payment schedules, research proposals. Ivy recognized the language of academic research grants and corporate consulting agreements. On the surface, it all looked reasonable.

"I've been looking into Zimmerman since you asked me to," Oliver continued. "Trying to find out about his professional background. What I found..." He trailed off, pulling out a different set of documents. "There are buried reports. Former patients complaining about memory loss after sessions with him. People who went to him for standard therapy and came out with gaps in their recollection."

Memory loss. Gaps in recollection. She thought about the blank spaces in her own mind, the way certain memories of her family's final days remained frustratingly out of reach.

"Are you saying…?"

"I think this may be what happened to you," he replied. "Why you can't remember. I was waiting to hear back from Jonathan so I could give him the information when you showed up. He was here. Looking for you."

Ivy sank onto his couch, the weight of this revelation settling over her. She'd always assumed her memory gaps were trauma-related, her mind's way of protecting her from the worst details of her family's death. But what if it wasn't natural? What if Zimmerman had deliberately stolen those memories from her?

"This is insane." Nat's voice carried a note of something that might have been sympathy. "If this is true, if he's been experimenting on people for fifteen years…"

"It explains how he's stayed hidden for so long," Oliver said. "How he's been able to manipulate situations, control narratives. If he can create memory gaps then he could be practically invisible."

Ivy thought about all the therapy sessions she'd attended over the years, all the well-meaning professionals who'd told her that healing meant accepting that some memories might never return. What if they hadn't been lost to trauma, but stolen outright?

"Can you prove this?" she asked.

"I wish. All we have are some client testimonies that have

been buried under a mountain of lawsuits or outright suppressed."

"And your clients—do they know what Zimmerman really does?"

"I don't know. Probably." Oliver sat heavily in his chair, exhaustion evident in every line of his body. "If they really are connected, there's no telling what information they might be sharing."

"Can you find out?"

His eyes went wide. "You want me to break into my employer's records *again*, after they nearly killed me last time?"

"You said you wanted a way out," Ivy said. She couldn't help but still feel the sting of betrayal, whether he had known about the connection or not. She had told him over and over again to stay away from working with illegal operations. And this was exactly why. Not only could they not be trusted, but there was no good way out. Once you were in that world, you were in it for life.

"Okay," Oliver finally said. "I'll do it."

Ivy raised her eyebrow. "Really?"

He nodded. "It's the least I can do. To make up for… well, for this."

"Seems like a lot of people are trying to make up for their pasts lately," Nat said, crossing her arms.

"Ivy. I swear to you, if I knew what this was, I would have found a way out a long time ago." Oliver gave her a look of desperation.

His sudden altruism surprised her. But maybe it shouldn't have. Oliver *had* always been on her side, even when they were little. And sure, their reunion had a few rough patches, but they'd worked through those. And if he was telling the truth— if he was attacked because he'd tried to get away from these people, maybe she needed to trust that he wasn't trying to stab her in the back. The whole event with Nat had made her more paranoid than usual.

"Can you do it without raising any flags?" Ivy asked. "I don't want…" She looked around the house. There were still signs from the last attack. And Oliver's back room was surely still a mess of server parts.

"Maybe. But it will be tricky," he said. "Can you give me a few hours? And if you can get me that information Alice pulled it would be helpful."

Ivy nodded. "Sure. We'll go over and grab it now."

"Ivy—" Nat started.

"No." She stood, gathering her composure. "We need to have some faith. We'll be back with the documentation."

They walked back to the Jeep in silence, the electronic lock on the gate engaging behind them with a sharp click. As they reached the vehicle, Nat spoke quietly. "You know this could all be an elaborate lie, right? He could be playing you. Seeing what we have on Zimmerman to report back to his bosses."

"He's not." Ivy stared at Oliver's house through the chain-link fence, his silhouette visible in the living room window. "I trust him."

"And if you're wrong?"

Ivy thought about Oliver's injuries, about the desperation in his voice when he'd talked about trying to escape his criminal clients. About the research he'd compiled on Zimmerman, the financial records that painted a picture of a vast network she was only beginning to understand.

"Then I'll deal with that when I have to," she said. "But right now, he's our best chance."

Chapter Nineteen

On the way back to Jonathan's place, the only thoughts Ivy could think were of all the times she'd leaned on Oliver, and he hadn't let her down. He wouldn't let her down this time either, she was sure of it.

"Duck down," Nat said, pulling Ivy from her thoughts.

"What?"

"Quick!"

Ivy did as she was told, ducking down into the footwell of the Jeep as much as she could. She glanced up at Nat for some kind of signal but the woman kept checking the rearview mirror every few seconds.

"Nat, what's—"

"Shit," Nat said. "He's gonna pull us over."

"Who is?"

"Looks like Cahill. Can't be sure though. Can you climb into the backseat without lifting above the back window?"

Ivy glanced around the center console to the small area behind Nat's seats. There wasn't a lot of space back there. "I don't know."

"Try," she said as flashing blue and red lights began reflecting off the surfaces of the cab.

Ivy wasn't a large person by any means, but it still meant squeezing into a very small area. She kept her head down, climbing over the center console as Nat began to slow the Jeep. And she had no idea if she was visible from the back window or not, but she kept as low as she possibly could.

"Hurry," Nat urged, the Jeep rolling along, not having stopped completely. It was obvious she was drawing out stopping completely in an effort to stall.

"I'm trying!" Ivy reached around to the back of Nat's seat. Her hands going first, she managed to pull herself all the way into the small space behind Nat's seat. "Scoot up."

Nat shifted the seat forward a little, giving Ivy enough room to get her hips and legs over too. There was an old jacket beneath her and Ivy pulled it out, covering herself and putting her back up against the frame of the Jeep, hoping she couldn't be spotted.

"I need to move the seat back again," Nat said. "It's too far forward." She shifted back and Ivy felt like she'd been squeezed in a vice. She could only take short, quick breaths as her lungs were completely compacted. Though she couldn't see, she heard Nat roll down the window.

"Lieutenant." That was Cahill alright. His Texas drawl was recognizable anywhere. He sounded surprised.

"Morning, Cahill," Nat said. "How's your day going?"

"Oh, you know, can't complain," he said. "I didn't realize that was you when I passed." There was a pause. "You didn't happen to have someone with you, did you?"

"Just me," Nat replied.

"You know, I think Armstrong is looking for you. There's been a lot of chatter since you left."

"I needed some personal time," Nat replied. "He wouldn't give it to me, so I left. Is that a crime?"

"No. 'Course not," he replied. "Just… surprisin' is all. Well, I threw my flashers on 'cause I thought I saw—we've got a watch out for Bishop. You haven't seen her, have you?"

"Not since I left the department," Nat replied without missing a beat. Ivy tried to take a breath, only to find she could barely get any air. Her blood pressure began to spike. If she didn't get out of this soon, she was going suffocate.

"Well, if she reaches out, let us know, willya? She's wanted in connection with the Quinn case."

"Yeah, I heard about that. With the little girl, right?" Nat said. "If I see her, I'll let you know."

"'preciate it, Lieutenant," Cahill said. Ivy could practically imagine him tipping his hat at her. "Have a good rest of your day."

"You too." Nat rolled the window back up, and Ivy felt the car pull away from the side of the road.

"Tight," she managed to squeak out.

Nat pulled the seat up, and air flooded Ivy's lungs as she took deep breaths. "What… happened?" she asked between breaths.

"He passed us coming the other way," Nat said. "Probably saw you in the passenger's seat. I didn't see it quickly enough. Now he's following us."

Cahill might have sounded like he was from the backwoods, but he was a sharp officer. "Can you lose him?"

"You just stay there," Nat said. "Let me see what I can do."

The next fifteen minutes were a series of quick turns and swerves, enough that even Ivy—who usually had an iron stomach—was beginning to feel the effects.

"I think we're clear," she finally said. "I was trying not to be obvious."

Ivy pulled the jacket off her head and started to wriggle out from behind the seat. "But you're sure he saw me?"

Nat nodded. "He wasn't going to try and search me, but he was shooting looks around the back. They're going to know we're in it together now."

"Great. Just when I was hoping to get back to my apartment tonight." Ivy pulled herself all the way back into the front seat again.

"We'll have to assume both our places are being watched twenty-four seven now," Nat replied.

That was standard procedure given the situation. Ivy had just made Nat an accessory, though she still thought the whole BOLO was ridiculous. The real problem was they had lost Zimmerman and been caught with their pants around their legs, and now they wanted a win just so they could feel better about themselves.

She wasn't prepared to give it to them.

They arrived back to Jonathan's apartment to find him asleep on the couch again, still sitting up. Thankfully Ivy had taken the key before they left because otherwise, they might have been knocking for a good ten minutes.

"Should we just take it now?" Nat asked, indicating the information Alice had left on Zimmerman.

Jonathan stirred, looking over at Ivy. "Oh. Hey," he said. "How'd it go?"

"He admitted to working with those organizations, but denied knowing Zimmerman had anything to do with them," Nat said before Ivy could answer. "Which is a nice, safe place to land."

Jonathan blinked a few more times as he struggled to wake up. "What do you think?"

Ivy took a deep breath. "I want to trust him… but it feels *too* convenient to be a coincidence."

"Then what's the play?"

"He's promised to help us find Zimmerman," Ivy said. "But he needs Alice's background work to speed up the process."

Alarm colored Jonathan's features. "Wait a second. You're taking her research to him? What if he's using you to find out what we know about Zimmerman already?"

"That's what I said," Nat replied.

"And what about the reports you're supposed to be looking for?" he asked her.

"It turns out Alice left a bigger swath than she indicated," Nat replied. "Getting anything from my contacts was already difficult. On the way back here we were spotted by Oakhurst PD. I'm sure Cahill is working on his report right now about how Ivy and I are in this together. Which means all my sources just dried up."

"You got pulled over?"

"We managed it, but Cahill's no fool. He knows what he saw," Nat replied.

"Damn," Jonathan said, leaning back.

Nat's eyebrows shot up before looking at Ivy. "Did you just hear that?"

"It's becoming more common," Ivy said, grinning. "Anyway. I trust Oliver isn't stabbing us in the back. And the sooner he can track down Zimmerman, the better. I don't know what the man is waiting for, but I don't like the idea that he's just out there somewhere, biding his time. We need to get a pinpoint on him and we need it *today*." She gathered up Alice's research, stacked it all together in a file folder and shoved it under her arm.

"Wait, you're going back over there now?" Jonathan asked.

"We sure are," Ivy said. "No time like the present."

Jonathan pushed himself off the couch with some difficulty. "Let me do it."

"Can you even drive?" Nat asked.

"Listen, I learned how to drive with one hand when I was seventeen," Jonathan replied. "I think I can handle it. If Oakhurst is out patrolling for you, you don't want to run the risk of being spotted on something simple like this. Let me get it to him so you don't have to worry about it."

Ivy hesitated, looking at Nat.

"Plus, it will give me something to do. I feel like I'm going stir crazy here."

"Fine," Ivy finally said. "As long as you're sure you won't wreck."

"I'll be fine," Jonathan replied, shooting Ivy a wink. "Don't worry about me."

"What are you doing here?" Oliver asked, standing in the open door, a grimace plastered across his face.

"Trying to decide if I should kick your ass or not," Jonthan rumbled. He'd wound himself up the whole way here, growing angrier and angrier at Oliver for getting involved in something that could hurt Ivy. And now that he stood in front of the man, he had a deep desire to knock him out cold.

Oliver's eyes slid down to Jonathan's arm in the sling.

"Don't let it fool you," he said. "I'm stronger than I look."

"You think I don't already feel awful about this?" Oliver said. "I've been racking my brain ever since Ivy left. How was I supposed to know Zimmerman was connected to…"

"Yes?" Jonathan asked.

"Maybe it's better I don't say," Oliver replied. "Plausible deniability and all that. The point is, I never had any idea. If I had, I wouldn't have started working with them in the first place. Plus, I *tried* to get out. And you see what good that did me."

"You didn't try hard enough," Jonathan replied.

"Did you just come over here to give me shit or is there a reason you're darkening my doorstep?"

"Ivy said you needed Alice's research."

Oliver nodded. "It will help me figure out this Zimmerman connection faster. Figure out what I missed."

Jonathan lowered his gaze. "I've seen you manipulate

security machines like they were tinker toys. You're telling me that you can't find anything on him without a little help?"

Oliver blanched. "I swear to you, I looked *everywhere*. If Zimmerman *is* connected to the people I work for, they have done an amazing job covering it up."

"Why would they cover it up?" Jonathan asked.

Oliver looked past him, out to the street. "Look, can you just come inside where we can talk about this? I don't feel comfortable with the door open this long."

Jonathan made his way in the house, allowing Oliver to close and lock the door behind him. If he was going to jump Jonathan, he'd have to be ready.

"You know, I should really be the one pissed at you. You were supposed to let me know Ivy was okay. And I hear nothing until she shows up at my door."

"Too bad for you," Jonathan replied.

Oliver made his way into one of the back bedrooms where he'd set up a new computer workstation. "I've run every possible search and scenario I can, looking in every crevice I can think of, and there is no mention of Zimmerman. I managed to find some of his records, but most have been redacted or destroyed from what I can tell. It's like his whole profile has been sanitized."

"How long would something like that take?" Jonathan asked.

"For someone like me who knows what they're doing? A few hours."

"Is it possible the information could have been sanitized *after* Alice did her research?"

Oliver frowned. "Unlikely. Because I started looking right after Zimmerman was arrested, after Ivy asked me to. And I still didn't come away with anything."

"Then how is it she managed to find incriminating evidence so quickly?"

Oliver sighed. "There is a drawback to how I work. I'm

alone. Isolated, which means I only rely on myself here. I'm sure Alice has all kinds of contacts, all sorts of favors. She's in the public eye. She's had years to build relationships with people. I… don't work that way."

Despite everything, Jonathan was beginning to feel sorry for the man. Here he was, alone in his home, and he couldn't even do what was necessary to keep his friend safe.

"Then you're telling the truth. You never knew about Zimmerman's connections and you weren't using them to undermine Ivy."

"Of course not," Oliver said. "I could never do that."

Jonathan saw something in the way he responded. Something that felt… familiar. "Why not?"

"What?"

"Why couldn't you do that?" he asked again, more insistent. Years of interrogating suspects told him that Freudian slips were more common than most people thought. And Oliver had just let something go without even realizing it.

"I don't know what you mean," he said, turning around in his chair.

"Yes, you do," Jonathan said, watching him intently. "Why couldn't you undermine her?"

"She's my friend," Oliver said, his gaze going to the empty corner of the room.

"That's not the reason."

"Look, I don't see what this has to do with anything," Oliver replied. "Did you bring the research or not?"

Jonathan considered continuing to press, but he'd gotten his answer, whether Oliver realized it or not. His stark refusal to address the question head on told Jonathan everything he needed to know. Oliver was in love with Ivy…which meant he probably *was* telling the truth about not knowing about Zimmerman. Ever since Alice had confronted Jonathan with the same fact, it had changed the way he thought about Ivy. Oliver's response didn't surprise him. They had known each other for a long time—it was only natural. The question was... did Ivy know?

"The research is in the car, I'll get it," Jonathan said. He headed back to the door, waiting for Oliver to unlock it remotely before heading outside, wincing with each step. He hated being hamstrung like this, not operating at a hundred percent. It drove him insane. But at least he'd gotten what he'd come for.

Back in the house, he handed over the research.

"Great, thank you," Oliver said, flipping through everything Alice had collated. "Hopefully with this I can nail something down."

"The sooner the better," Jonathan said. "Ivy's still AWOL and until Zimmerman is found and captured again, I don't think my bosses are about to let her off the hook."

Oliver nodded. "I got it. I'll be in touch as soon I have something solid." He hesitated like he wanted to say something else. "And... um... thanks for not beating me up. I've had enough physical altercations to last me a while."

"I just needed to be sure," Jonathan said. "This whole thing has turned into a mess."

"Ivy will find a way out," Oliver said. "She always does. Especially with your help."

Was that... a compliment?

"Just let me know as soon as you have something. Ivy doesn't have a phone at the moment."

As he turned to leave he could feel Oliver's gaze on him. The two of them had never gotten along, but it seemed like Oliver's brush with death had changed his demeanor somewhat. Gone was the combative man-child and in his place was someone who seemed to understand the gravity of what was happening. That was an improvement, at least.

As Jonathan drove back to his place, his shoulder aching worse than ever, he thought back to the look Oliver had given him when he'd confronted him directly with the one question he couldn't answer.

The problem was, when he thought about Oliver being in love with Ivy… it triggered feelings of deep jealousy in his own core.

And *that* was something he wasn't prepared for.

Chapter Twenty

Ivy sat at Jonathan's small dining table, her fingers wrapped around a coffee mug that had gone cold an hour ago, staring at Jonathan's cell phone as if she could will it to ring through sheer force of concentration.

Three calls to Oliver. Three times hearing his voice, each more strained than the last, telling her the same thing: *I'm working on it.*

"You're going to bore a hole through that phone if you keep staring at it like that," Nat said from the living room, where she'd been pacing for the better part of an hour. Her restlessness wasn't helping matters any, only making Ivy more anxious.

Considering they'd been clocked together by Oakhurst PD, it would have been foolish for either Nat or Ivy to leave Jonathan's place. Even Aunt Carol's felt distant. Collectively they'd agreed to stay here for the time being, but it meant Ivy wouldn't get to sleep in her own bed again tonight. For lack of something better to do, she'd taken to making everyone lunch because it kept her busy and active.

Jonathan emerged from his bedroom, having lain down for a few hours.

"I'm guessing no updates," he said, heading over and grabbing a sandwich Ivy had made using his panini press.

"Trust me, you'll know," Ivy said, getting up to make him a plate, much in the same way Carol had done for her. "How's the arm?"

"Better," he admitted. "Stiff, but I think those anti-inflammatory meds are working. Just gotta wean myself off the pain pills." He caught Ivy's gaze. "How are you holding up?"

She found she couldn't look him in the eye for fear of getting lost in there. She scraped some chips on a plate. "Fine."

"Thanks," he said, taking the plate over to the table and sitting in the seat adjacent to Ivy's. "I guess we should talk about sleeping arrangements tonight?"

Ivy wasn't sure what it was, but the way he said *sleeping arrangements* made her heart flutter. Jonathan only had one bedroom.

"I call the couch," Nat said.

"I have a sleeping bag and a cot," Jonathan said. "I can camp out in the spare room down the hall."

"I'm not kicking you out of your bed," Ivy said. "*I'll* take the cot. You're injured."

"But—"

"Or you two could just act like grownups and sleep in the same bed," Nat said, cutting him off. "Figure it out."

Ivy caught Jonathan's surprised look and immediately turned away. Suddenly the room was too warm and Ivy went to the sink, getting a glass of water. "I just wish we could do *something*," she said, hoping to change the subject. The air had become stifling in here. "We're just sitting here while Zimmerman could be anywhere, doing anything. This is exactly what he wants—us paralyzed, waiting for someone else to make the first move." The truth was all this waiting was starting to get to her. And she couldn't keep those dark images at bay forever. She needed to bring this to an end, and soon.

"Sometimes waiting is the smart play," Jonathan said gently, but Ivy could see the concern in his eyes.

Ivy moved to the window, looking out at the quiet suburban street. "I've been thinking about Zimmerman, trying to get into his head. He's methodical. Patient. He's been planning this for years, probably decades. But he's also reactive—he responds to threats, to changes in his environment."

She turned back to face them both. "He knows we're looking for him. He has to do something."

"Okay, so?" Nat asked, though her tone suggested she already suspected where Ivy's thoughts were leading.

"We've already exhausted the cabin," Ivy said. "But that wasn't where it *really* started. It started at my old house."

Nat furrowed her brow. "Your house was the first place you looked the day you became an officer. Remember? I had to practically drag you out of there?"

"I know. But I didn't know then what we know now," Ivy said. "We didn't know about the Vapoxil. We didn't know about *Zimmerman*. What if he decided to go back to the original scene of the crime too? The house has been abandoned for what, three years now?"

She could see the hesitation from both of them. And honestly, she couldn't blame them. More than likely there was nothing to be found there. But it had to be better than sitting around here doing nothing all day. Better than sitting here… imagining horrible things.

"I'm going," Ivy said simply. "I'm sure you're right. But it's worth checking out. I can be back in a few hours."

Nat sighed, running her hands through her hair. "You're not going alone."

"She's right," Jonathan said. "It either needs to be all of us or none of us. Give me a few minutes to get ready." He gobbled up the rest of his sandwich before heading back to his bedroom.

Ivy caught Nat looking at her and when she narrowed her

gaze, Nat wiggled her eyebrows at her, then motioned towards Jonathan's closed door. Ivy just huffed and turned away, but she heard Nat snicker.

Five minutes later, Jonathan emerged, put together as always, his hair combed and pristine and he was back in a suit, though the sling interrupted the look a bit. He grabbed his keys from the counter. "If we're going to do this, we need to be smart. We park a few blocks away, go in quiet, and if anything feels off—anything at all—we leave immediately."

"Agreed." Ivy felt a surge of relief and anticipation. At least they were doing something.

The drive to her old neighborhood took twenty minutes, but it felt like hours. Ivy sat in the back seat with Nat, both of them crouched low to avoid being seen, while Jonathan navigated the familiar streets.

It all looked smaller than she remembered, more ordinary, just as it had when they came to speak to Mrs. Crane. But as they approached her old house, Ivy felt her chest tighten with an emotion she couldn't quite name. Not fear, exactly, but something deeper. Recognition, maybe. Or inevitability.

"Who owns the house now?" Jonathan asked quietly, pulling into a parking spot two blocks away.

"No idea," Ivy said, getting out of the car. The last time she'd been here, a family had been renting the home from a local property management company. Only one other family had owned the home after it was sold when Ivy was young, and they had left almost eight years ago. She'd kept tabs on the place. Apparently it was difficult to sell or even rent the house where an entire family had disappeared.

In some cases, not all publicity was good publicity.

"Great, then they won't care if we break and enter," Nat muttered.

They walked the remaining blocks in silence, taking a circuitous route that kept them hidden from the main street. The house looked exactly as Ivy remembered it from her previous visit—empty windows staring out like dead eyes, overgrown yard suggesting abandonment. But now, approaching it with purpose rather than emotion, she noticed details that had escaped her before.

The mailbox was new, despite the house's obvious vacancy. The lawn, while overgrown, showed signs of recent maintenance—patches where weeds had been cleared, edges that had been trimmed. Someone was taking care of this place, even if they weren't living in it.

"Side door," Jonathan said quietly, leading them around to the back of the house. "Less visible from the street." He tried the door, but it was locked.

"Here," Nat said. "I got it." She produced the small tool kit from her jacket pocket, and within minutes they were inside. The house smelled musty and closed-up, but underneath that was something else—something unfamiliar that made Ivy's skin crawl.

"This is weird," Ivy said. The last time she'd been here, the family's things had been scattered around the house, which had in a way been like a shroud, masking it—making it look like somewhere else. But now that it was empty, it was easy to recognize all the landmarks she'd become so used to as a kid.

Ivy made her way through the living room, past the stairs where she'd run up to her bedroom every night, past the spot where the couch had been, where her family had watched movies together. The furniture was gone, but the layout remained the same. She closed her eyes and tried to remember that last night, the night her world had ended.

She'd gone to bed late, after staying up to finish a book.

And then… nothing. A blank space where her memories should be.

"Ivy." Jonathan's voice came from the kitchen, tight with concern. "Come look at this."

She found him kneeling beside the central air vent, the metal grate removed and set aside. He was shining his phone's flashlight into the ductwork, and even from several feet away, Ivy could see what had caught his attention.

The inside of the vent was coated with a thin, blue-tinged residue.

"Vapoxil," Nat breathed, crouching beside Jonathan. "He used it here too."

She'd been right. That's how he'd done it. He'd drugged them to sleep before moving them to that cabin.

"He gassed the whole house," she said, her voice barely a whisper.

They moved through the house meticulously, finding the same blue residue in every vent they checked. Zimmerman had been thorough, ensuring that no one in the house could have escaped whatever he'd done to them. Ivy went back outside to double check the space beside the air conditioning units, but if there had been a Vapoxil canister there, it had long since vanished.

Returning to the house, she headed back upstairs to her old bedroom, the place where she'd once felt safer than anywhere else in the world. She stood in the same place where her bed had once been and tried to push past the chemical fog that had stolen her memories and reach the truth that lay beneath.

A sound. Movement in the house when there shouldn't have been. The smell of something wrong.

"There's something else," she said, her voice strange to her own ears. "Something about being touched. Or grabbed? I can almost remember..."

The memory hovered just out of reach, like a word on the tip of her tongue. She knew it was there, knew it was important, but every time she tried to grasp it, it slipped away.

Nat reached out then, her hand cold and clinical as it touched Ivy's shoulder. The contact sent a shock through her system that was different from her usual phobic response—sharper, more specific. For a moment, she wasn't in her childhood bedroom but somewhere else entirely. Somewhere dark and terrifying, where gentle hands became weapons and comfort became betrayal.

She jerked away so violently that she nearly fell, her stomach lurching with a nausea that had nothing to do with the chemical residue in the air. Her vision grayed at the edges, and she fought to stay conscious as panic clawed at her chest.

"Ivy!" Jonathan's voice seemed to come from very far away. "Ivy, look at me. You're safe. You're here with us."

She forced herself to focus on his face, using it as an anchor while her world slowly stopped spinning. His eyes were warm with concern, steady and real in a way that made her feel less like she was drowning.

"I'm okay," she managed. "I think... I think I remember him grabbing me. Lifting me off my bed."

Jonathan helped her to her feet, his touch careful and brief. Even through her distress, Ivy noticed that his contact didn't trigger the same violent response as Nat's had. With him, there was almost no discomfort at all. It was something that felt almost like relief.

"Do you want to leave?" he asked.

"No, let me just... just give me a few minutes. I feel like there's something here I'm missing. I just don't know what."

She spent the next thirty minutes methodically moving through the house, trying to catch the elusive memories of that night. Of trying to find something, *anything* that could bring them one step closer to Zimmerman. But other than the residue in the vents, there was no remaining physical evidence after fifteen years.

But Ivy found as she moved through the spaces where she used to live, she recalled a lot of *other* memories from her former life. Happy family memories long forgotten, or buried. Of slightly burned popcorn before the four of them would sit down for movie night. Of muddy footprints through the house that her mother would lose her shit about, of a Christmas tree that was slightly too tall and scraped the living room ceiling because her dad had misjudged the height. She could even still see the marks on the ceiling from all those years ago.

It painted a pretty picture. Sure, there had been bad times too. The arguments Ivy would hear on occasion when she cracked her door. Or when her brother broke her lamp then tried to blame it on her. But those times had been few and far between.

Ivy stood at the base of the stairs, her hand on the railing. There was something—she screwed up her features.

The arguments.

The more she thought the more she remembered. Her parents hardly ever argued... *ever*. Except, Ivy started hearing the shouting matches downstairs. They hadn't been angry with each other, but it had been about *something*. And they'd become more frequent as time had gone on. At the time Ivy had figured they'd always done that and she'd just never noticed. But now she realized that no, that *hadn't* been the case at all.

"Ivy?" Nat said carefully. "Are you okay?"

Ivy realized her cheek was wet. She wiped away the tear. "Yeah, fine."

"What's going on?"

"I think... I remember my parents having fights," she said. "And I think they might have been about Zimmerman."

"What?" Jonathan asked.

"Remember how Mr. Lane said we were getting a lot of hand-written letters right up until that night? Assume those letters had been from Zimmerman, and they're what caused my mom to go to the police. He said my dad had been nervous about them... anxious even."

"Your parents had arguments about the letters," Jonathan said. "Because they knew he was threatening her."

"I remember one night, maybe a week or two before everything happened," Ivy said, getting lost in the memory.

"Dad was asking her why *he* kept contacting her. What did he want? And she was adamant that she didn't know. She hadn't even seen him in years."

"Zimmerman knew your mother," Jonathan said. "*Before.*"

Ivy nodded. "I think so. I think he might have known her for a long time."

"Then we need to go into your mom's past," Nat replied. "Figure out how they're connected."

Ivy's heart practically leapt at the revelation. This was it. This is what they'd been looking for. Now all they needed to do was find that last connecting piece, and they'd be able to find Zimmerman.

The sound of his phone vibrating came from Jonathan's pocket. "It's Oliver," he said, glancing at the screen. He answered it and put it on speaker. "Found something?"

"I did," he replied. "And I think I have a plan."

Chapter Twenty-One

"Okay, so here's the deal," Oliver said, pointing to the upper-left corner of the wall he had decided to use as a makeshift bulletin board. All of Alice's research had been taped to the wall, along with hundreds of other documents he'd discovered and printed off. The whole thing looked like a massive Rubik's Cube of information and Ivy couldn't make heads or tails of it. The only thing she did recognize was a picture of Zimmerman pinned at the top.

"Zimmerman is invested with Pacific Research Associates, which is a shell company that operates out of the Bahamas," Oliver said, drawing a line across the sheets with a highlighter from Zimmerman's picture to a statement from PRA. "The company that controls PRA is called Regional Holdings, LLC, which is a property firm that buys and sells condos and timeshares to people stupid enough to buy those." He made another line from the PRA document to a separate document showing a bunch of advertisements for homes along crystal blue waters. "Now, Regional Holdings is itself another shell company. This one—"

"Can we just get to the point?" Nat asked, scowling as she watched Oliver's performance. The three of them had made their way over from Ivy's old house directly here, given the urgency in Oliver's voice, though Ivy and Nat had needed to duck down in the back again.

"I'm getting there if you'll let me finish," he said. "Regional is a shell company for something called *Proprietary Allies*, which is the official name of the company I'm involved with. It's run by a woman named Cor Constantine—" He drew another line from a smart-looking woman with platinum blonde hair down to the Regional document. "—and she is the person from whom I have been trying to get out from under for the past six months."

"Who is she?" Jonathan asked, leaning forward.

"She's kind of like a Caribbean warlord," Oliver said. "Runs all sorts of shady businesses down there, most have to do with import/export. You know, getting illegal goods into the country and back out again. And before you ask, yes, that includes drugs. She's also worth approximately eight hundred million dollars. And that's money I can actually find. No telling how much it really is."

"This is the person bankrolling Zimmerman?" Ivy asked.

"I can't tell the nature of their relationship yet," Oliver replied. "It's possible Zimmerman is a partner, an investor, or he could be some kind of independent contractor. What I do know is it's a symbiotic relationship. They're both benefitting."

"Benefitting how?" Nat asked.

"Zimmerman is providing Proprietary Allies with research material. The type and nature of which I can't say as I can't get into the databases necessary to take a look. But whatever he's doing for them, they're paying him a lot of money. Not only that, but it seems they were behind his breakout the other day."

"That makes sense," Jonathan said. "Only someone with those kind of resources could have pulled off something so professional. And given that even the FBI hasn't been able to track them down, they obviously know what they're doing."

"How does this help us?" Nat asked. "Zimmerman could be sipping mai tais on a beach in the South Pacific for all we know."

"No," Ivy said. "Not until he's done. Whatever he started he wants to finish. And it's obvious that ends with me. He isn't done until…"

"Until what?" Oliver asked.

She wished she could say. The truth was she didn't know what Zimmerman's endgame was. "We need to find the connection between him and my mother. That's the key."

"In the meantime, I think I've figured out a way to put a wrench in the gears," Oliver said. "Cor has been keeping a close eye on me since… since my little 'tantrum,' as she calls it. But I think I can backdoor my way into their systems and start introducing some chaos."

"What kind of chaos?" Jonathan asked.

"The kind that screws up their payment systems. Locks down their financial accounts. Keeps them from accessing any of their money. I may not be able to steal it, but I have enough clearance and know-how to be able to gum up the works, temporarily at least. Maybe that will force Zimmerman to make his move."

"Won't that put you in danger again?" Ivy asked.

"Probably. But I don't think we have many other options, do you? It's either that or wait around for Zimmerman to come after you and I'd much rather be on offense rather than defense."

Ivy glanced at the others, unsure. She didn't want anyone putting themselves in harm's way for her.

"I agree with Oliver," Nat finally said. "It's the quickest way to get their attention."

"But if this… Cor… has a literal army at her disposal…" The implications were clear. Jonathan's run-in with those people had been bad enough. But to willfully invite them to strike?

"I don't like the thought of going up against those goons again either," he said. "We've already lost two good officers and we don't need to lose any more. On the other hand, what's the alternative? You and Nat keep hiding out at my place in the hopes that Zimmerman makes a move? How long can you keep that up?"

"Do you think he's hoping I'll be arrested?" Ivy asked.

"I think it would make you an easy target."

She sighed. Nothing about this felt right. Oliver sticking his neck out for her—again, poking the proverbial bear hoping to get the right reaction. What if they were wrong and Zimmerman had no interest in Ivy at all? Maybe all he'd wanted was to get out of custody and really did fly off to some tropical island somewhere.

But that didn't feel right either. This had all started with Ivy's family. She felt certain it would end that way too.

She sighed. "I guess we don't have much of a choice."

"Is that a yes?" Oliver asked.

Could she really ask this of him? He'd already suffered so much and he was just starting to heal. In fact, both he and Jonathan had suffered injuries that related back to her involvement with this case.

She could feel everyone's eyes on her, waiting for her to make a decision that would impact all their lives. And probably in the worst possible way.

"Excuse me," Ivy said and headed down the hall towards the kitchen. She felt like she had been suffocating in that bedroom, surrounded by everyone else and Oliver's "tactical board." She needed air.

Ivy noted the new sliding doors that had replaced the shattered ones when Oliver had been attacked. She pushed one side open and stepped outside, breathing in the cool Oregon air. It was like a refreshing bath for her lungs. Some people got tired of the constant rain and dreariness, but not Ivy. It fueled her soul in some way, like this place was a part of something special—unique that couldn't be found anywhere else.

But now it almost felt like there was a dark cloud over the town, over the whole area. She felt Zimmerman's presence wherever she went, like he was in the shadows, always watching. He was a poison to this place. And until they got rid of him, she would never know peace again.

"Hey."

She turned to see Jonathan standing at the door, carefully observing her. "You okay?"

She nodded. "Just needed some air. It's… a lot."

"I agree," he replied. "What are you feeling?"

She shook her head. "I don't know. Nothing. Everything. It feels like no matter what we do it's the wrong move. Like he's just out there waiting for us to jump so he can smash us down with a big hammer."

"We can wait," Jonathan suggested. "Maybe he'll come to us on his own."

She shook her head. "He's been planning this for years. He enjoys the game. Whatever is going on, he's prepared for it. This… silence is all part of some ploy. I'm sure of it."

"Did you remember anything else from the house?" he asked carefully.

"No. And it doesn't really matter. But on the flip side I can't ask Oliver to put himself in danger like that again. Not after what happened last time. They could kill him. I mean, look what happened to you."

He nodded. "But if he's willing to take that risk?"

She shot him a look. "I know you don't like each other, but you can't seriously think this is the best idea. I can't ask him to do that."

"I think Oliver would go to the moon and back for you if you asked him," Jonathan said.

Something tugged deep within Ivy. "What does that mean?"

"Never mind," he said. "I shouldn't have said anything." He turned to go back inside.

"Jonathan, wait a second," she said, moving in front of him so he couldn't get back in. "What did that mean?"

"Can't you see it?" he asked. "He's infatuated with you."

Ivy winced. On some level she'd always known Oliver's feelings for her were deeper than just friendship, even when they were kids. When they'd reconnected she'd hoped that he'd gotten over it for the most part, because as close as she felt to him, it wasn't *that* kind of closeness.

"You knew, didn't you?" Jonathan asked. "That's why you're so hesitant to ask him."

"I don't want anyone risking their lives for me," she said. "Especially if they're not necessarily thinking straight."

"Then what? The rest of us are supposed to wait around for him to ambush you? It's the same problem, Ivy. We don't want you to risk your life for us either."

She turned and headed back for the fence again. "I just wish I knew what this was all about. Why me? Why my family?"

"There's only one way to find out. And that's to ask Zimmerman himself."

He was right. If Ivy wanted answers, they needed to make a move. She wasn't going to wait around for him to keep psychologically torturing her. The man was a trained professional, he had to know that by staying just out of reach he was only making things worse for Ivy.

She set her jaw and returned to the others, still in the bedroom looking at data Oliver had collected from Proprietary Allies.

"Okay," Ivy said. "Let's do it."

Chapter Twenty-Two

THEY'D CONSIDERED STAYING AT OLIVER'S, BUT GIVEN HOW long this could take, they elected to go back to Jonathan's for the time being. Nat was being uncharacteristically quiet, seemingly lost in her thoughts while Ivy kept thinking about what Jonathan had said about Oliver. Even though she had known about Oliver's feelings, hearing someone else put them into words made it all that more real. As much as she hated to disappoint him, she just didn't feel the same way. And that was a conversation they'd have to have once all this was over.

Jonathan had turned on the TV, the channel tuned to some cooking show that none of them were watching. Nat continued to watch out the window with the excuse she needed to keep a lookout for any suspicious vehicles, but Ivy could tell something else was going on with her. Ever since they'd finished interrogating the suspects, she had been uncharacteristically quiet. Ivy felt like something was brewing, she just couldn't tell what.

Still, despite everything, they had made some progress. Jonathan had heard from Alice via a text, letting him know she would be unavailable for a few days. Her mother had finally passed and she was in the process of making arrangements.

She hated this for Alice. But as macabre as it was, it reminded Ivy she needed to keep Carol in the loop. More than that, she just wanted to hear the woman's reassuring voice again. She'd been so compassionate the other day... in a way Ivy had either never realized or never fully appreciated.

"Can I borrow your phone again?" she held her hand out to Jonathan.

"Tell her hi," Jonathan said, shooting Ivy a wink as he handed over his device.

Ivy dialed Carol's number, listening to it ring once, twice, three times. On the fourth ring, it went to voicemail. Carol's familiar voice filled the kitchen: *"You've reached Carol and Hero. We can't come to the phone right now, but leave a message and we'll get back to you as soon as possible."*

Ivy hung up without leaving a message, trying to shake off the immediate spike of anxiety. Carol could be anywhere—grocery shopping, taking Hero for a walk, working in her garden. Just because she didn't answer the phone didn't mean anything was wrong.

But the feeling lingered, a cold knot in her stomach that refused to dissolve.

"Everything okay?" Nat asked, silently monitoring from the large window in the living room.

"She didn't pick up. Probably just busy." Ivy tried to keep her voice casual, but she caught the sharp look Nat gave her. After fifteen years of being studied by this woman, Ivy knew when her poker face was failing.

"I'll try again later," Ivy said, but as the words left her mouth, the phone buzzed in her hand, showing Carol's number.

Instantly she felt relief. "Hello?"

"This is what happens when you poke the bear."

A chill ran through Ivy. The voice was unfamiliar, having

used an electronic voice modulator so she wouldn't be able to recognize it. But they were gone before she could say anything else or respond. Ivy frantically dialed the number back, but it immediately went to Carol's voicemail again.

"What?" Nat said, coming into the kitchen.

"It wasn't her..." Ivy yelped. "It was... I think it was *them*. Maybe Zimmerman himself."

"What?" Jonathan said, pushing himself out of the chair and joining her in the kitchen.

"They used a voice modulator," Ivy said, her heart nearly beating out of her chest. "But they knew who they were talking to. They said '*this is what happens when you poke the bear*'."

"What the hell does that mean?" Nat asked.

"Could they know about what Oliver is doing?" Ivy was beginning to panic.

"How? It's only been a few hours."

"I don't know, but we need to get over there right away," Ivy said. Not only was Carol in danger, but Hero too. *Damnit*, why hadn't she just stayed with her?

Nat was already grabbing her jacket. "Jonathan, you should stay here. Rest that shoulder."

"Like hell," Jonathan said. "If something's wrong, you'll need backup."

Ivy dialed the number again even as they were heading out of the house but it went back to voicemail. She called Oliver instead.

"Yo," he answered.

"Are you okay?" she asked, getting in the passenger seat as Nat got behind the wheel. Jonathan argued with her for a minute before getting in the back.

"I mean, that's a—"

"I'm serious Oliver, is everything okay there?" Ivy shouted.

"Yeah, everything's fine, why?"

She quickly explained about Carol. "You need to be on alert. I think they know what you're doing."

"That's impossible," he replied. "I'm being as careful as possible. Even the US Government wouldn't know what I'm doing if I was breaking into the CIA."

"They know," Ivy said. "We're heading to Carol's place and then we're coming by to pick you up."

Nat pulled out of the driveway and floored it, pointing the car in the direction of Carol's house.

"Ivy, you need to give me time to work. This stuff takes a while. If you really want me to slow Cor and Zimmerman down, I need—"

"I need you not to be dead," Ivy replied. "We're picking you up."

He huffed. "Fine. Give me thirty minutes."

Ivy hung up and turned back to Jonathan. "You agree, right?"

He sighed. "As much as I didn't want my house to become a zoo, I do. They obviously know how to get to him. If they're targeting people you know, it's better if no one is isolated."

"That means Alice too." She handed his phone back to him.

The drive to Carol's house felt endless despite taking less than fifteen minutes. Ivy gripped the passenger door handle so tightly her knuckles went white, watching familiar neighborhoods blur past the window. She tried not to think of the worst-case scenario, that they would arrive and find Carol's body somewhere in the house. But she knew what they were capable of, what they'd already managed. And she couldn't keep the ominous images out of her head.

Carol's street looked normal when they turned onto it. A few kids playing in front yards, an elderly man walking his dog, the usual suburban tranquility that had always made Ivy feel safe. But as they approached Carol's house, something felt wrong.

The front yard was too still. Carol's car sat in the driveway, and the porch light was on despite it being mid-afternoon.

"Park on the street," Ivy said as they approached. "Caution."

Nat pulled to the curb, and they sat for a moment studying the house. The front door was closed, curtains drawn, no sign of movement inside. It looked like any other house on a quiet Tuesday afternoon, but Ivy's instincts were screaming warnings.

"Do we go?" Nat asked.

Ivy scanned the surrounding area. If Zimmerman was springing a trap for them, this was the perfect opportunity. He could have people lying in wait, invisible until the last second.

But every second that passed was one where Carol could be bleeding out. And Ivy couldn't wait any longer.

"Go. Quickly."

They approached the house cautiously, Ivy leading despite Jonathan's protests. The front porch creaked under their weight. Ivy pulled out Jonathan's spare sidearm that he'd let her borrow. Nat's was out as well.

Ivy tried the door handle and found it unlocked. Carol never left her door unlocked, not since the day she'd taken custody of a traumatized thirteen-year-old who'd taught her that the world could be dangerous in ways she'd never imagined.

Silence greeted them, heavy and wrong. The living room looked normal at first glance—Carol's reading chair in its usual position, Hero's toys scattered across the carpet. But as Ivy's eyes adjusted to the dimmer light inside, she began to notice the mess.

A lamp was knocked over behind the couch. One of the throw pillows lay on the floor. The coffee table had been shifted several inches from its usual position, the magazines now scattered rather than stacked.

"Stay alert," Ivy hissed. Her pulse was flying.

The kitchen showed more signs of disturbance. Cabinet doors hung open, their contents partially pulled out as if someone had been searching for something. A coffee mug lay shattered on the floor, dark stains spreading across the tile. But it was the sight of the kitchen chair overturned by the back door that made Ivy's blood run cold.

The three of them split up, moving quickly through the house. Every time Ivy turned a corner she expected to see her adoptive mother lying in a pool of blood. But so far there had been no sign of her anywhere.

"Ivy," Nat called from one of the back bedrooms.

Ivy kept her weapon down, but moved with surprising speed down the hallway. The guest room that Carol used as an office had been thoroughly ransacked. Desk drawers pulled out, papers scattered everywhere, the computer monitor cracked. But it was what she found on the floor behind the bed that stopped her breath entirely.

Carol's shotgun lay broken in two pieces, the barrel separated from the stock. Spent shells scattered across the carpet showed that it had been fired at least twice before whatever happened here had ended.

"She fought," Jonathan said from the doorway, his voice grim. "Whatever happened, she didn't go quietly."

Ivy knelt beside the broken weapon, her hands shaking as she picked up one of the spent shells.

She had done as Ivy had told her, and it hadn't mattered at all.

"Where's Hero?" Ivy asked.

A soft whimper from under the bed made them all freeze.

"Hero?" Ivy called softly, dropping to her knees. "Come here, boy."

A small brown nose appeared first, followed by the rest of Oliver's little dog. Hero was trembling, his usual exuberant energy replaced by cowering fear. When he saw Ivy, he crawled out and pressed himself against her legs, shaking so hard she could feel it through her jeans.

"It's okay," she murmured, stroking his fur. "You're safe now."

But as she looked around the destroyed room, at the evidence of violence and struggle, she knew that *safe* was a relative term. Zimmerman had gotten to Carol. Maybe not directly, but he'd still gotten to her.

"We need to call this in," Jonathan said, though his voice lacked conviction.

"No." Ivy's response was immediate and sharp. "If we bring in the police, he might kill her. This is about me—he's trying to draw me out."

"Ivy, she might already be dead," Nat said, an edge to her voice.

Jonathan kneeled down in front of her, stroking Hero's back. "And we can't handle this alone—"

"Can't we?" She looked up, still holding Hero, and faced Jonathan with a determination that surprised even her. "Tell me the police are going to be able to find her before he decides she's served her purpose."

Nat was studying the scattered papers, her expression grim. "He definitely wanted to send you a message."

"We have to find her," Ivy said, though even as the words left her mouth, she knew how impossible it sounded. "He can't have taken her far, not with her fighting back. Someone would have heard the shots."

"I'll check with the neighbors," Nat said, excusing herself without another word.

Jonathan reached out for Ivy, but seemed to think better of it and retracted his hand. "We'll find her. If he wanted her dead, she'd still be here."

Ivy nodded. "He's using her to get me to come to him. But you would think..." she looked around.

"What?"

"If he knew we'd be coming after her, wouldn't he have left some way to find him? Some cryptic clue that we needed to find? He obviously sees this as a game."

Hero whimpered in her arms, and Ivy realized she'd been gripping him too tightly. She loosened her hold, but the dog still pressed against her as if he understood that she was the only safe harbor in a suddenly dangerous world.

"What kind of clue?" Jonathan asked.

She shook her head, unable to answer her own question. Why call her back if he hadn't wanted her to come here and find Carol missing? Jonathan and Ivy moved through the house methodically, searching every crevice, every drawer. Hero stayed close by Ivy's feet, not wanting to leave her side.

Finally, when they got to Ivy's childhood room, the place she always stayed when she slept over at Carol's, they found what they'd been looking for.

Underneath her pillow was an envelope with Ivy's name—her *given* name written in a sharp script.

Ivy could barely keep her hands from shaking as she opened the envelope, pulling out the letter. Her breath caught in her throat as she read it.

Dear Ivy,

It's been a long time. I wondered how long it would take you to finally make your move and now I have my answer. How do you like my response? I was disappointed we never got to share that cell, but I'm anything if not adaptable. I look forward to a little trip down memory lane with you. Won't you join me?

- *Dr. Z*

"A trip down memory lane? What does that mean?" Jonathan asked.

"I… don't know," Ivy admitted. She turned the letter over. There seemed to be no other clue as to his whereabouts.

Nat returned a few moments later, out of breath. "Only one of the neighbors was home this afternoon and her hearing aid is on the fritz. She didn't hear or see a thing." She glanced at the paper in Ivy's hands. "Find something?"

Ivy handed it over. "Any idea what it means?"

"I'm not sure," Nat said. "But first I think we need to do as Jonathan suggests. Talk to Ayford. Get Oakhurst PD involved. We need every able-bodied officer out there looking for Carol instead of us."

"And if they decide not to trust us?" Ivy asked.

"At this point, I don't think we have a choice."

Chapter Twenty-Three

Oliver's fingers moved across the keyboard with practiced precision, executing the final commands that would lock down Cor's payment systems. After Ivy's call, Oliver had begun to work more frantically, feeling like there was a wolf nipping on his heels as he worked. The lines of code scrolled past on his monitor, meaningless to most but beautiful in their destructive simplicity to him.

It all had to be a coincidence, no one could have picked up on his efforts, not yet anyway. Sure, in a few hours it would be plainly obvious what he'd done—Cor didn't go more than a few hours without initiating or receiving payments from *somewhere*. And as soon as the pattern emerged, they would know.

Part of him didn't care. This was what he'd wanted for months now; a way to get back at them, to break their operations. While not his only client, they were his biggest, and what had seemed like a series of easy and high-paying jobs in the beginning had turned into a ball and chain that Oliver couldn't break free from to save his life.

Until today.

He paused, his hands hovering over the keys. Once he pressed enter, there would be no going back. Cor would find out exactly who had sabotaged her operations, and she wouldn't hesitate to retaliate. But the image of Ivy's face when she'd learned about his connection to these people—the betrayal in her eyes, the way she'd looked at him like he was a stranger—made his decision easy.

Enter.

The screen flashed green. Financial accounts frozen. Payment processors disabled. Wire transfers halted mid-transaction. Oliver leaned back in his chair, a grim satisfaction settling over him. Let Cor try to fund Zimmerman's twisted games now.

His secure phone buzzed almost immediately. Oliver stared at the device, knowing who was calling before he even looked at the display. That wasn't good. Cor's name appeared on the screen, and for a moment he considered not answering. But hiding from her would only delay the inevitable.

"Hello, Cor."

"Oliver." Her voice was silk wrapped around steel, as always. "I just received some very interesting alerts from our financial department."

Shit. That was fast.

"Did you?" He kept his tone neutral, professional. The same voice he'd used in countless business calls over the years.

"It seems someone with high-level access has been playing games with our systems. Someone who knows exactly where to hit us to cause maximum damage." A pause. "Someone we thought we could trust."

Oliver's jaw tightened. "Trust is a funny word coming from you."

"Is it?" Her laugh was cold. "When have I ever lied to you, Oliver? When have I ever promised you something I didn't deliver?"

"You failed to mention working with Dr. Jason Zimmerman. A man whose activities have become very concerning to me."

"Now, Oliver," she said, that silky voice of hers grating against his nerves. "We work with a lot of people. How was I to know you had a problem with a very specific vendor?"

"This man tormented a friend of mine. And it's hard for me to accept it's just coincidence that he works for you."

"Ah." Her voice shifted, becoming almost conversational. "So this is about your little detective crush. I should have known."

Oliver's blood ran cold at the casual way she dismissed Ivy. "What do you mean?"

He could hear the smile in her voice as she spoke. "Tell me, Oliver, do you remember when you first came to work for us? Do you remember how that arrangement began?"

The question sent an unexpected chill down his spine. Of course he remembered. Cor had approached him through intermediaries after he'd pulled off a federal database hacking job. She'd offered him a good deal of money for a similar job, with less risk. It had been an easy decision at the time.

"What kind of question is that?"

"Humor me. What was your first assignment?"

Oliver frowned, searching his memory. That was over a decade ago now. He'd been young, arrogant, convinced he was smarter than everyone around him. "Financial systems analysis for some of your shell companies. Basic stuff."

"Before that."

"There wasn't a 'before that.'"

"Think harder, Oliver."

A strange sensation washed over him, like trying to remember a dream that kept slipping away. There had been something else, hadn't there? Something before the financial work. But every time he tried to focus on it, the memory seemed to dissolve.

"I don't know what game you're playing, but—"

"No game. Just helping you remember who you really are." Cor's voice took on an almost maternal quality. "Dr.

Zimmerman was so fond of you in the beginning. He had such high hopes."

The phone nearly slipped from Oliver's fingers. "What are you talking about?"

"You were his first choice, Oliver. His preferred candidate for keeping tabs on Detective Bishop. After all, you'd known her since childhood. You had history together. Trust. It would have been so simple."

Oliver's mind reeled. The memories were there, just beyond his reach, like shapes moving through fog. Sessions with Zimmerman. Commands that felt like suggestions, suggestions that felt like his own thoughts.

"That's impossible." But even as he said it, fragments were surfacing. A sterile room. Zimmerman's voice, calm and authoritative. The feeling of his thoughts being rearranged, reorganized, refined.

"You disappointed him, you know. All that careful conditioning, all those sessions to make you the perfect observer, and what did you do? You fell in love with her." Cor's voice carried genuine amusement now. "Love, it turns out, is quite resilient against psychological manipulation. Who would have thought?"

Oliver's breathing became shallow. "You're lying."

"Am I? Think about your falling-out with Ivy. What caused it, exactly? Can you remember the details, or just the emotions? The hurt, the anger, the sense that you'd lost something precious?"

He tried to focus, but the memory was like looking through water. He remembered the pain of losing Ivy's friendship. He remembered the years of regret that followed. But the actual cause felt... manufactured. Artificial.

"Zimmerman had to improvise after that. Find someone else who could get close to her. Someone who wouldn't be compromised by inconvenient feelings." Cor's voice hardened. "His solution wasn't elegant, but effective enough."

"You bastards." The words came out as a whisper.

"Now, now. No need for name-calling. You served your purpose in other ways. Your technical skills proved quite valuable to me, even if you couldn't fulfill your original function."

Oliver's hands were shaking now, whether from rage or fear he couldn't tell. "What do you want?"

"What I've always wanted. Cooperation. Did you seriously think we'd let you operate unchecked after last time? All your work. It's meaningless."

Instantly the images on his screen shifted, the accounts acting as if they hadn't been frozen at all. "You've outlived your usefulness, Oliver. I hate to say it, because you had talent. Talent that could have made you rich beyond your wildest dreams. And now… now it's all down the drain. Enjoy your life. What's left of it, anyway." She hung up without waiting for a reply, leaving Oliver with the breath knocked out of him.

He tried getting back into her systems, but he'd been locked out, his credentials pulled. Ivy was right, they *had* known what he was doing all along. They'd been watching, waiting to see if he'd actually pull the trigger. And it had all been for nothing.

Oliver stared at the phone, his entire world tilting on its axis. Everything he thought he knew about his life, his choices, his relationship with Ivy—all of it had been a lie. Or rather, all of it had been engineered by people who saw him as nothing more than a tool.

He looked at his computer screen, now displaying an access denied message. All his carefully constructed backdoors into Cor's systems had been closed. They were blown, and he needed to warn Ivy.

Oliver reached for his regular phone to call, but before he could dial, he realized something that made his blood freeze.

If Cor knew about his feelings for Ivy, if she'd been monitoring him all these years, then she might know where Ivy was right now. She would know about Jonathan's house; about every move they'd made. And sending all that information back to one person.

They weren't hunting Zimmerman.

Zimmerman was hunting them.

Oliver jumped up from his chair, his injured leg protesting the sudden movement. He needed to get to Ivy, needed to warn her that their entire investigation had been compromised from the beginning. He grabbed his keys and headed for the door.

Three measured knocks echoed through his apartment.

Oliver froze, his hand on the doorknob. He took a careful step back, images of the last time someone knocked on his door speeding through his mind. He knew what he'd find if we went back to check the security feeds from the cameras looking at that door.

He backed away from the door slowly, his mind racing through possible escape routes. Out back was his only way. Could he climb the fence in his condition? Did he even have a choice?

Three more knocks, identical to the first. Patient. Professional.

He no longer had a choice. Oliver turned and ran for the back just as the door behind him splintered into a thousand pieces.

Chapter Twenty-Four

THE DECISION TO WALK INTO OAKHURST POLICE DEPARTMENT felt like stepping into the tiger's lair. Ivy's hands trembled as she pushed through the glass doors, Jonathan flanking her left side while Nat hung back, her face a mask of resigned determination. The familiar scent of industrial coffee and worn leather hit Ivy immediately, triggering a thousand memories of better days when this place had felt like sanctuary rather than a potential trap.

Hero padded alongside them, his presence the only thing keeping Ivy's anxiety from spiraling completely out of control. The desk sergeant looked up with surprise that quickly shifted to wariness when he recognized her face.

"Detective Bishop," Sergeant Morrison said carefully. "You're supposed to be—"

"I know what I'm supposed to be," Ivy interrupted, her voice steadier than she felt. "I need to speak with Lieutenant Ayford immediately. And Captain Armstrong. I'm voluntarily surrendering."

"I'll call them down," Morrison said, already reaching for his phone.

While they waited in the main lobby, Ivy caught fragments

of whispered conversations from officers passing by. Some stared openly, their expressions ranging from curiosity to barely concealed hostility. She understood their confusion. From their perspective, she'd vanished during a critical investigation, abandoned her job without explanation, left her partner to handle everything alone and was a potential suspect in an operation that had gotten two officers killed.

Nat seemed to be receiving a similar amount of attention, though it was more curiosity given that she was sitting right beside Ivy and Jonathan.

Lieutenant Ayford appeared first, his usually immaculate appearance slightly rumpled, stress lines deeper than she remembered. Behind him came Captain Armstrong, whose expression could have frozen molten steel. Ivy's stomach clenched as she recognized the look of a man who'd been personally betrayed by someone he'd trusted.

"Detective Bishop," Ayford said, his voice professionally neutral but carrying an undercurrent of relief. "Let's have a chat."

They were escorted to Interview Room Two, the same room where she'd questioned countless suspects. The irony wasn't lost on her as she settled into the hard plastic chair across from her superiors, Jonathan beside her, Nat taking the remaining seat with visible reluctance.

It was strange, alien almost, sitting on this side of the table. Ivy could see why it was intimidating. Hero settled at Ivy's feet, his warm weight against her legs a reminder that not everything in her world had shifted beyond recognition.

"Before we begin," Ayford said, pulling out a small digital recorder, "I need to inform you that this conversation is being recorded. You have the right to have an attorney present—"

"Waived," Ivy said quickly. "I need you to listen."

Armstrong leaned forward, his weathered hands flat on the metal table. "You're not in charge here, detective. I am. Let's start with where you've been for the past six days. And why you have been MIA during a critical investigation." He shot a glance at Jonathan.

"Listen, we don't have time—"

"Answer the question, Detective. Unless you want to do it in handcuffs."

"She's not under arrest," Jonathan said.

"And if she wants to keep it that way, she will tell us everything we want to know," Ayford replied. "Explain yourself. Now."

Ivy gritted her teeth, looking over her shoulder at Nat who wouldn't meet her gaze. She didn't want to incriminate her, but at the same time, she needed a satisfying explanation.

"You were right. I *am* part of Zimmerman's operation," Ivy finally said. Ayford and Armstrong exchanged glances. "I am the man's primary target, and I have been for over fifteen years. He spent God knows how much time stalking my family only to kill them in cold blood and now he's trying to finish the job. He wants *me* specifically and he'll go to any length to get me. Including kidnapping my mother."

Ayford furrowed his brow. "He kidnapped your mother?"

"Her adoptive mother. We just came from her place," Jonathan said. "It had been turned over and she was gone. Show them the note."

Ivy pulled out the envelope they'd found in her room, holding it out for Ayford. He took it and unfolded the letter inside, reading it carefully. "You found this?"

"Not more than an hour ago," Ivy said.

Ayford turned to the camera. "Carter, get in here." A second later the door opened to reveal a man in a haphazard suit with the tie askew. Ayford handed him the letter which Carter took and placed into a plastic bag. "Get this down to evidence. See if they can pull anything from it."

"Yes, sir," Carter said and disappeared through the door again.

"That doesn't explain where you've been," Armstrong

rumbled. "I've given you more than your fair share of leeway, young lady, and—"

"Oh come off it," Nat said, standing behind them. "You never believed in Ivy. I had to practically beg you to let me promote her. So don't sit there and pretend you've been supporting her all along. You would have transferred her by now if you could."

"Careful, Lieutenant," Armstrong said. "You're not exactly in the clear here either. Abandoning your post, disappearing without a word. Leaving your fellow officers to pick up the slack. It's enough for a termination."

"Fire me then. I don't care," Nat replied. "Ivy missed her psych eval because of me, okay? Because I made a bad judgement call. I put her in a situation where she couldn't leave, couldn't contact anyone because at the time I thought it was the right call. I've since tried to make up for that mistake. But don't come down on her. Because you can bet your ass if she could have been here, she would have been."

"Hold on a second," Ayford said. "What do you mean you put her in a situation where she couldn't leave?"

"I kidnapped her," Nat replied, exasperated. "I kidnapped and held her."

Both men stared at her with a mix of shock and confusion. "Why?" Armstrong asked.

"Because I believed she might be a threat… to the public." Nat sat back down, and all the air went out of her like a deflating balloon. Ivy wanted to comfort her, but she knew Nat well enough to know she would just push her away if she tried.

"I incorrectly believed Ivy was responsible for the death of her family fifteen years ago."

"Death?" Ayford said, turning to Ivy. "The record shows your family disappeared. Now you say Zimmerman killed them." He turned his attention back to Nat. "How did you know they died?"

Ivy could see the walls inside Nat begin to crumble. The secret she had held so long, the one that had changed and defined her life was now out in the open. "I found their bodies... and I covered it up."

"You *what?*" Armstrong bellowed.

"Why?" Ayford asked.

She took another deep breath. "Given the evidence at the time, I had a strong suspicion Ivy was the one who committed the murders. I... have since learned that couldn't have been the case."

"Even so," Ayford said. "Why not bring her in for questioning at the time?"

"I can't believe this," Armstrong said, standing and pacing in the small room. "All this time."

"Because she had just come out of a traumatic coma and had no memory of the event," Nat explained. "I couldn't in good conscience commit her to even more trauma, no matter the circumstances."

"So you just decided to take the law into your own hands and cover up a triple homicide?" Armstrong yelled.

"Yes, sir."

"Buckley, you're fired. And you're under arrest for conspiracy."

Ivy stood. "No."

Armstrong turned to her, an amused look on his face. "I'm sorry?"

"We do not have time for this right now. Zimmerman is out there with another hostage. Nat isn't going anywhere. If you want to bring charges against her, fine. But we do it after we have Zimmerman in custody. She has been invaluable in helping us get this far. We've managed to uncover far more about the man and his operation on our own than the entire department managed after he was arrested."

"Now you listen to me," Armstrong said, lowering his voice and getting right in Ivy's face. "You don't have any authority here. You are on the cusp of losing your job yourself so if you want a future in law enforcement, I suggest you shut your mouth and sit down."

Ivy stared him down. "You can't bully me. Not anymore. I don't care if I'm a detective or not. The whole reason I became a detective in the first place was to find out what happened to my family. Now I know. And I know the person responsible is still out there, ready to strike. He has my mother and he will *kill her* unless I find him. We came to you for help, not to be browbeaten."

Ayford stood as well, attempting to place himself between Ivy and Armstrong, which was difficult, given there was a table in the way. "Let's all just take a minute," he said before turning to Ivy. "You said you discovered information about Zimmerman. What kind of information?"

Ivy shook her head. "Not until he backs off."

"I will *not*—"

"Sir," Ayford interrupted again, drawing Armstrong's attention. He motioned to the corner of the room where Armstrong reluctantly followed. The two of them spoke in hushed tones for a few moments before Armstrong blew out a frustrated breath and left through the door, slamming it behind him. Hero raised his head at the loud noise, but put his chin back on Ivy's boot a moment later.

Ivy glanced up at the camera that was still rolling on them, its little red light on.

"Now, Detective. Tell me what you and Lieutenant Buckley discovered," Ayford said, returning to the table.

"What about Nat?" Ivy asked.

The man took a breath, then looked over Ivy's shoulder. "You have to admit it's a… complicated situation. And I can't guarantee you won't face consequences for your actions," he said to Nat. "But for the time being, I think we can all agree it's in our collective best interests to work together. Not only for ourselves, but for the safety of the general public."

Ivy nodded. That was good enough for now. "Zimmerman has ties to a crime ring in the Bahamas," she said. "We believe they were the ones who were responsible for his escape as well as who has been providing him with resources to remain hidden."

"What kind of ties?" Ayford asked, leaning back.

"Financial for sure," Jonathan said. "But we believe there is more, we're just not sure yet. Alice Blair has managed to do some digging for us and has uncovered his connection to a number of shell companies that all lead back to something called *Proprietary Allies*, which we believe is a front for this organization. They are well-funded, resource heavy and clearly have no qualms about who they kill."

"You think this organization is protecting Zimmerman?" Ayford asked.

"Protecting. Working with. Taking orders from," Ivy said. "We still don't know the full extent of their relationship. But a friend of mine is currently working to disrupt their operations. At least temporarily."

"For what reason?"

"To hopefully draw Zimmerman out," Ivy admitted. "But... that was before we realized he'd already taken another victim."

Ayford leaned back again, rubbing his temples with both hands. "Jesus, Bishop. You don't make this easy." He glanced back at Nat. "I'm starting to see why you left." For the first time, Nat cracked a smile. "What's your projected success rate with this... disruption?"

"Honestly?" Jonathan said. "It's a shot in the dark. But it was the only way we could think to draw Zimmerman out before being ambushed again. If Proprietary Allies or whoever is funding him, he could have serious firepower. And he's just waiting to unleash it on Ivy."

"Bishop. What's your take on this?"

"He's kidnapped Carol because he wants me to chase

him," Ivy said. "That's what he's always wanted. We found evidence that he knew my birth mother *before* he attacked my family. I don't know what's behind it all, but I know he's fixated on me."

"I can back that up," Jonthan said. "The only reason I'm alive was to deliver a message to Ivy. And he admitted he was disappointed Ivy wasn't at his hearing. In fact, we believe he allowed himself to be arrested on purpose."

"On purpose? For what reason?"

"To torment me," Ivy replied. "Because he thought I would be in there with him. He didn't anticipate—" She turned and shot a quick glance at Nat. "—me being away for a while. So when I wasn't there, he decided to break out and now this is how he's decided to get me to come to him again."

"But if he wants you to find him, why not leave a clearer clue?" Ayford asked. "If that letter is all you have—"

Before he could finish the door to the room flew open, startling Hero again. "Sir, we've got a house fire out of control over on Roslyndale Ave. Should I send additional units?"

Ivy's stomach bottomed out. "Roslyndale? Which address?"

"4486," the officer said. "The flames are burning so hot they're threatening to jump to the nearby homes. We could have an out-of-control forest fire in less than an hour."

Ayford jumped up, yelling orders at the officer and running to gather a response team to help the fire department.

But Ivy couldn't hear a word any of them were saying. It was like the world had fallen away.

4486… Oliver's home address.

Chapter Twenty-Five

IVY SAW THE SMOKE BEFORE THEY EVEN TURNED INTO THE neighborhood. It billowed up behind the tree line like a volcano spewing debris into the air, thick and black, darkening the sky. Another fire truck screamed by as she and Jonathan drove to the site.

Given the connection with the current case, Jonathan had managed to convince Lieutenant Ayford to allow him and Ivy to assist on what was almost certainly connected to Zimmerman. Ivy had barely heard any of their discussion; she'd been so lost in the terror of what was happening it felt nearly debilitating. First Carol and now Oliver? They had just spoken on the phone a couple hours ago. Could Zimmerman have gotten to him that quickly? She couldn't even bring herself to consider that it might be a coincidence. No, this was calculated to deliver the maximum impact, and it had done its job.

Ivy felt very much the way she had the night she and Alice had first encountered the cabin. Almost as if she were experiencing reality *outside* herself, watching everything as it happened from somewhere else. She watched as she and Jonathan got into one of the patrol cars and followed Officer Carter and Lieutenant Ayford out to the scene of the fire. She also watched as Nat stayed behind, a condition Ayford insisted upon, most likely due to whatever verbal agreement he'd made with Armstrong.

But none of that mattered. They needed to get to Oliver's place, finding him alive and not burned to death inside his own home. Thank God Hero hadn't been there.

As they turned the corner, the full view of the house came into view. The entire structure was a complete blaze, the fire burning through the windows and doorways, and even out into the grass. Three fire trucks had set up and were dousing the area with water, attempting to keep the flames from jumping to the next-door neighbors or any of the surrounding trees.

"Holy shit," Jonathan whispered as they approached. It was like driving up to the world's largest bonfire. He parked the car four houses down, but Ivy could feel the heat even through the windows. People had gathered outside their homes, while other firefighters were busy evacuating the houses closest to the fire.

"He'll be okay," Jonathan said before getting out. "Let's just get control of the situation. Okay?"

Ivy nodded, still feeling like she wasn't really there. "Okay."

They got out and immediately Jonathan began working crowd control. Ivy's gaze was pinned to the blaze a moment longer before her training snapped her out of it and into action to get civilians away from the fire as quickly as possible. She, Jonathan and two other officers helped set up a large perimeter around the homes while the fire department continued to work, strategically dousing the home with water and taking turns with the hoses.

There was no way this was an ordinary fire. It was burning much too hot and fast for accelerants not to have been used.

Finally, after what seemed like an eternity, the fire department seemed to be gaining the upper hand. They contained the flames to Oliver's home, preventing the quick spread of an uncontrollable blaze that could have taken out half the neighborhood and within another hour, had all the flames out.

Ivy and Jonathan watched the men and women work, putting their lives at risk to keep the public safe. That was what Ivy had sworn as well—to protect and serve. And she hadn't felt like she'd been doing a very good job of it lately. Especially after what happened with Jasmine Quinn. Maybe she wasn't cut out to be a police detective... she obviously had too much emotional baggage. It was why she wasn't upset to miss her psych eval. They had always taken a great amount of preparation and care for her to navigate those without throwing up any red flags, and to be honest, she was tired of it all. She was tired of pretending, of trying to fit in. Of feeling like there was something wrong with her deep down.

But there was something wrong with her. Because she hadn't been able to save Jasmine. She hadn't been able to keep Carol safe. And now... she may have lost Oliver as well.

"Any sign of anyone inside?" Jonathan asked as the fire chief came over to speak with Ayford, his face covered in soot.

He removed his helmet, revealing a shock of white hair. "Too early to tell. We're still putting out the hot spots."

"How long until we can get in there?" Ayford asked.

"Maybe a few hours. We gotta make sure there aren't any more pockets—give the fire time to fully burn out."

"Any indication of the cause?"

"It was intentional, that much I know. I expect we'll find kerosene or gasoline was used. Maybe even propane."

Ayford turned back to Ivy and the others. "Let's start working the neighborhood, see if anyone saw or heard anything."

Ivy felt that deep pit within her open again. Oliver could already be dead. But Carol might still be out there. And the more time they spent on this, the less time she had.

"Lieutenant, maybe I should get back, so I can—"

"Bishop, we don't have time to argue. You wanted to be here, you're here. We can only deal with one thing at a time."

Ivy nodded. She headed over to begin speaking to some of the homeowners when a hand caught her arm. Normally something like that would cause her to freeze up, but she knew without looking it was Jonathan. His touch had become a gentle reminder that maybe not everything in her was broken.

"Nat's still working on it," he said.

"Not with Armstrong breathing down her neck," Ivy replied.

"When have you known Nat to back down from anyone?"

She had to concede the point. But still, she was here, and Carol was out there. Somewhere.

She'd thought by coming here she might be able to do something... that she would be able to somehow stop it all from happening, as if by magic. But now she saw how foolish and naïve that had been. What if this was nothing more than a distraction to keep her from Carol? What if Zimmerman wasn't involved at all? There was that Cor woman, after all. Her people could have been behind this whole thing... though, if they had found out what Oliver had been up to that quickly, it only further cemented that Zimmerman had taken Carol *because* of their actions. Which meant he was still one step ahead.

It also meant that Ivy was responsible for losing two of the most important people in her life.

"Ivy," Jonathan said, looking at his phone.

It vibrated, showing *Blocked number* on the screen. She nodded and when he put it on speaker, that same electronic voice spoke again.

"Quite the bonfire, isn't it?"

"Is he alive?" Ivy demanded.

"Right to the point. I like that about you, Detective," the voice replied.

"Answer the question. Are they both ok? What did you do with Carol?"

"You're not in any position to be demanding anything," the voice replied.

"I found your note. It's obvious you want me so just tell me where and when and I'll be there," she spat.

Jonathan shook his head adamantly but she ignored him.

"Oh. So brave. So... willing to sacrifice. Too bad you couldn't do that for poor Jasmine. You just weren't fast enough."

It was like driving an ice spike through Ivy's heart. "Tell me where you are."

"Unfortunately, it's not going to be that easy for you," he replied. "If you want answers, you have to *earn* them."

"How?" Ivy asked.

"If you must ask, then maybe you're not meant to know." The line went dead.

"FUCK!" Ivy yelled, startling some people standing nearby. "He might have left him in there to die."

Jonathan looked back in the direction of the house. "Are you sure?"

"This is what he wants," she said. "To torture me. And he's doing a hell of a job at it."

"That doesn't mean Oliver was in there when the house burned," Jonathan said. "He could just as easily have him as well as Carol."

"I don't understand," Ivy said, pacing down the road and back. "Why not just tell me where he wants me to go? I don't care if it is a trap. At this point I'd do anything."

"Maybe that's the point. He wants you so desperate you can't even consider fighting back," Jonathan replied.

"Then he's got me," she said, slumping down on the curb. Ivy dropped her head between her knees. "What am I supposed to do?"

Jonathan leaned down beside her. "I don't know. But you can't give up. There has to be a way to find him."

"We'll only find him once he wants to be found," Ivy replied. "In the meantime he'll keep taking and taking from me until there's nothing left."

"He won't get me," Jonathan replied. "And I'm pretty sure he can't get to Nat. As long as she's still in the station anyway."

"Did you ever get in contact with Alice?" Ivy asked. Even though she wouldn't necessarily call herself and Alice close friends, she had been an integral part of this investigation ever since she'd helped discover the cabin. It was very possible Zimmerman could target her as well.

Jonathan screwed up his features and put the phone on speaker again as he dialed Alice's number. A worried mask came over his face as the phone rang two... then three times.

"Hello?"

Jonathan sighed. "Uh... hey. Is everything okay?"

"Yeah, I'm at the funeral home. Why?" she asked, seemingly annoyed.

"Alice, it's Ivy," Ivy said. "I don't want to alarm you, but there's a possibility you've been identified as a potential target."

"Target for what? And way to not alarm me."

"We just discovered Oliver's house burned to the ground," Jonathan said. "And Carol is missing from her home. He seems to be targeting people that have been or are close to Ivy."

"I'm sorry," she said, humor in her voice. "Want to run that by me again?"

"He's targeting people I care about!" Ivy yelled. "Oliver might be dead; we can't get in there for another few hours. I don't know what he's done with Carol. But he just called, taunting me again. I just... I wanted to let you know."

There was silence on the other end for a moment. "Thank

you. I appreciate that… but I don't know what I'm supposed to do about it. I have arrangements to make, creditors to deal with. A pile of half-finished crocheted scarves to donate. I don't have time to be someone's target."

"Alice, *please*," Ivy said.

"Look, I can take care of myself," she replied. "And I'll make sure to watch out for any scary men in white vans."

"Alice—" Jonthan said but she cut him off before he could finish.

"Thanks for the call." She hung up before they could say anything else.

Jonathan stared at the phone a few moments longer. "Her mother's death… I think it's hitting her harder than she's willing to admit."

Ivy shook her head. "I just don't want her to get mixed up in this. Let me speak to Ayford. Maybe he can at least put some kind of a detail on her to watch her back."

"She won't like that."

"Who cares? As long as she's safe," Ivy said, heading for the Lieutenant.

"Hey! Over here!" The voice carried the urgency of discovery, cutting through the ambient noise of diesel engines and radio chatter. "We got something!"

Ayford's head snapped toward the sound, his weathered face immediately shifting into crisis mode. Ivy felt her stomach drop even before they began moving toward the firefighter who'd called out, already knowing with that terrible certainty that comes from experience that whatever they'd found would change everything.

The fire chief emerged from what had been Oliver's living room, his protective gear streaked with soot and ash, his expression grim in the way that spoke of years dealing with tragedy. "We found a body," he announced, his professional tone wavering at the weight of the discovery. "Male, appears to be adult. But the thermal damage is extensive—the accelerants used made this fire burn hotter than anything we typically see in residential structures."

Ivy's vision tunneled. Oliver—brilliant, complicated Oliver who'd been trying to help her despite everything that had gone wrong between them. Oliver, who loved her.

"Can you determine identity?" Ayford asked, though Ivy could hear in his voice that he already suspected the answer.

The fire chief shook his head slowly. "Not from visual examination. We'll need dental records, DNA analysis. The damage is too severe for immediate identification. Could take days, maybe weeks."

Ivy could only focus on one terrible certainty. Zimmerman had done this. Whatever doubts she might have harbored about coincidence or alternative explanations evaporated in the heat still radiating from Oliver's destroyed home. This was calculated, personal, designed to destroy her from the inside out by targeting everyone who mattered to her.

Jonathan placed a supportive hand on her shoulder. "Come on," he said. "There's nothing else we can do here."

If this really was Oliver—if Zimmerman had killed the one friend Ivy had made during all her time in that foster home—she would make him pay. No matter what it took; if it cost her everything she owned, she would see to it that the man could never hurt anyone ever again.

Chapter Twenty-Six

"WHAT DO YOU MEAN SHE LEFT?" IVY SHOUTED AT THE DESK sergeant as soon as they arrived back at the station.

"She left," the man reiterated. "I don't know how much plainer to make it. She ducked her escort and made it out the side door."

Ivy couldn't believe this. She turned to Jonathan. "Call her." She returned her attention to the sergeant. "Did she say where she was going?"

"Not to me."

"To anyone?"

"Bishop, I don't know, okay? I didn't think to question it. No one told me Buckley was on lockdown until after she was gone."

Ivy ran her hand down her face. What was going on here? "Where's Captain Armstrong?"

"He's due to speak to the media in thirty minutes about updates to the Zimmerman case. He's probably in his office."

"I need to speak to him," Ivy said, heading for the security door. The sergeant hesitated a second before buzzing her through, with Jonathan close on her heels.

"Where the hell could she have gone?" Ivy muttered. "Why would she leave?"

"She's not picking up," Jonathan said. "I've tried three times."

Ivy burst into Armstrong's office, interrupting the man as he was attempting to fix his tie in the mirror. "Bishop, what—"

"Where is she?" Ivy demanded.

"I should ask you the same thing," he replied. "You two are obviously in this thing together." He abandoned the tie, throwing it off and circling back around his desk, staring at Ivy like a bull who had seen the red cape and was about to charge. "Or did you think I'd buy that 'turning yourself in' act?"

"What are you even talking about?" Ivy said. "*We've* been over on Roslyndale... the house fire?" She added when Armstrong didn't reply. "He killed my—" she choked back her hitched breath, unable to bring herself to say it aloud.

He glared at her, not an ounce of empathy in his eyes. "I don't know what game you're playing, but as of this minute, consider yourself under arrest for accessory."

"Sir," Jonathan said. "Ivy didn't—"

"White, shut your mouth right now unless you want to join her. Both of you have demonstrated a serious lack in your decision making. And the fact that Buckley has gone AWOL only reinforces that fact."

"Begging your pardon, sir," Ivy said, unable to help herself. "But she left on your watch. Not mine."

Armstrong's visage darkened before he picked up his phone. "Sergeant. Come in here."

A moment later the door opened to reveal Sergeant Walsh.

"Take these two into custody," Armstrong said. "I want them held until further notice."

"Sir!" Jonathan said.

"Get out. Now." Ivy didn't bother arguing. She followed Walsh along with Jonathan.

"He's taking it out on us because he knows we're right," Ivy muttered. Armstong had always been a hothead, and he'd never had any love for Ivy. Nat had shielded a lot of that. It seemed now that he had the opportunity to take his frustrations out on Ivy, he wasn't going to miss it. "Walsh, you know this is bullshit."

"I'm not getting involved," she said. "I'm just following orders."

"Mercedes, come on," Jonathan said. "We're not the enemy here."

The woman stopped, the three of them standing in the middle of the station.

"What happened to Nat?" Ivy asked.

Walsh took a deep breath. "Armstrong had her waiting in his office. She asked to go to the restroom and just… walked out. I guess he took her leaving on his watch personally."

"Did she say anything to anyone or…" Ivy looked around, grasping for straws. "Anything?"

Walsh shook her head. "I wish I could help. But I only saw her leave and she looked like she was on a mission."

Ivy couldn't believe this. Her entire world was caving in around her at once. First Carol, then Oliver and now Nat… what was going on?

"Look," Walsh said, lowering her voice. "Armstrong has been on the warpath ever since that girl died. He's been more of a terror than normal. I could… leave you in interrogation two and forget to lock the door. Just so long as it doesn't come back on me."

Relief flooded through Ivy. "Mercedes, thank you."

"Don't thank me," she replied. "I don't know what you two have gotten yourselves into and I don't want any part of it. But I don't think keeping you here will do anyone any good either. You are both good cops. You don't deserve to be treated like criminals."

Ivy pursed her lips and found herself reaching for Jonathan's hand, though she pulled it back as Walsh turned and they followed her to interrogation two. "Just wait about five minutes," Walsh said. "I'll make sure the way is clear to the east exit."

"Thank you again," Jonathan said. "We owe you big time."

"Just don't come back without something concrete," she replied. "Otherwise Armstrong will throw away the key without even so much as a second thought."

She left them alone in the interrogation room. Ivy glanced up and noticed the red light on the camera was off. Which meant there wasn't anyone in the surveillance room. "Where could she have gone?" she asked. "She knows how serious this is."

"You don't think she would have gone back to California," Jonathan suggested. "Maybe it's all been too much for her."

"No, not Nat. Not the woman I know. I've been fighting with her for so long, I thought she was someone else. That she didn't have the same moral center that I did, or that I saw when she first rescued me. But now that everything is out in the open I think I finally understand her. And she isn't the kind of person who backs down. She's not just going to tuck tail and run. She'll want to do something."

"What can she do?" he asked. "She's as clueless as the rest of us."

Ivy furrowed her brow. "Is she?" She thought back to her short conversation after showing Nat the letter from Zimmerman. She recalled asking Nat if she knew what it meant, and Nat dodging the question. "Maybe she's only been acting clueless, so she could make amends for what she thinks she's done."

"You think she's going after Zimmerman herself?"

"It makes sense," Ivy replied. "She's been beating herself up over the last fifteen years, that guilt burying itself inside her. Maybe she figures the only way to get rid of it is to track him down on her own and do what she should have done fifteen years ago."

"But how would she know where to start?" he asked. "The clues haven't exactly been ironclad."

"Not to us," Ivy said. "But I think maybe Nat has one last secret."

"Okay," he said. "So what do we do? How do we find her?"

Ivy's brain was buzzing with emotions, the stress of losing two of the most important people in the world in one day bearing down on her. But at her heart she was still an investigator. And that drive managed to cut through some of that pain, to show her a way forward. "We need to talk to the one resource we have left."

Alice opened the door to her home, her eyes going wide seeing Ivy and Jonathan standing on her doorstep.

"You can't be serious," she said. "Look, I've got my gun right here. I'm being careful." She opened her blazer to reveal a 9MM tucked into her waistband.

"And yet you opened the door without knowing who was behind it," Jonathan said. Alice pursed her lips and pointed to the little doorbell camera.

"I have a doorbell camera, dumbass. I knew it was you. Doesn't mean I need to like it."

"Oh," Jonathan said.

"Care to tell me why you're darkening my doorstep?"

Ivy grimaced. "Can we come in? It'll be easier to talk inside."

Alice sighed and moved so they could both come in. She

closed and locked the door behind them, removing the gun from her waistband and placing it on the small table near the entryway. At least she had taken their warning to heart.

"Sorry for the mess," she said. "I haven't exactly had time to clean." There were papers stacked all over her living room table and old takeout boxes laid haphazardly around the room.

"How's it all going with your mom's stuff?" Jonathan asked.

Alice cleared off the table, moving all her papers and documents to a desk in the corner. "Let's just cut the formalities, huh? What's going on?"

"Alice," Ivy said, drawing the woman's attention. "I'm really sorry about your mother."

That stern gaze of hers, honed by years of staring into a camera and reporting the news didn't crack. Alice had learned how to bury things deep. So deep no one could ever touch them. "Thanks."

"We…" Ivy found it hard to know where to start. "We need to find Nat. She's missing."

"Missing how?" Alice asked.

"She walked right out of the station about an hour ago and no one seems to know where she went," Jonathan said.

Alice shrugged, taking a seat on the couch. "So?"

"So we think she's going after Zimmerman," Ivy replied. "By herself."

Alice paused. "Is that a bad thing?"

"Look," Ivy replied. "I know you've been through a lot. And I know this is terrible timing. But two people are already missing and if you don't help us, we might lose a third."

Alice's gaze darkened. "*Two* people? Did they find—."

"A burned male body was found inside the home. We don't know if it's him or not."

Something in Alice softened. "Oh. I'm… sorry. I didn't know."

"We weren't kidding when we told you to be on the lookout," Ivy said. "The people I know are being targeted. And if we don't find out where Nat went, she could be next."

Alice nodded, seemingly lost in thought. "Okay, yeah. That makes sense. Um… let me get my computer." She stood and left the room, heading down the hallway. The faint smell of antiseptic and bleach reached Ivy's nose, causing irritation.

"It was never supposed to be permanent," Jonathan said in a low voice. "Her mother. She was only supposed to be here a few weeks. Which turned into months. Which turned into…"

"Yeah," Ivy said.

Alice returned a moment later with the laptop and set it on the living room table. "You realize we only set up surveillance in a small part of the city," she said. "This is by no means comprehensive."

"I know," Ivy said. "If these were normal circumstances, I'd have gone to—" She stopped. "We have to start somewhere."

"I understand," Alice said. She pulled up the feeds, which showed real-time images from the city's industrial area. "Here's where Jonathan and I saw you the other day." She pointed at the street where Ivy and Nat had stopped, where Nat had shown Ivy the knife that had killed her family.

"Okay, let's start looking," Ivy said, scanning through each of the camera's images. She started with the first one and wound it back to before Nat would have left the station, then played it again at double speed, looking for any trace of her or her Jeep.

"Do you really think you'll find anything?" Alice asked. "I mean, this can only be what, five, ten percent of the city?"

"Right now it's all we have," Jonathan replied. "Oakhurst PD isn't being very cooperative."

"There's a shocker," Alice replied. "Let me guess. Ayford?"

"Armstrong," Ivy said, scanning through the next camera. "We're to be arrested if seen again. Ayford is still dealing with the house fire."

"That man needs an enema," Alice muttered. "Maybe it would calm him down a little. Don't feel bad, though. He's been on my ass for years too. Even back when Jon and I were dating."

"He *especially* didn't like you then," Jonathan said.

Alice smiled. "I like to think of my presence as death by a thousand cuts around Armstrong," she said. "He sure as hell wasn't happy to see me the other day."

"What do you mean?" Jonathan asked.

"When I grabbed those files. He practically threatened to shoot me if I didn't put them back down."

Ivy turned to her. "Then how did you get them out of the building?"

Alice gave her that signature reporter grin of hers. "I just had to manufacture a small crisis, something to distract him long enough that I could make quick copies and be on my way. I had Beatrix unlock two of the cells. He owed me big time so I guess now we're even."

"You let two prisoners escape?" Jonathan asked.

"I knew they wouldn't get out of the building. I just needed a little controlled chaos for about five minutes. And it was more than sufficient."

Jonathan chuckled. "You really are something, you know that?"

"I do."

Ivy had been only half listening as she scanned the video. While extreme, she could absolutely believe Alice would do something like that to achieve her goals. It was what Ivy admired about her, despite her causing Ivy plenty of headaches in the past.

After about ten minutes her eyes began to blur, scanning through video after video. And the more she listened to

Jonathan and Alice reminisce and banter, the more a strange feeling pulled at her gut. It wasn't a feeling she felt often, but she knew jealousy when it arrived. Maybe it was just because the two of them had such a history, or maybe it was because part of her thought Alice might be better for Jonathan than—

"Wait a second," she said, her focus returning completely to the video. Something had blurred by on the bottom of one of the cameras. She rewound it as Jonathan peered over her shoulder. As Ivy paused the camera, she realized she was looking at the back corner of Nat's Jeep. The color was a perfect match.

"That's her."

"Fourteenth and Century," Jonathan said. "What's out there?"

"A bunch of warehouses as far as I know," Ivy replied. "But that's only two streets over from where... where she found me."

"Check the other feeds," Alice said.

Ivy did, but the Jeep didn't appear anywhere else. There were no other cameras that focused on that particular area.

"Think she's still there?" Jonathan asked.

"Maybe. There's only one way to find out." Ivy stood and headed for the door. "Thanks Alice. I know this isn't a great time. We appreciate your help."

Alice nodded. "Yeah. I hope you find her."

"Me too."

Chapter Twenty-Seven

Ivy could barely stop her heart from thumping as they approached the city's industrial district. Old, abandoned smokestacks defined this part of town, replaced by newer towers that billowed white smoke into the sky instead of black. There weren't many working industries left in Oakhurst, but the few that remained worked almost nonstop, the factories never shutting down.

"What do we do if we don't find her?" Jonathan asked, rubbing his shoulder which was still in the sling. Ivy realized he hadn't had a pain pill in a while.

"I think the bigger question is what do we do if we *do* find her," Ivy replied. "I just hope we can reach her before she does something stupid."

"Stupid like trying to take on Zimmerman alone?"

Ivy nodded. "What I can't figure out is what she knew that I missed. How could she have known where he would be? I get why she wouldn't say anything—she feels like she's failed me too many times already and wouldn't want me in harm's way. But how did she know where to go in the first place?"

"I think that's a very good question," Jonathan said. Ivy could tell it was an automatic response, that his mind was on other things. And given everything that had happened, she couldn't exactly blame him.

"Where are you?" she asked gently.

"Hmm?" he asked.

"What are you thinking about?"

"Oh," he said, readjusting himself in the passenger seat. "Nothing. Just... all this stuff with Alice's mother has made me think of my own. I know she's just doing what she thinks is best, in her own, annoying and infuriating way. I think... I may need to go back up there. Sooner than later. I need to calm the waters."

Ivy nodded. "And there's your sister too."

"Yeah," he replied. "There's that."

"Do you think..." she paused. "Would that be a permanent move?"

"I don't know," he said. "I hope not. But... it's hard to say."

She couldn't exactly blame him. He'd come to Oakhurst to find some time and peace from everything going on with his family. And instead he'd been forced to deal with headless bodies, kidnapped victims, a drug ring and now a homicidal maniac out for blood. Not exactly the getaway he had planned, she was sure.

"Fourteenth and Century," Ivy said, coming to the intersection. A large dump truck pulled through and headed past them, the engine roaring through the street. Ivy looked behind her; the camera was mounted on a pole about ten feet up, looking at the intersection. If she followed Nat's Jeep, it meant she'd need to turn right, which she did, putting her on Century Avenue itself.

"You know, just because she drove by here, doesn't mean she stayed here," Jonathan said as they headed down the thoroughfare. It was a wide, four-lane road where a tractor trailer was in the process of pulling out about a hundred feet away.

"I know," Ivy said, scanning the spaces between the buildings and side roads. "But it's all we have." She knew Jonathan was just trying to be realistic, but finding Nat before something else terrible happened had become her singular focus. She couldn't think about Carol or Oliver, not right now. Not until—

"There," Ivy said, spotting Nat's Jeep parked in a small pullout between two large warehouses. From the looks of it, both buildings were abandoned as there was a large gate around both, overgrown weeds poking out between the cracks in the concrete beyond.

Ivy pulled in behind Nat's vehicle and hopped out, checking the interior. There was no sign of anyone inside, but no sign of a struggle either. She looked around as Jonathan joined her, hoping to see something that would give them a direction.

"She's here. Somewhere," Ivy said. She thought about telling Jonathan to try calling her again, but if Nat was in a compromised position, that would only make things worse.

Jonathan pulled on the gates, which were locked with a large padlock. "Think there's another way in?" He glanced up at the spiral barbed wire that ran along the top of the fence. "I don't think we're getting in this way."

Ivy scanned the length of the fence. About fifty feet down there looked to be a break in the fence itself. She jogged down, finding it wasn't exactly a break, but instead the fence had been partially cut away, allowing access.

"Ivy," Jonathan said as she ducked down to go through. "Maybe we should call for backup."

"From whom?" she asked. "Armstrong will just send someone to arrest us, or worse, come himself," she replied. "We're on our own."

"What if Zimmerman is in there?" he asked.

"Then we don't have any time to waste," Ivy replied. "Because it means he has Nat. If she's not already dead too." She crawled through the fence, standing on the other side mentally pleading with Jonathan to join her. She wouldn't force him. But she couldn't stand by either.

The man sighed. "Hang on." He returned to the car and retrieved his backup firearm, handing it to Ivy before managing his way through the fence himself. Given he could only use three limbs, it took him considerably longer.

The giant warehouse loomed huge before them.

"How do you want to do this?" he asked.

Ivy spotted a set of stairs that led to a door about thirty feet up. "We need to get the high ground." She rushed forward, taking the stairs two at a time as Jonathan followed. When she reached the door, she found the lock had already been broken. She pulled out the weapon Jonathan had given her, unlatched the safety, and slowly opened the door.

There was no movement from the other side. She turned back to Jonathan and nodded, indicating she was taking point. He had his weapon out in his good hand and nodded back.

Ivy made her way around the doorway, checking the dark corners just inside the building. Nothing. She moved slowly and stayed low, looking for anything that might be out of place. Jonathan stayed close behind her, bringing up the rear. The whole place was incredibly dark, the only light filtering through some dirty skylights that ran the length of the warehouse. Ivy thought she could see something on the floor of the building, but without more light she couldn't tell what it was.

It was then she heard the cocking of a gun.

"Don't move, Detective."

Ivy froze; her weapon still raised in front of her. She felt a hand remove the weapon from her hand as the muzzle of another weapon pressed against her skull. *Shit.*

"Delta four, we have them," the voice said again, with a peculiar accent. She would have to place it as Spanish, maybe Bolivian.

"Switch to six," another voice said through the radio.

"Clear," the voice said.

"Clear," another voice behind Jonathan that Ivy hadn't even realized was there repeated.

Light flooded the space.

Ivy found herself staring at the length of a long catwalk with stairs going back down to the warehouse floor every fifty feet or so. A man in dark fatigues stood behind her, goggles over his eyes that she recognized as night-vision. He pulled them up to reveal a tanned face. Behind Jonathan stood an identical-looking man, also in dark fatigues. Each of them were armed with automatic rifles.

But that wasn't what drew Ivy's attention the most. Because there on the floor of the warehouse, each tied to a chair, were Carol, Oliver and Nat.

Chapter Twenty-Eight

Relief flooded Ivy as she and Jonathan were led down one of the staircases, each of them with a "guard" behind their backs, urging them on with the ends of their weapons like they were nothing more than cattle being led to a slaughter. Ivy had been forced to raise her hands, though Jonathan had only managed to get one hand up after he'd been disarmed.

Oliver was still alive. He hadn't died in his house. That was something, at least.

They—no, *she* had been too hasty. They should have taken a better look at the property, figured out what they were dealing with here. And Nat was still alive, though even from a distance Ivy could tell her face was bruised and slightly bloody. Oliver sat tied to the chair beside her. He looked fine, otherwise, apparently not having received the same beating as Nat.

As for Carol, she looked more tired than anything else, but otherwise seemed okay. Had she been here this entire time since she'd been taken from her home? Ivy wasn't sure. But she *was* sure she would do whatever was necessary to secure their release. If Zimmerman wanted her unconditional surrender, he had it. If it meant the three of them could go free.

"Vee," Oliver muttered as Ivy and Jonathan were marched out onto the middle of the bright concrete floor. Nat barely looked up, but when she did, she winced upon seeing Ivy. Carol smiled, though she was clearly in pain from the way she'd been restrained to the chair.

"I'm going to fix this," Ivy said to all three of them.

"Shut up and stand here," the guard behind her ordered, pushing Ivy to a spot right in front of the three of them. She turned to see another guard had appeared and they'd taken Jonathan off to the side, keeping their weapons trained on him.

Ivy looked around the massive space. More guards lined the catwalks above. She counted at least fifteen. Maybe more.

"Zimmerman!" she yelled, her voice echoing through the building. "You wanted me. I'm here. So let's get on with this!"

In a darkened area under one of the staircases, a flame appeared, which then turned into a bright red ember. A moment later the man himself emerged, a cigar hanging from his mouth and a grin a mile wide on his lips. He sauntered towards Ivy, removing the cigar and blowing out the smoke.

"A celebratory treat for myself," he said, making a large arc around Ivy and the others as he continued to smoke. "Nothing like a good, quality cigar to soothe the soul. Would you like one?"

"Cut the shit," Ivy said. "You got me. Great job. Now let them go."

Zimmerman only gave her a toothy smile, holding the cigar between his teeth before continuing his large circle. "I'm afraid it's not that simple, Detective Bishop. Or maybe I should just call you Ivy? Ivy Katherine Stanford. The girl who tried to disappear."

Ivy bristled at her given name.

"Vee, I'm sorry. This is all my fault," Oliver said. Zimmerman walked up to him and plucked his ear with his finger.

"Now, now. No commentary from the peanut gallery," he said. "Next time you speak I'll cut it off."

"Ivy," Carol said. "Is Hero—"

"He's fine," she said. "He's at the station. A K9 officer is watching him."

Carol nodded. "Thank God. I tried—" She stopped talking as soon as she saw the blade appear between her and Oliver. Carol's eyes grew wide with terror.

"Now what did I just say about speaking?" Zimmerman asked.

"Stop it," Ivy demanded. "Your fight is with me. Not them."

"You're right," Zimmerman said, still holding the knife between Carol and Oliver, it was only when he retracted it that Ivy took a breath. "Still. I've been waiting for this moment a long time, Ivy. I should get to enjoy it at least a little." He held up the knife. "You know what this is, don't you?"

"The knife you used to kill my family," Ivy said.

He gave her a sly smile. "The knife used to kill your family, yes. Lovingly preserved by the dutiful Natasha Buckley." He turned to Nat. "*Thank you,* Lieutenant, for keeping this for me. Having it here means a lot."

Nat didn't reply, just stared at the ground. She looked like she'd been worked over a good bit, but Nat had always been the kind of person who could take a punch and keep on coming.

"This knife... it's what changed the trajectory of both our lives, wouldn't you say?" He held it up so it caught the light, reflecting it back into Ivy's eyes, causing her to turn away. "It changed everything that night."

"You talk about it like it's alive," Ivy said, training her gaze on him again. "When it was really *you* who were behind all this. *You* were the one who stalked my mother. *You* were the one who used the Vapoxil to incapacitate and kidnap us. And you were the one who finally used it to kill everyone I ever cared about."

"Well," he said, still inspecting the blade with one hand while he took the cigar and blew out another puff of smoke with the other. "You've certainly done your homework. But you're wrong about one thing. *I* didn't kill your family, Ivy. *You* did that."

Ivy locked eyes with Nat.

No. It couldn't be true.

"That's a lie," she growled.

He shrugged. "Doesn't matter if you believe me or not. The fact we're both here is something of a miracle. I figured you wouldn't last one day out there with the evidence piled up against you. I figured you'd be picked up—or run over on that deserted street, and eventually justice would prevail. A family murdered by their own daughter. Who would have thought?" He circled around the chairs again, standing behind the others while keeping his attention on Ivy. "But I neglected to consider how soft some people are inside." He brought the butt of the knife down on the back of Nat's head, causing her to grunt in response.

"Stop!" Ivy yelled.

"If it weren't for this woman here, you would have been in jail for your parents' murder within *hours*," Zimmerman said. "Who could have ever predicted that she would have just... let you go out into the world. A killer, a *murderer*, roaming free." He leaned down and blew a puff of smoke into Nat's face, causing her to wince. "Bold move."

"I didn't kill them!" Ivy yelled.

"It caused me quite the consternation," Zimmerman said. "I couldn't figure it out. But I also realized there was an opportunity there. I am, after all, a scientist. And I thought this could make for a very interesting experiment. But I needed someone to keep a close eye on you. Someone who could provide me with updates." He turned to Oliver, flicking his ear again. "Unfortunately, he turned out to be very disappointing."

Wait, what was he saying? Oliver was meant to spy on her?

"There's just no getting good help these days. I'll admit my work with Oliver was primitive, but he never had the true drive I needed. The *desire* to please that so many of my patients strive for. That and the fact he was lovestruck made him completely useless to me."

Ivy stilled, watching Oliver for his reaction. But there was none. He only continued to stare at the ground, much like Nat.

"I needed someone with more... creativity, we'll say."

"Kieran Woodward," Ivy replied.

He nodded. "Exactly. Took me *years* to get him just right. Countless hours of work, of building memory blocks and breaking them down, of creating someone so desperate for love that he was willing to do anything for me. And that's when I knew I was ready to get your attention again."

"You used him to kill those people," Ivy said, recalling her first case.

Zimmerman grinned. "I'd been gone a while, Ivy. Working with my partners, building something great together. And I needed to know what I was up against. After my failure with Oliver, I knew I couldn't just brute force my way in. I needed to draw you out. Make you vulnerable."

"That's what all this has been about," Ivy said. "You orchestrated all this, just to see how I would respond?"

"Well, I can't say I wasn't hoping you wouldn't just snap one day and go on a rampage. That would have been a bonus." He shot her a wink. "But no, you played the role of a good detective, doing your job, protecting the public, blah, blah, blah. And I realized I could only ever get you to break if I put you in the same position you were in before. And that's where the Quinn family came in."

"*That's* what you were trying to do? Get me to snap so I'd become what? Some kind of weapon for you?"

"In a manner of speaking, yes," he replied. "But it still didn't take. I'll admit, Ivy. You are one hard nut to crack. And I mean that pun sincerely. Which brings us here." He held his hands out, indicating all three of his victims. "You see, I finally realized that not just any old victim would do. It has to be someone you're connected to. Someone you really care about. Only then will your true nature come back out. Only then would I be able to mold you into the perfect killer you were always meant to be: the one who doesn't even know what she is."

Ivy's eyes went wide as she realized what he was saying. "No. I won't do it," she said.

"Oh, you will," he replied. "You will kill one of them. Or I will kill all of them."

She shook her head. This couldn't be happening. How could she hurt any of the people before her? They were her family. The people she loved most in the world. How was she supposed to choose?

Zimmerman held out the knife to Ivy while one of his goons kept a weapon trained on her. The message was clear: step one foot out of line and take a bullet. But she couldn't do it. It was impossible.

"I refuse," she whispered.

"Kill White," Zimmerman said.

"No!" Ivy yelled, turning to see the man who'd escorted them down place the muzzle of his gun against Jonathan's head.

"Take it, Ivy. Do what you need to do. Or watch your partner, and the people you love, die before your very eyes."

It was as if she was frozen. But she didn't have a choice. She couldn't let them shoot Jonathan.

Ivy took the knife from Zimmerman and in its cleaned and sharpened blade, she saw her own reflection.

The reflection of a killer.

Chapter Twenty-Nine

THE KNIFE FELT HEAVY, BUT WELL-BALANCED. AS IVY WRAPPED her fingers around the grip, something familiar tugged at the back of her brain. It was like the ghost of a memory, the memory of being here once before, of feeling this weapon in her hand. It was familiar, and that scared her.

When Nat first told Ivy she had killed her own family, the idea had seemed ludicrous. For her entire adult life and beyond, Ivy had wanted nothing more than to discover the truth about what happened to them. She had built a career around that question, doing everything she could to dig up the past and uncover the secrets buried in time.

It seemed that her past had finally caught up with her.

As Ivy examined the weapon in her hand, she tried to imagine using it. Tried to picture what that would have been like to actually end a life. Of driving the blade through the flesh of her mother, her father… her brother. But she couldn't. Even though the knife itself felt familiar, the action didn't.

"Why?" she asked.

"Now, now, no stalling," Zimmerman chided.

"No. Why me?" she repeated. "Why did I kill them?"

The man flashed her a wicked grin. "Because I told you

to. Because deep down you've always known you're different, haven't you? That you don't really fit in with other people? That the world seems strange and you feel disconnected from it, like you're nothing more than an observer, looking in. I saw that within you and I could tell, you wouldn't blink an eye at snuffing out the lives of people, even those you pretended to care about. You are unique, Ivy, able to take a life and move on as easily as someone else would step on and off a bus."

"Don't you believe him, Ivy," Carol said. "It isn't true."

"Oh, but it is," Zimmerman said. "Look how you treat the people you say are closest to you. You can't even bring yourself to touch them. To offer them compassion. You may pretend like you care, but we both know that's nothing more than a show. What is there in everyone else is missing in you, Ivy. I've seen what you can do. Take the action now. Free yourself. You don't have to be part of this world any longer."

"He's wrong," Nat uttered. "I was wrong."

"See how they try to beg for their lives?" Zimmerman asked, coming up beside Ivy. "See how pathetic they are? They'll say anything to get you to drop that knife. They will lie straight to your face. Like they've been doing your entire life."

Ivy turned to Zimmerman. "You know I'm right. Your beloved adopted mother, watching you struggle all these years and telling you there was nothing wrong with you. *Lie.*"

He stepped beside Nat. "Your former boss and friend, who knew you were a killer deep in her bones and she kept it from you for fifteen years. *Lie.*"

Finally he moved to Oliver. "And your purported best friend who has been in love with you ever since the day he met you. Who never told you because he knew you'd never reciprocate. Because you're incapable. One. More. Lie."

Zimmerman stepped in front of the three of them. "You say you care about these people. You think they care about you. But the truth is, you are an anomaly to them. A curiosity and a nuisance. Do it now. Rid yourself of the biggest liar of the bunch. Prove to yourself that you are better than they are, that you are more, just like you did all those years ago. That was your first step. It is time to take the next."

All three of them were looking at Ivy now, and she searched their eyes for the truth. What kind of daughter couldn't even hug her own mother? And what kind of friend cut off contact with her best friend for ten years? And what kind of detective selfishly used the one person she knew in the department to get her promotions?

The kind of person who didn't care about other people… who saw them as tools more than anything else, there to be used up and discarded.

Was that what happened fifteen years ago? Had Ivy seen her family as nothing more than baggage… and decided to rid herself of them?

A tear fell down her cheek, startling her. She hadn't even realized her eyes had begun to well.

"Yes, let it out," Zimmerman said softly. "Let go of the pain. Become the person you were meant to be."

Ivy squeezed her eyes shut, seeing the blood running down her arm. It was the same as in her dreams, the coppery tang filling the air.

Kill one of them… or I will kill them all.

The words reverberated through her thoughts and time seemed to slow, the memory blossoming in her brain. She stood in the room beneath the cabin, having woken up in the strange place with her family. Her brother sat beside her, terrified, her mother and father trying to reassure them everything would be okay.

And Zimmerman was there. He approached them, yanking Ivy from her mother's arms.

"No! Take me!" her mother yelled. *"It's me you want, leave my daughter alone!"*

"You had your chance," Zimmerman had said to her. "Time's up." He dragged Ivy over to the small table in the cabin, where a large knife sat on the table. Zimmerman picked it up, holding it above Ivy as her mother screamed at him.

"Choose," he told Ivy.

But she didn't understand. Ivy didn't understand any of this. She had just been in her bed, in her house... she didn't know what was going on or who this strange man was. Or why he was holding a knife out in front of her.

"Ch-choose?"

"Kill one of them," he said. "Or I'll kill them all."

Ivy's throat had gone dry. She didn't understand what he was saying. She was supposed to kill one of her own family? How could she? All she knew was this wasn't right. She shook her head, tears falling down her cheeks.

"Very well," he said and walked back over to them.

"Wait!" Ivy cried, unable to believe this was happening to her. Her breaths were fast and it felt like she was going to throw up. She looked in her mother's eyes, seeing the terror there. The pain. She couldn't. She turned to her brother, absolutely horrified at what was happening. He'd always been so strong, and now he was cradled in their father's arms, the man protecting him from this strange person threatening them with the knife.

Then she found her father's gaze. Measured, determined. He nodded to Ivy. Was he saying...? No, she couldn't.

"This has gone far enough, Jason," her father said. "Let our children go." He glanced at Ivy again.

"You had your chance, *Michael*," Zimmerman said. "You forced my hand. Or more accurately, your whore of a wife did."

"You son of a bitch," Ivy's mother said.

Zimmerman turned on his heel to Ivy. "*Choose! Right now!*"

Ivy's father nodded at her again, mouthing *It's okay.*

"Daddy," she whimpered, the word coming through tears.

Zimmerman almost seemed surprised. "The child has spoken."

"No!" her mother yelled as Zimmerman drove the knife into her father's chest. Blood erupted from his mouth as he gurgled his final breaths. Her mother and brother screamed. Ivy ran to her mother, grabbing hold of her, cradled in her arms.

Zimmerman turned to the three of them. "You know," he said, fury on his face. "I didn't actually think you'd do it. No matter." He then yanked her brother away, and before Ivy could process what was happening, her brother's lifeless body fell next to her father's.

"You son of a bitch," her mother cried. "You *monster*."

"You made me this way, Rebecca," Zimmerman said. "We could have had a good life together. This is *your* fault."

Ivy grabbed hold of her mother, squeezing her tight and closing her eyes. If this was how she was going to die, at least she would be with them.

She felt something hot and wet against her pajamas. When she opened her eyes and looked down, her mother's blood was seeping out from the stab wounds and into her clothes. Ivy locked eyes with her mother, watching the light fade from them.

A hand grabbed her from behind, yanking her away and in that instant, something broke inside Ivy.

Her entire body went numb.

Zimmerman stood over her, breathing hard, the bloody knife in his hand. He was practically seething. But Ivy just watched him, all emotion having left her body. She was watching the scene from somewhere else, somewhere above. It was like she really had died and her body just hadn't gotten the news yet.

Zimmerman continued to watch her, though he cocked his head. "You're not scared," he finally said. He then seemed to come back to himself, looking around at the massacre. "Well... it seems this is quite..." He ran a hand through his long hair. "This is quite the mess." He leaned down, looking at Ivy, but her eyes were glassy. He made a motion like he was going to stab her too, but she didn't even flinch.

"Interesting," Zimmerman said. "But maybe we can use this." He surveyed the room, then began the process of staging the scene, cleaning the blood off certain areas, while keeping it on others. Finally, he took the knife and placed it in Ivy's hand, wrapping her little fingers around the handle. He then gingerly removed it by the blade with a gloved hand and placed it next to the body of Ivy's mother.

He then moved behind Ivy, standing her up. He seemed pleased she could stand under her own power. "Yes, this will work nicely," he said, snapping his fingers in front of her face. She didn't even blink. "Catatonic state as a result of extreme personal trauma. And open to suggestion." It was like he had switched into clinical mode. "Ivy," he said, snapping his fingers again in front of her face. She both looked at him and past him at the same time. "When they find you, you will admit to doing this. All of it, do you understand?"

She continued to look at him.

"Tell me you understand. You killed your family, didn't you?"

She gave him a subtle nod.

"There we go. You won't recall the details. It was done in a fit of rage. But no one blames you. You're not in trouble. You did what you had to do." He snapped his fingers a few more times, but it didn't seem to matter.

"Here," he said, leading her out of the underground room, through the tunnel and into the garage beneath the cabin. He opened the door for her, leading her outside where it was beginning to rain. "Off you go. Just keep walking," he said.

So Ivy walked, the rain cooling her skin. She recalled

looking down at her arm, at the rain mixing with the blood, washing it away slowly.

She walked and walked until she found herself on a street. And headlights ahead of her. And after that... nothing.

Ivy opened her eyes, looking into the eager face of Zimmerman. Into the eyes of the man who had murdered her family right in front of her own eyes, then tried to frame her for it. She wasn't a killer and there was nothing wrong with her.

"*You* did it," she whispered.

"What?" he demanded.

"*You* killed them, not me. You're not letting any of us walk out of here alive, no matter what I do. No matter who I choose."

"Ivy, what are you talking about?" Zimmerman asked, though she saw the façade breaking.

"Fifteen years ago, you made me make a terrible choice. And you killed them all anyway. And you tried to convince me it was my fault. But it wasn't."

The man's face darkened.

"You wanted me to choose my mother, didn't you? You wanted her dead most of all."

Zimmerman winced and Ivy could see in his reaction it was the truth. Her mother had been his original target. "The stalking reports, the strange letters. You... wanted her to love you. And you couldn't deal with the fact she'd chosen someone else. Made a life, a family with someone else."

"You don't know what you're talking about," he growled.

"And you thought what better way to disgrace her than to turn her own daughter into her killer. Because then whatever goodwill she'd built, whatever reputation she'd cultivated, it would all be overshadowed by the fact her own daughter killed her and her husband and son. Isn't that right?"

He only continued to glower at her.

"And yet, despite all your plans, it fell apart when Nat got involved," Ivy said. She glanced at Nat. "Because no one could predict someone would give a child killer a second chance."

"You're right," Zimmerman said. "I should have finished what I started years ago."

He grabbed the knife, still in Ivy's hand and twisted it, plunging it into her midsection.

Chapter Thirty

Ivy's sharp intake of breath cut through the warehouse air. She staggered backward, her hands moving instinctively to her torso where Zimmerman's blade had found its home.

Blood seeped between her fingers, dark against her pale skin in the harsh warehouse lighting. She looked down at the spreading stain with an expression Jonathan recognized from crime scenes—that peculiar combination of shock and analytical assessment that came when the mind struggled to process sudden violence. Her knees buckled, and she collapsed to the concrete floor with an echo that reverberated through the cavernous space.

Jonathan's world contracted to that single moment of impact. Every tactical consideration, every procedural protocol, every rational thought evaporated in the face of watching someone he cared about crumple to the ground. The muzzle pushed against his head, the automatic rifles trained on the hostages, even his own survival—none of it mattered compared to the growing pool of crimson spreading beneath Ivy's still form.

"Disappointing," Zimmerman said, examining the blood on his knife with clinical detachment. He pulled a handkerchief from his pocket and began cleaning the blade with methodical precision. "All that time waiting... for this. Had I known I would have saved myself a lot of headache. No matter."

He turned to his men with the casual authority of someone discussing a change in dinner plans. "Execute the rest of them. We're leaving."

The mercenaries responded with professional efficiency, raising their automatic rifles toward Carol, Oliver, and Nat. Jonathan felt the cold rush of absolute panic—that primal terror when death approaches with mechanical certainty. They were going to die here, in this anonymous warehouse, and there wasn't a goddamned thing he could do about it.

That's when the world exploded in light and sound.

The first flashbang detonated somewhere behind Jonathan, followed immediately by two more in rapid succession. The warehouse filled with blinding white radiance that burned through his closed eyelids, accompanied by a concussive blast that seemed to liquefy his inner ears. His temporary blindness was absolute—a whiteout that left him completely disoriented and helpless.

"POLICE! DROP YOUR WEAPONS!"

The shouted commands echoed through the chaos, distorted by his damaged hearing but unmistakably authoritative. SWAT teams had breached multiple entry points simultaneously, their tactical precision cutting through Zimmerman's carefully orchestrated endgame like a scalpel through tissue.

Automatic weapons fire erupted from all directions. Muzzle flashes strobed through Jonathan's slowly returning vision like deadly fireworks. The mercenaries, their vision compromised by the flashbangs, stumbled and cursed in what sounded like Spanish. One of them crashed into industrial equipment near Jonathan's position, his rifle clattering across the concrete.

This was his chance.

Jonathan threw his body weight against the mercenary guarding him, the man's disorientation providing the split-second advantage he needed. They hit the floor together, Jonathan's injured arm screaming in protest as they rolled. His good hand found the rifle strap, and he used his leverage to swing the weapon like a club into the mercenary's temple. The man went limp.

The handgun was in a tactical holster on the unconscious man's belt. Jonathan's fingers, still numb from the restraints, fumbled with the retention mechanism before finally freeing the weapon. He couldn't use the rifle with his arm in the condition it was in, but he could handle a handgun.

Bullets whined past his head as he dropped low, using the concrete floor as cover. The warehouse had become a war zone, with SWAT officers advancing from multiple positions while Zimmerman's mercenaries fought a desperate holding action. The air filled with the acrid stench of cordite and the ringing percussion of high-powered weapons in an enclosed space.

But Jonathan had only one objective: reaching Ivy.

He began crawling across the warehouse floor, keeping as low as possible while gunfire erupted overhead. The concrete scraped against his knees and palms, leaving bloody tracks in his wake. Every few feet, he had to duck behind industrial equipment as bullets sparked off metal with angry whines. The distance to where Ivy lay seemed endless, each yard an eternity of exposed vulnerability.

A line of bullet holes stitched across the floor inches from his face, concrete fragments stinging his cheek. Someone was targeting his movement, trying to pin him down. Jonathan rolled behind a heavy support column, his heart hammering against his ribs. He could see Ivy now, maybe thirty feet away, motionless on the blood-stained concrete.

Move. Keep moving.

He broke from cover, sprinting in a crouch toward her position. More gunfire tracked his movement, but the chaos was working in his favor—too many targets, too much confusion for accurate aimed fire. He dove the last ten feet, sliding across the rough concrete on his stomach until he reached her side.

Ivy's eyes fluttered open as he grabbed her shoulders. They were unfocused, pupils dilated from shock and blood loss, but aware. Alive. The relief that flooded through him was almost paralyzing in its intensity.

"Jonathan?" Her voice was barely a whisper, nearly lost in the surrounding gunfire.

"Just hang on." He pressed his hands against the wound in her abdomen, feeling warm blood pulse between his fingers. The injury was serious—the blade had penetrated deep. She needed an ambulance immediately. But he didn't want to leave her alone.

Buckley. He needed to get to the Lieutenant. She could help him get her out of here.

He placed the pistol on the concrete beside her. "Keep this close. I need to get the others."

Ivy didn't reply, it was only the staggered raising and lowering of her chest that told him she was still alive.

Jonathan sprinted toward the chairs where the hostages remained tied, staying low as bullets continued to crack overhead. The SWAT officers were gaining ground, their superior training and equipment beginning to win out against Zimmerman's mercenaries. But the firefight was far from over.

Nat was closest. Jonathan's fingers worked frantically at her rope bonds, muscle memory from his academy training kicking in despite the chaos. The knots were professional—tight and layered—but not impossible.

"How bad is she?" Nat asked the moment her hands were free, her medical training overriding everything else.

"Bad. We need to move fast."

Nat nodded grimly and immediately began crawling toward Ivy's position, keeping low to avoid the crossfire. Jonathan moved to Carol next, her face pale with terror but her eyes alert and focused. Her restraints came loose more easily—whoever had tied her hadn't been as thorough.

"Stay down," he told her, guiding her toward better cover behind a concrete support pillar. "Don't move until this is over."

Oliver was last, his bonds professionally secured like Nat's had been. His face showed the strain of captivity but his movements were steady as Jonathan freed his hands.

"Thanks," Oliver said simply, then moved immediately to help Carol into a more protected position.

Jonathan turned back toward Ivy, intending to provide whatever assistance Nat might need, when movement in his peripheral vision made him spin around. Zimmerman emerged from the smoke and chaos like a specter, the knife still gripped in his right hand. His face was twisted with rage at seeing his carefully orchestrated plan disintegrating around him.

Some instinct—maybe the change in air pressure, maybe the soft sound of footsteps on concrete—had made him glance over his shoulder at the last possible second. Zimmerman was already lunging, the knife raised high for a killing stroke aimed at the base of Jonathan's neck.

Jonathan threw his injured arm up defensively, attempting to block the blow. Pain exploded through his shoulder as Zimmerman's momentum drove his arm down against the injured muscle. They crashed to the ground together, Zimmerman's weight driving Jonathan onto his back.

The knife hovered inches from Jonathan's face, Zimmerman pressing down with desperate strength while Jonathan fought to keep the blade at bay. His injured arm was useless—every movement sent lightning bolts of agony through his shoulder. His good arm strained against Zimmerman's wrist, muscles burning with the effort, but he could feel his strength beginning to fail.

Zimmerman smiled down at him, an expression of pure malevolent satisfaction. "I didn't wait fifteen years to watch you destroy everything I've built. You are insignificant, and you'll always be insignificant. Do you want to know why I didn't bother trying to capture you? To make Ivy choose you from the others? It was because you were never that important to her. Just another stepping stone for her to use and discard."

The knife edge moved closer, the point now mere inches from Jonathan's left eye. His arm shook with the strain of holding it back. He could smell Zimmerman's breath, feel the man's sweat dripping onto his face. This was how it would end—not in some heroic confrontation, but pinned helplessly while a madman carved him apart.

The gunshot was different from the others—sharper, closer, with a distinctive crack that cut through the ambient noise of automatic weapons fire. Zimmerman's body went rigid, his eyes widening in surprise before the strength left his arms entirely. The knife tumbled from nerveless fingers as he collapsed forward onto Jonathan's chest.

Jonathan struggled to push the dead weight off him, rolling Zimmerman's body aside with a grunt of effort. When he looked up, he saw Ivy across the warehouse, the pistol extended in her trembling hand despite her weakened condition. Smoke curled from the barrel, and her arm shook with the effort of maintaining her aim.

Their eyes met across the chaos of the firefight. Even from a distance, Jonathan could see the fierce determination in her gaze—the same look he'd seen when she'd crawled through that tunnel to save Jasmine Quinn, the same unwavering resolve that had made her such an exceptional detective. She'd used what might have been her last reserves of strength to save his life.

She fell back into Nat's arms, the pistol clattering beside her as consciousness began to ebb. But she'd done it. Whatever else happened, she'd eliminated the threat that had haunted them for weeks.

"CLEAR! ALL CLEAR!"

Lieutenant Ayford's voice cut through the diminishing gunfire, his command presence bringing order to the chaos. The remaining mercenaries were surrendering or had been subdued, their resistance finally broken by superior firepower and tactical coordination.

Jonathan grabbed a police radio from one of the SWAT officers. "This is Detective White. I need medical assistance immediately. Officer down, stab wound, significant blood loss."

"Medical is already en route," came the reply. "ETA two minutes."

Two minutes felt like an eternity.

Jonathan knelt beside Ivy, taking her hand in both of his. Her pulse was weak but steady beneath his fingertips—a thread of life that he clung to with desperate hope. Her eyes opened and closed in slow cycles, fighting to maintain awareness as shock and blood loss took their toll. He felt others behind him, Carol, Oliver, even some of the officers.

"Help's coming," he whispered, though he wasn't sure she could hear him. "Just hold on. You did it, Ivy. It's over."

Her lips moved, forming words he couldn't quite make out over the ringing in his ears. He leaned closer, straining to hear whatever she was trying to say.

"It's over," she whispered, a smile appearing on her lips.

"Yeah," Jonathan said, squeezing her hand gently.

Her breathing continued, shallow but regular, and her pulse remained steady under his touch. Outside, the wail of approaching sirens grew louder, emergency medical technicians racing toward them with the equipment and expertise that might save her life.

Jonathan held her hand and waited, listening to each breath she drew as if it were a promise that she would still be there for the next one. The warehouse fell silent around them, time stretching into an unending eternity.

Chapter Thirty-One

ALL SHE COULD SEE WAS HER MOTHER'S FACE.

Ivy was in her bed, safe in her room as her mother came to tuck her in.

"G'nite, ladybug," she said. "Sleep tight."

"Mom, you don't have to tuck me in anymore," Ivy said. "I'm twelve."

Her mother smiled. "I know. But I can't help it. I'll stop when you move out."

Ivy giggled. "Mom."

Her mother leaned down and kissed her on the forehead. "Goodnight. Sleep tight."

The next thing Ivy remembered was being in the horrible room. Waking up on the floor covered in dirt and debris. Looking up at the man with the crazy eyes.

She watched as he killed her father. Then her brother.

"Ivy, you listen to me," her mother said, holding her tight. "I love you, more than anything I love you. Survive. Whatever it takes. Survive, and I'll always be with you."

She felt her mother shudder one last time, and she was gone.

Ivy's eyes snapped open.

She was staring at a dim fluorescent light above, the soft sounds of an IV drip and heart rate monitor doing their rhythmic march off somewhere to her left.

Carol appeared in her field of vision. "Ivy?"

She tried to speak but her throat was as dry as the desert. She tried to swallow, then reached for her throat, noting her finger was encased in a monitoring device.

A cup of water found her hand and Ivy drank it down as fast as possible, holding it out for another. Once she'd gone through two more cups she finally felt like she might be able to form words again.

"You're...okay?" she asked.

Carol nodded. "Thanks to you."

Her throat was still scratchy. "What's—"

"You've been out for almost a week," Carol said. "The doctors weren't sure they could save you. And even if they did, they weren't sure you'd wake back up. You got stabbed, remember?"

A week? It felt like it had only been a few minutes since Zimmerman had plunged that knife into her. "How could I forget?" She tried to sit up, but Carol kept her on the bed.

"You need to not move. You're still healing."

"The others?" she asked.

"Jonathan went down to the cafeteria," Carol said. "He hasn't left your side."

"What about—"

"They're...okay, but it's complicated. I'll let Jonathan explain when he gets back."

Ivy closed her eyes and relaxed into the bed, trying to go through everything that had happened. "I remembered," she said. "I remembered what happened that night."

Carol nodded. "Are you... okay?"

Ivy smiled. "I think so." She realized Carol's hand was on

her arm, stroking it supportively. When Carol looked down, she realized what she was doing.

"Oh, I'm so sorry, I didn't—"

"No, it's okay," Ivy said. "It doesn't hurt. The... sensations... they're gone." She reached up and placed her palm against Carol's cheek. Nothing. No pain. No agony.

"I don't understand," Carol said.

Ivy didn't either, but now that she had her memories back, maybe she could find the answer somewhere in there. Maybe it had something to do with her final moments with her mother... when she uttered those last words to her.

"He was wrong," Ivy said. "Zimmerman. He never covered up my memories. I did that. After she told me to. My mother."

Carol took her seat, still holding Ivy's hand.

"She said *survive*," Ivy said. "It was the last thing she said to me before he..." She took a deep breath, finding it hard to fill her lungs completely without a dull ache in her midsection. "I buried the memories so I could survive."

Carol nodded. "And you did."

The door opened to reveal Jonathan, his arm still in a sling but also carrying a to-go bag. "Ivy!" He nearly dropped the bag when he saw her before Carol rushed over and helped him. "Are you—"

"I'm okay," she replied.

He came to the other side of the bed as Carol put the bag away. "We weren't sure you'd wake up. The doctors didn't know what would happen."

Ivy reached for his hand. He hesitated. "It's okay," she said, taking his hand in hers. It was warm.

"I don't—"

"I'm still figuring it out too," she replied. "I think it's going to take a long time for me to process everything that's happened."

He nodded. "Take as much time as you need."

"Where are Nat and Oliver?" Ivy asked. "Carol said you'd explain."

Jonathan shot a quick look at Carol. "Oliver has been by a few times, but right now he's in a meeting with Ayford and the FBI. He's been cooperating with them all week to expose Cor's operations and hopefully has enough useful dirt on them to keep him out of prison." He sighed. "Nat is another story."

"Why?"

"Currently she's sitting in county lockup. She pled guilty to covering up your family's murders fifteen years ago. And since no one can find her old partner, she's taking the brunt of the punishment alone."

"But… she was just—"

"I know," Jonathan said. "She's also cooperated fully. But someone had to take the fall for all this. I think the DA will be lenient on her and give her a good plea deal. Hopefully she'll be out in less than five years."

"It's not right," Ivy said.

"Maybe not," Carol replied. "But that's what we have to deal with."

"And Zimmerman?" Ivy asked.

"Dead and buried. Or, actually, his body is still in the morgue until the case is closed. Lieutenant Ayford will want to speak to you. As will Captain Armstrong."

Ivy furrowed her brow. "How did they know?" She didn't recall exactly what happened. One minute Zimmerman was telling his men to shoot them, the next she saw SWAT officers swarming the place.

A rueful smile came over Jonathan's face. "You can thank Alice for that."

"Alice?"

"She got worried after we left and when I wasn't picking up my phone, she called in the last set of favors she had in the department, including one very—" He glanced at Carol. "—compromising one on Captain Armstrong. They had no choice but to respond. And since she knew where we were going, they managed to find us easily. I just wish they'd blown the doors about twenty seconds earlier. Then you wouldn't be lying here."

"Remind me to send her a thank-you basket," Ivy said.

There was a soft knock at the door. "Ms. Bishop?" A nurse entered the room, a stethoscope around his neck. "Glad to see you're awake."

"I pressed the call button," Carol said.

"I'll let the doctor know and he should be in here in a few minutes," the nurse said. "How are you feeling?"

Jonathan moved to the side so the nurse could check Ivy's vitals. "Other than some soreness in my abdomen, I feel okay."

"That's excellent," he replied. "Your family may have already told you, but the surgery went well and we don't expect any complications. In fact, you being immobile for almost a week has given your body ample time to heal. I don't want to get your hopes up, but I don't think you'll need to stay here too much longer."

That was welcome news for sure. But it wasn't what Ivy had fixated on. The nurse had called Carol and Jonathan her *family*. Nothing felt more right to her.

"Okay if I stay in my old room?" she asked Carol as the nurse checked her pulse. It was so strange for someone to touch her and for Ivy not to pull away. But it felt as natural as anything. "I'm not sure I can go back to my apartment. Not yet."

"Of course," Carol said. "Hero will be happy to have someone else to snuggle with."

"I'll be back in a few minutes with the doctor," the nurse said. "Hang tight."

Jonathan leaned down after he'd left and Ivy felt her

heartrate pick up as he got closer. "I need to head out of town for a few days. But I'll be back."

"Your sister?" Ivy asked. Jonathan nodded. "Everything okay?"

"It will be. I just need to take care of some things." He turned to Carol. "You okay watching her until Sunday?"

"It's always a pleasure for me," Carol replied with a smile.

Jonathan nodded. He then leaned down and before Ivy knew what was happening, his lips were on hers. Instead of a shock though, she felt a different kind of electricity running through her. The kind that lit her up in ways she never thought possible. "I've been wanting to do that for a while now," he said as he pulled away. "I'll see you in a few days."

With that he grinned and left the two women alone, stunned in silence.

"What... just happened?" Ivy asked, touching her lips, still feeling the impression of his kiss there.

"I believe Jonathan decided to take a chance. Maybe he finally figured out life is too short to wait for things to happen," Carol replied. "You have to make the good things happen for yourself."

Ivy couldn't believe it. She had long ago abandoned the idea of a physical relationship... with anyone. But now that her... phobia... was gone, the possibilities were endless. And a future with Jonathan... that didn't sound too bad at all.

The large metal door opened and Nat shuffled through, dressed in a drab beige jumpsuit with black slip-on shoes. She saw Ivy and turned away, stopping for a moment before finally heading over and joining her at the communal table.

"You shouldn't be here," Nat said, sitting down across from Ivy.

"You weren't taking my calls," Ivy said. It had been a week

since she was discharged from the hospital, and she'd spent a majority of that time at Carol's recuperating with Hero. It had taken a lot of effort to walk without the wheelchair, but as soon as she had been able, she'd set up an appointment with the county lockup to meet with Nat. She hadn't spoken to the woman since that day in the warehouse and they needed to clear a few things up.

"How are you feeling?" Nat asked. "I asked someone at the station to keep me updated on your progress."

"Better," Ivy said. "Still feel like I was kicked in the gut by someone with a steel-toed boot, but it's a little better every day. The doctor said I can start light exercises next week."

Nat nodded, her face drawn with worry and anguish. "That's good."

"Nat, you don't have to be in here," Ivy said, leaning forward, even though it caused her midsection to ache.

"Someone needs to be held responsible. For you. Your family. For what I put you through," Nat said.

"But—"

"No buts," she replied. "I broke the law. I have to answer for it."

Ivy sighed. Technically she was correct. But if Nat had turned Ivy in back then, she would have gone to juvie, or worse, been charged with a triple homicide. Nat's actions saved Ivy's life, one way or the other. She didn't deserve to sit behind bars because of it.

"I talked to the D.A., told him I wasn't pursuing any charges. That whatever they were holding on you was not because I wanted it."

"I know," Nat said. "But this is my burden to bear, Ivy. I knew what I was doing back then and I did it anyway. And I knew one day it would come back to haunt me. I'm just glad I was wrong… and you weren't what I first assumed you to be."

"Nat, there is something I need to ask you. My family…

where are they buried? I want—I *need* to give them a proper burial."

She nodded. "I already gave the information to Ayford. Talk to him, I'm sure he can help you exhume their bodies and have them properly laid to rest." She dropped her head. "I'm just so sorry for it. For all of it."

Ivy reached across the table and took Nat's hands in her own, surprising the woman. "It's okay," Ivy replied. "You saved my life. That's something I can never repay."

"No physical contact," the guard called out, causing Ivy to pull back again.

Nat nodded at her hands. "Your affliction?"

"Gone," Ivy said. "My therapist thinks it all started that night, when Zimmerman physically tore me from my mother. I always thought it was something that I developed at the foster home. But he believes it started that night. It was why I was so averse to any kind of touch. But now that I remember and can process it, not to mention the son of a bitch is dead, my body doesn't have to go into full protective mode all the time."

"Ivy," Nat said. "That's... amazing."

She nodded. "I know."

"I'm so happy for you."

"Nat," Ivy began. "You are the sister I never had. And you were there for me when no one else was. Everything you did, to protect me, to keep me safe... I can't—I don't know how to thank you for that."

"You don't have to," Nat replied.

"I know. But I just want you to know I'm grateful. And I'll be here, standing right out there the day you're released." She pointed behind her towards the front gates of the prison. "Until then, expect a lot of phone calls. I'd visit more, but it would be too long of a drive."

Nat pulled her brows together. "You're leaving? What about your job?"

"I'm handing in my resignation tomorrow," Ivy said. "I think I've had enough of chasing down killers and psychopaths."

Nat inclined her head. "I can't fault you there. So what are you going to do?"

"Still working on that part," Ivy said. "But I'll be sure to let you know."

Chapter 32

TWO WEEKS LATER

"You ready to do this?"

Ivy looked over at Jonathan. Her heart had been beating hard all morning, but now it was threatening to break through her ribs. Still, she gave his hand a squeeze. It was a sensation she was quickly warming to. She never knew touch could be so... pleasurable. "Yeah. I'm ready."

They stepped out of the car into the morning sun and Ivy found it was warm enough she could remove her jacket. With Jonathan at her side, she made her way across the grass to the area where a large number of people were already gathered.

"Thought you two might not show up."

Ivy turned to see Alice approaching, dressed in an immaculate black dress, complete with a wide-brimmed black hat and sunglasses. She removed the glasses as she appraised Ivy. "But I'm glad you did."

Ivy approached her and wrapped the woman in a hug, something she'd only started to get used to doing. Usually the person on the receiving end was as surprised as Ivy, but she found Alice actually hugged her back. "Thanks for coming."

"Of course," Alice replied. "I couldn't miss this. I think most of the town has shown up."

"I didn't mean to make a big deal about it," Ivy said. "I just wanted to do the right thing."

Alice nodded. "Unfortunately, word travels. And the media has been all over this for the past month. But lucky for you I pulled some strings. All the reporters are staying a respectful distance away and I've instructed that no one is to bother either of you." Alice's eyes traveled down to Ivy's hand clasped in Jonathan's. "You two make a good-looking pair."

"Thanks," Jonathan said. "We wouldn't be here without you."

"Don't I know it," Alice replied, giving them a sly smile. "Don't worry, you can repay me by allowing me to interview you for the book."

"What book?" Ivy asked.

Alice grinned. "Everyone needs to know the truth about what really happened to your family. About what that monster did to you. No one will be able to doubt you and your family were the victims of a crazed man. You should see some of the stuff I've managed to dig up on him. Apparently he was *obsessed* with your mother when they were young. Thought they were soul mates or some shit. And he just couldn't handle her being with someone else. That combined with the fact he was a classic narcissist and a manipulator—"

"Alice, maybe now isn't the time," Jonathan said.

She gave him a terse smile. "Right. *Anyway.* I just wanted to let you know there's no rush. Whenever you're ready to talk, I'll be there. And just to show you I'm not such a bitch, I negotiated it so you'd get half the sales revenue."

"What?" Ivy asked, incredulous.

"Well, it's your story after all," Alice replied. She leaned closer. "But only if you want it to be. You say the word, and we never have to talk about it again. Up to you."

Ivy couldn't believe Alice would be willing to give up something so lucrative. But then again, the two women had grown closer over the past few weeks, with Alice making constant visits to see how Ivy was doing, all the while teasing that she had something big in the works. Ivy supposed this was it.

"Think about it, no rush," Alice added. "I know today will be hard. But I just wanted you to know."

"Thanks, Alice. See you over there," Jonathan said.

She nodded. "Yep."

Ivy and Jonathan continued to make their way to the site. "Never thought I'd see the day Alice Blair shared a story," Jonathan said. "You must be really softening her up."

"She's always been that way," Ivy replied. "She just had a lot of armor on." Ivy was more than familiar with that tactic. But ever since she'd been working on not hiding behind her own armor anymore, she'd started to see things a little differently.

"There's Carol," Jonathan said, nodding to the front row where Carol sat with Hero on her lap. The little dog was excitedly looking around at all the people, though he was remaining where he was.

"Ivy?"

She turned to see Oliver standing off to the side, the tie of his suit askew.

"I'll go make the rounds," Jonathan said, giving Oliver a nod. "Just let us know when you're ready."

"Thanks," Ivy said, watching him walk towards the crowd.

"Hey," Oliver said.

"Hey." She hesitated. "Ayford said you've been helping the FBI. That you're working as a consultant of some kind?"

He nodded. "Yeah. Been working directly with D.C. This spitfire agent... Special Agent Zara Foley. She's...keeping me on my toes."

"And out of jail," Ivy said.

He chuckled. "So far. We'll see. I just hope I can make up for... well, for everything." He cleared his throat. "I just wanted to tell you how… sorry I am… for everything I put you through."

"You don't have anything to be sorry about," Ivy said.

"I should have told you how I felt when you first contacted me again," he said. "Instead, I let it stew… I made decisions thinking I could impress you or… I don't know. Maybe make you feel about me the way I felt about you."

"Oliver—"

"No, it's okay," he said, glancing over at Jonathan. "You two are good together. You and me… it would never have worked. I just wish I had known what Zimmerman tried to do to me. I could have warned you."

"I don't think any of us could have seen that coming," Ivy said.

"Still. I should have been man enough to accept that you would have said no. And I should have trusted you… about Cor… about all of it."

"We all have our own secrets," she said. "It's okay." She reached out and took his hand in hers. "You'll always be the person who kept me from falling down a dark hole in that foster home. And I'll still be here, if you should ever need a friend."

He glanced over to where Carol sat with Hero. "Please tell her thank you again for me. For taking Hero. For caring for him."

Ivy let go of his hand, furrowing her brow. "You're not staying for the service?"

"I have a plane to catch in half an hour," he said. "They want me in D.C. in person."

"Wow, look at you. Full-on government lackey."

He grinned. "Try not to rub it in. I probably won't be back to Oakhurst for a few months, assuming that agent doesn't kill me first."

"That makes two of us," Ivy said.

His eyes went wide. "Does that mean you got accepted?"

She nodded. "Yep. It's going to be a lot of work and certification, not to mention a lot of time with a therapist, but I really want to help trauma survivors. I want to be there for them in the way Nat was with me, just on a more official capacity. And by not covering up crimes." She leaned closer, whispering. "It's something I'm an expert on."

Oliver motioned to Jonathan. "What about White?"

"He's going back to work for Portland PD," she said. "That way he's close to his family, should they need him, *and* he gets to keep doing what he loves."

"No more investigative work for you?" Oliver asked.

Ivy turned to look at the three caskets suspended above their respective plots in the ground. It had taken her fifteen years and an unending obsession to figure out what really happened one dark night in August, the year she turned twelve. But now that she had, she no longer felt that same drive, that same pull to uncover every mystery that confronted her. And while she would miss the work, she believed she could do more for the victims of crimes than she could trying to track down the perpetrators. After everything she'd witnessed, after everything she'd experienced, it was time to turn the page and start looking at life a little differently.

"No," she said as they walked over to the caskets as the service was about to start. "That chapter of my life is closed. It's time to start a new one."

The End

New Series Alert!
A twisted killer lies in wait…

I hope you enjoyed *One Dark Night*! While this may be the end of Ivy's story (for now at least!), I'd like to introduce you to Charlotte and Mona, two amazing detectives who are after a very twisted killer.

When a woman's body is discovered in Oak Creek, local police quickly dismiss it as an accidental drowning from years ago. Brought in from Chicago to help with the case, Detective Charlotte Dawes has worked on more murder investigations than she'd like to remember. An examination of the body tells her what local police refuse to see – somebody moved the victim to this remote location.

After a local artist is found murdered, her body positioned to match one of her final paintings, the sinister truth can't be ignored. More disturbing still, the artist's other works seem to predict who in the small town will be next to die, in increasingly macabre ways.

As fear grips the town, Charlotte discovers a link between the first victim and a local cop, and it's clear the killer has planned their moves meticulously. In a community where everyone guards their secrets, Charlotte must determine who's truly playing on her side, before she becomes the next target...

What readers are saying about *The Darkest Game*:

'This is the start of something special... prepare to fall in love with this new world and its darkly addictive pace.' Reader review, ★★★★★

'I was completely held hostage by my Kindle the whole way til the end.' Reader review, ★★★★★

'Okay, wow! This book was just... whoosh! Mind blown... a masterclass in suspense. Gripping, intelligent, and so compelling, I reread it the moment I finished. I haven't been able to stop thinking about it since.' Reader review, ★★★★★

'I'm kind of fangirling right now. Honestly, I was blown away by how much I enjoyed it.' Reader review, ★★★★★

Interested? CLICK HERE to snag your copy of THE DARKEST GAME!

Now Available

I can't wait for you to read it!

CLICK HERE or scan the code below to get yours now!

ALEX SIGMORE

The Ivy Bishop Mystery Thriller Series

Free Prequel - Bishop's Edge (Ivy Bishop Bonus Story)
Her Dark Secret - (Ivy Bishop Series Book One)
The Girl Without a Clue - (Ivy Bishop Series Book Two)
The Buried Faces - (Ivy Bishop Series Book Three)
Her Hidden Lies - (Ivy Bishop Series Book Four)
One Dark Night - (Ivy Bishop Series Book Five)

The Emily Slate FBI Mystery Series

Free Prequel - Her Last Shot (Emily Slate Bonus Story)
His Perfect Crime - (Emily Slate Series Book One)
The Collection Girls - (Emily Slate Series Book Two)
Smoke and Ashes - (Emily Slate Series Book Three)
Her Final Words - (Emily Slate Series Book Four)
Can't Miss Her - (Emily Slate Series Book Five)
The Lost Daughter - (Emily Slate Series Book Six)
The Secret Seven - (Emily Slate Series Book Seven)
A Liar's Grave - (Emily Slate Series Book Eight)
Oh What Fun - (Emily Slate Series Holiday Special)
The Girl in the Wall - (Emily Slate Series Book Nine)
His Final Act - (Emily Slate Series Book Ten)
The Vanishing Eyes - (Emily Slate Series Book Eleven)
Edge of the Woods - (Emily Slate Series Book Twelve)
Ties That Bind - (Emily Slate Series Book Thirteen)
The Missing Bones - (Emily Slate Series Book Fourteen)
Blood in the Sand - (Emily Slate Series Book Fifteen)
The Passage - (Emily Slate Series Book Sixteen)

Fire in the Sky - (Emily Slate Series Book Seventeen)
The Killing Jar - (Emily Slate Series Book Eighteen)

The Oak Creek Thriller Series

The Darkest Game - (Oak Creek Thriller Book One)
Never Strike Twice - (Oak Creek Thriller Book Two)

A Note from Alex

Dear reader,

After five books and countless twists and turns, we've finally reached the end of Ivy's story. I really hope you've enjoyed this journey as much as I enjoyed writing it.

Ivy was born out of a desire to explore the darker sides of ourselves, in those moments when we question who we truly are and what we're capable of, which you've now seen how that plays out for Ivy. I've always been aware that Ivy is a deeply flawed character, but I think that's what makes us root for her even more. And while this may be the end for Ivy's story, I won't say some of the characters won't pop up in other books :)

But for now, I'd like to thank you for your time and attention, I've always known that is the most valuable thing of all and the fact that you spend it on my books warms my heart like nothing else.

If you enjoyed this book, please leave a review or recommend to your friends. Writing is my passion and I want to continue to bring you many more books in the future!

Thank you for being a loyal reader,
Alex

Made in United States
North Haven, CT
14 October 2025